Walking By Faith

ALEXANDRA T ARMSTRONG

PARABLE PRINT

PARABLE PRINT

For my precious granddaughter,
Adelaide James Grace Smith

For we walk by faith, not by sight.
1 Corinthians 5:7

Character Recap

Jonathan Jefferson: Pastor of Grace Fellowship Church. Wife, Kesha. Father of four young, rowdy sons.

Joe Jacobs: Faircourt attorney who Grant witnessed to at the golf course and invited to church. Running for state office. Wife, Allison.

Shorty Ortiz: Employee of McBride Motor Mart. Formerly shared an apartment with his father who had to be placed in a care facility in Louisville. Had a short-term roommate who moved on after just a couple months. Shorty is struggling financially to keep up with his monthly bills.

Silas: A high-school freshman and son of Will the postman. He's Chase Norman's best friend and step-cousin since Will and Shelby married.

Five: Formerly pink-haired barista at Latte Da who was befriended by Will and Shelby and has come to faith in Christ. Her transformation, both inward and outward, continues.

Tom Farmer: Former part-time custodian at Grace Fellowship Church. Wife, Patty. Tom is working off his debt to the church part time, and working at McBride Motor Mart full-time.

(Louisa Renniger) G-Lu: Grant's mother who lives at Pleasant Pond Retirement Village.

CHAPTER ONE

"Hey, Dad! I've been working on a little project upstairs, and I want you to come see it and tell me what you think," DeShawn requested, bending over the back of the living room couch where his father was stretched out watching television.

Bobby picked up the remote and turned the TV off. "Reds are going to lose this one anyway," he grumbled, then followed his son up the staircase, using the handrail for assistance.

They entered DeShawn's upstairs office, where Mariana sat and smiled behind the desk in a white tank top that showed off her summer tan. When his father cleared the doorway, DeShawn tossed his head toward a newly assembled white-lacquered crib in the room's corner. Bobby's jaw dropped, and his eyes widened when he saw it.

"A baby? Miss Banana is going to have our baby?" Bobby was floored and turned away from the crib to stare at his daughter-in-law.

"Well, Dad, she's going to have my baby," DeShawn chuckled.

"Congratulations, son! I'm so happy for you...for you both. I'm so happy for me!" Bobby gushed. "Oh, come here and let me hug your neck, little momma!" he pleaded to Mariana.

As she embraced her father-in-law, Mariana felt a teardrop fall on her bare shoulder and then another.

"Dad, you're going to drown us both!" she joked, dropping her arms to her sides.

Bobby stepped back to look at her figure. "When?" he asked, now discerning a slight bump in her abdomen.

"Early February. The 6th, the doctor said."

"I'm no good with numbers anymore. So, how far along are you?"

"Eighteen weeks," Mariana beamed.

Bobby smiled, pretending the information clarified instead of muddied his calculations. "You've known for a while?" he asked what he really wanted to know.

"We have," DeShawn answered for the couple. "Mariana didn't want to steal any of Shelby's limelight with the wedding coming up. And honestly, it was bonding for us to have this special little secret to ourselves for a while. But the wedding's done, and now it's time to share our happy news."

"I can't get over it," Bobby said as he sunk into the rocking chair at the desk's corner. "Ah! So, this is why you got a rocking chair!" he was putting clues together. "And it was more than your job that was making you tired and wanting to go to bed early. Have you been sick?"

"Not a bit, just the tired," Mariana moved next to her husband, who put his arm around her shoulder.

"A baby," Bobby repeated the news to himself, grinning broadly. "Who else knows?" he asked.

"Besides us and Mariana's obstetrician, just you. You're the first one we've told," DeShawn confessed.

"As it should be!" Mariana added. "Family first."

"Boy or girl? Did you find out?" the questions in Bobby's mind were stacking up.

"Not yet. We can find out at my next appointment if we want."

"Do you want to?"

"We've talked about it, and I think so," Mariana's eyes twinkled as she answered.

Bobby put his hand to his face and squeezed his chin. "This is life-changing," he said suddenly somber. "You'll want to leave and have your own place."

"Are you putting us out, Dad?" DeShawn raised his eyebrows and lowered the corners of his mouth, a hint of mirth in his question.

"No! I..." Bobby began, fearing he was misunderstood.

"This is home," Mariana cut him off. "You, DeShawn, me, and baby makes four. We're a family, and this is our home." She planted her feet to emphasize her point.

Bobby's eyes welled again. "I don't even know what to say except I'm so happy!"

"Dad, Mariana and I have done a lot of talking – about life, family, and about our plans. I've dropped all but one of my Bible classes. One is all I can handle as I'm trying to learn the business, be a husband and now a father, and spend a little time with you. My life is here, and I know my ministry is here, too. It's different from what I imagined it would be, but it's good. God is good, and I'm content. We hope you can be content and keep your sanity when we bring a crying infant into this house. We understand this wasn't part of the plan when you invited us to live here."

"I'm not sure why, but it never even occurred to me that the two of you would have children. I was so full of happiness that you were here – under my roof again, where I could see you every day – I never thought to hope for more. But now that our baby is on the way, all I can say is if the poor thing cries, I might cry, too, from pity. Then there will be two of us wailing!" Bobby admitted.

A smile washed over his face. "You know, it was just this time last year, around Labor Day, that Jonathan Jefferson knocked on my door to tell me you'd welcome a visit from me. I felt then like I do now – excited but nervous. Happy for sure! Labor Day weekends have been good to me lately," Bobby chuckled.

DeShawn gazed out the window, gathering his thoughts. "Yeah, Dad, a lot has happened in a year. Time in prison drags by, but time out here flies – I'm still getting used to that. And I'm so incredibly blessed with you, my wife, and now a little one. I've got old friends and new friends. And I've got a job I find satisfying. Sheesh! I never thought I'd say that about the car lot. I'm so rich when it comes to major life blessings now; sometimes, I'm afraid it won't last."

"None of it is meant to last," Mariana spoke jarring words.

Bobby and DeShawn turned their heads toward her, wearing opposite expressions – DeShawn's peace and Bobby's confusion.

"We're meant to enjoy the good gifts our Heavenly Father gives us, but none of them are ours eternally. The knowledge that His gifts are temporary makes us long for His permanent, eternal kingdom. I can't wait to hold my baby in my arms. But I also want to know that when this child outgrows my arms, as he surely will, he'll never outgrow eternal life in Christ. That's what will last. So, Dad, expect this child will hear and know the gospel as long as I'm his momma," Mariana asserted.

DeShawn shifted on his feet. "You're right, babe. I shouldn't worry about trying to keep temporary things permanent. That's a lost cause. I need reminding to focus on the eternal."

"Sometimes, when I listen to the two of you, it seems like eternity is more real than the present. I spend a lot of time ruminating on the past I can't change. But I'm sure of one thing – our baby has got me excited about the future now!" Bobby grinned and began rocking in the chair.

"That's a start," DeShawn whispered to his wife with a wink.

Chapter Two

Driving down Main Street on her way home from a hair appointment, Kesha Jefferson almost rear-ended a delivery van when she saw the large sign in the window of Latte Da. "FOR SALE," the red block letters announced. She shared the news with her husband while making the family lunch.

"We can't lose our coffee shop! If someone doesn't buy the business, we'll probably get another vape shop or something equally unwanted and unnecessary," Kesha whined to Jonathan.

"I use Latte Da when Ava Van Zant isn't in the office and I have to meet with female congregation members. It's public, yet quiet enough to have a private conversation. I have no backup plan if we lose the coffee shop," Jonathan complained to DeShawn.

"Hey, Freshman! Did you see that Latte Da is being sold? The high schoolers will have to find another place to take their little dates," DeShawn pointed out to Chase as they rode Blue Beauty down Main Street.

"Aw, Dad, Latte Da bit the dust! What a bummer," Chase complained to his father at supper.

"It's closed?" Micah asked, cocking his head in disbelief.

"Not yet, but there's a sign in the window that says it's for sale," Chase clarified.

After supper, Micah came to the back porch and saw Grant changing the flood light on his garage. He walked over to put a stabilizing hand on the ladder and pass along the community news.

"Hey, Grant! How ya doing? Did you hear Latte Da is on the chopping block? Got a FOR SALE sign on her, I'm told."

"I'm a tea drinker myself and have never set foot in the place other than the upstairs for Will and Shelby's rehearsal dinner. But I know some people who might have a bawling cry over this development," Grant tossed his head toward his house.

"I just heard Latte Da is for sale," Grant announced as he entered the kitchen from the back door.

A chorus of groans erupted from the household assembled at the kitchen table, devouring June's low-sugar cheesecake – a recipe she developed for her diabetic husband with a sweet tooth.

"Please tell me you're kidding," Marie, dropping her fork, begged.

"Cal and I should have gone more often for iced coffees," June lamented as if they could have single-handedly saved the business.

"Dat's a shame," Marcus processed, rubbing a hand over his head.

"I drink home-brewed 'cause I won't pay those outrageous prices for a cup of coffee. But they made some delicious lemon-poppyseed muffins. Those were worth every penny," Elodie acknowledged.

"Let's buy it!" Ava suggested, clapping her hands together.

"Please tell me *you're* kidding," Grant tilted his chair back on two legs.

A gleam rose in Marie's eyes. "It would be so much fun to redecorate."

"We could run it under a 'business as mission' model," Marcus considered the idea.

"I'd be willing to bake," June offered.

"Don't look at me," Cal mumbled, shoveling cheesecake into his mouth.

Elodie looked at Grant and thought a vein running near his temple was near to rupturing. She caught his eye, winked, and mouthed to him: "I got you."

"Yeah, this could work," Elodie began, rubbing her chin thoughtfully.

"Of course, customers prefer their baked goods to be fresh. So, June, you'll be getting' up at 3:30 AM to open the store to get bakin' instead of sleepin' in like you do now? I understand we might not open on Sundays, but for sure, six days a week, right?" She watched June's blue eyes widen with realization and then continued.

"Marie, after you redecorate...by the way, whose money are you spendin' on that? Never mind; you can talk to your husband about that later. When the redecoratin's done, will you take shifts waitressin' or workin' behind the counter? Those jobs are a minimum of four to six hours on your feet, I'm guessin'." Marie's mouth pursed into an 'O'.

Elodie wasn't done. "And you, Calgary..."

"Don't look at me," Cal repeated, taking another bite of dessert.

"Marcus!" Elodie turned her shoulders and attention toward him. "You're our natural barista since you already know how to work a fancy machine. How much mission you gonna do when you're tryin' to keep up with orders in the mornings? Or do you prefer workin' evenings when we're having our supper here? Maybe it would be best to rotate your shifts around now that I think about it. That way, when you are able to get out from behind the counter, all our customers can tell you their problems. It'd be just like bein' a full-time pastor again. That's what you wanted, right?" She noticed his gray head sag as the reality she highlighted settled on him.

The kitchen was quiet for several moments until Ava broke the silence.

"El, do you remember when we were kids, and I was sick at camp, and my grandpa came with that giant Get Well Soon balloon, which you accidentally popped when you slammed the door on it? I just want you to know you've burst my lovely balloon again – only this time, it was on purpose."

Elodie smirked, pleased with herself.

"I guess it's one of those ideas that's better in our fantasy than in reality," June conceded, shielding the remaining cheesecake on her plate from her husband's fork. "You've met your carb allotment, dear," she chided Cal with a whisper.

"Yeah, dere's not too much flexibility in da schedule when your business has to be profitable," Marcus admitted.

"None of us wants a full-time job at this stage in our lives. I have no idea what got into your heads," Elodie admonished.

"Don't look at me," Cal reiterated, wiping his mouth on the sleeve of his white t-shirt.

"Well, it's true I'd prefer my current part-time job at the church, where I get to sit at a desk, to standing on my feet in a coffee shop for endless hours. But I still hate the thought of seeing Latte Da go under. What if no one buys it and keeps it as it is?" Ava wondered.

"We can't rescue everything as if it were a stray dog," Grant spoke up as he saw the tide turning his way.

"Says the man who rescued a stray dog," Marie shot back with a laughing snort.

With nothing left on his plate and June guarding her own, Cal stood to rinse his dish and stack it in the dishwasher. His wife and friends glumly followed suit, dispersing to the living room, study, or upstairs.

Rinsing his plate in the sink, Grant turned to Elodie, who was about to leave the kitchen.

"I could hug your neck for what you said," he thanked her.

"Do not do that," Elodie grimaced. She departed through the archway, cotton skirt swirling, and added over her shoulder: "Ever! Please and thank you."

Further down the hallway, Elodie grinned. She was pleased with herself for talking the dreamers of the household – Ava, June, Marie, and Marcus - out of a dumb idea.

CHAPTER THREE

"Girl, you need to button one more button on that blouse before you give the men of this church a cleavage show!" Kesha greeted Mariana in the vestibule with a whisper and a laugh.

Mariana smirked, handed Kesha her purse and Bible, and discreetly fastened another button on her pink, flowered-print blouse. Suddenly, Kesha's eyes grew large.

"You've never had cleavage before! You're pregnant!" the mom of four pronounced, forcing herself to whisper again.

"Shhhh! But, yes," Mariana confirmed. "My belly's still not showing much, but my top sure is."

Kesha looked across the vestibule and saw her husband shaking De-Shawn's hand and grinning. "Looks like your husband just shared the news with Jonathan. When are you due?

"February 6th," Mariana answered, expecting flak for keeping it secret so long.

"You're halfway through!" Kesha exclaimed, handing back Mariana's belongings.

"Nearly."

"Shelby's wedding. I get it. But girl, you kept that secret locked up tight. What a selfless friend you are! Me? I'm not that good. When I found out I was pregnant with my first, I told half a dozen people before I even told Jonathan!" Kesha confessed.

"We're letting the news out now, but I'd like you to keep it on the down-low this morning. DeShawn and I are going to tell our neighborhood walking crew on the way home."

"You got it, girl. I'm so happy for you guys. Congratulations! Your father-in-law is probably pleased."

"You could say that. He keeps referring to it as "our baby," Mariana giggled.

"Ut oh! Time to set some boundaries," Kesha advised, growing serious.

"No. Not yet, anyway. I can't deflate Dad's happiness after he's been so good to us. Just saying 'our baby' is harmless. We'll save boundaries for big issues if any arise," Mariana responded.

"I respect that," Kesha nodded.

"So, do I look appropriately modest now?"

"Like a pioneer woman on the Oregon Trail!" Kesha affirmed.

"What's for lunch?" Grant wanted to know as he walked home from church alongside his wife.

"No clue. Ava's in charge today. Ask her," Marie suggested.

"Ava!" Grant yelled over his shoulder. "What's on the lunch menu?"

"Glad you asked. I've got potato salad in the fridge, and you're grilling hot dogs," Ava answered.

"Really, Grant? We're not past the church parkin' lot, and you're already thinkin' about your stomach," Elodie chastised.

"I was thinking about my stomach when we were still in the church," Lovie, who came to church for the sole purpose of having somewhere to wear her junior bridesmaid dress again, admitted.

"I was thinking about my wife's stomach while we were still in the church," DeShawn saw his segway to the news he and Mariana wanted to share.

"That's weird! Even for you," Chase responded to his neighbor with a sour face.

"It's not weird if there's a baby there," Mariana defended her husband's comment.

"What?" Ava and Marie shrieked simultaneously.

"I believe she said dere's a bun in da oven," Marcus translated dryly.

"I heard what she said!" Ava poked her husband.

The procession came to a halt as the women and children surrounded Mariana. Marcus and Grant, receiving the news more casually than the others, moved to the outside. They might have kept walking if it weren't impolite.

"Congratulations!" June offered.

"Such wonderful news!" Ava exclaimed.

"When's her birthday?" Marie mixed her question with a guess.

DeShawn picked up on it. "Boy or girl, we don't know yet, but February 6th is the due date," he beamed.

"I'm sure your daddy's happy," Elodie assured DeShawn.

"Oh, you don't know the half of it! I never saw a man with baby fever like Dad's got it," DeShawn laughed.

"What did you want to have a baby for?" Chase asked.

"Who wouldn't want a sweet child like you?" Mariana answered. She reached out and patted the boy's head.

"True," Chase responded with sassy confidence.

Lovie said nothing as the group started walking toward home again but placed herself next to Mariana, keeping her eyes focused on her.

"It'll be wonderful having a neighbor baby. I hope he or she will be a frequent visitor to our porch glider," Marie wished.

"Have you considered what a masculine, powerful name 'Marcus' is?"

Marcus asked as he led the group across Cedar Street.

DeShawn moved from his place in the center of the women toward Marcus and Grant at the front of the pack.

"Personally, I was leaning toward Spurgeon or Wilberforce for a boy's name, but Mariana's not having either of those," DeShawn whined.

"Ha! Now 'Marcus' doesn't sound so strong and manly compared to those pillars of the faith, does it, Marcus?" Grant ribbed.

"How did a baby get in there?" Lovie addressed Mariana at last, sincerely perplexed.

Overhearing the child's question, Grant yelled over his shoulder: "We'll just be getting the grill started."

He yanked Marcus' arm and walked double-time, pulling away from the group. DeShawn matched their pace. Chase was torn. He snickered and wanted to hear how the ladies would explain the situation to his little sister, but he also wanted to identify with the men. The latter desire won out, and he jogged to catch up with them.

Mariana looked helplessly at the older women, and June rescued her.

"Babies are God's gift to mommies, Lovie, just like you were to your Mommy."

"That's what I thought," Lovie bobbed her eight-year-old head, satisfied. For now.

Chapter Four

"Welcome home, guys. I didn't burn down the love nest while you were gone," Micah greeted his sister and new brother-in-law as they walked through the front door of the gray rental house.

"We can see that, and you have our thanks for it," Shelby leaned in to give her brother a hug.

"Aunt Shelby, Uncle Will!" Lovie yelled as she darted across Cedar Street. She'd been watching out the front window of her house, anticipating their arrival, and lit out as soon as she spied them. She ran up the front steps of the house and through the still-open front door.

"Whoa, girl! Did someone set your hair on fire? You must be the fastest runner at your school," Will, standing closest to the door, intercepted Lovie and scooped her up in his arms.

"I'm not the fastest. But I'm not the slowest either," Lovie grinned at him. "Did you bring something back in your bags for me?

"Lovie! That's rude to ask. If someone has something for you, they'll give it to you when they're ready. You need to wait patiently," Micah corrected his daughter.

Lovie lowered her head, embarrassed, and squirmed for Will to put her down.

"How was Niagara Falls?" Micah changed the subject.

"Kitschy, crowded, fun," Shelby answered, smiling at Will.

"Everyone should go once and check it off the bucket list," Will agreed.

"Daddy, Miss Elodie said she's going back to her house today. Are Chase and I moving over here and you back to our house?" Lovie inquired, hoping she wouldn't get in trouble for asking this question.

Sensing Micah's discomfort, Shelby jumped in.

"I think you and your brother will be our first houseguests now that we're home. But I'm pretty sure it's only going to be for one night."

Micah, surprised, cast a quizzical glance at Shelby, who reached for Lovie's hand and led her toward the kitchen.

"We took a call from Joe Jacobs on Friday. He said everything should be ironed out tomorrow. But you'll probably get one, maybe two follow-up visits from CPS at the most," Will informed in a low voice.

Micah let out a deep sigh. "That's a relief."

"For everyone," Will agreed.

"Sorry you have to have kids over on your first night together in your home," Micah apologized for the inconvenience.

"Nah, don't be. We got that all out of our system in Niagara Falls," Will assured.

"Really?" Micah stared at him, stunned by such an admission.

"No," Will responded stone-faced, burst out laughing, then punched his brother-in-law's arm.

For the first time since he started dating Shelby, Will felt he and Micah shared a genuine, light-hearted, male-bonding moment as Micah's laughter joined his.

"What's so funny out there?" Shelby shouted from the kitchen.

"Nothing," rang the chorus of the guy's simultaneous reply.

"So, what breaking news from Faircourt did we miss while we were away?" Will asked, shutting the front door and moving suitcases toward the staircase.

"Well, no bank robberies or house-swallowing sinkholes, but Latte Da has a FOR SALE sign in the window," Micah answered.

"Aw, really?" Will expressed genuine disappointment.

"No," Micah copied Will's previous stone-faced fib before admitting, "but, yes. I'm afraid so. Everyone is in mourning because if the owners don't want it, and nobody else does either, then who knows what will go in its place? What town's Main Street doesn't have a coffee shop?"

"Shelby will join the mourners; you can count on that. We had our first date there. She was converted there. And I proposed to her there. Latte Da is a special place to both of us," Will responded, raking fingers through his dark hair.

"Perhaps someone with such an attachment should buy the place," Micah hinted.

"Ha! I might think about it if your sister didn't just marry me for my government health insurance," Will brushed off the suggestion.

"Well, then, say your prayers for the place," Micah responded. "You need a hand getting your bags upstairs? My sister's not a light packer."

"I will not turn down your offer. Matter of fact, that one's hers. Grab that one," Will chuckled and nodded toward the larger suitcase.

In the kitchen, Lovie was working on her second Ding Dong treat, listening to her Aunt talk about riding up to Niagara Falls on The Maid of the Mist in a large group of other tourists, all wearing yellow plastic ponchos.

"They must have a lot of sizes of those things for all the different people," Lovie guessed.

"Actually, I think there's just one size. You could fit two people in them!" Shelby corrected as she loaded dishes Micah had accumulated into the dishwasher.

"Mariana has two people in her clothes," Lovie revealed with a shy smile.

"Is she pregnant?" Shelby whirled around to face her niece.

"Yup," Lovie confirmed, licking chocolate from her fingers and proud to be telling an adult something they didn't know.

Unprepared to hide her emotions, Shelby involuntarily extended her lower lip, and Lovie noted the expression.

"Don't you like babies, Aunt Shelby?"

"No, I love babies. I'm thrilled Mariana is going to have one. Maybe in a few years, you'll get to be their babysitter!" Shelby diverted to Lovie's self-interest to take the focus off her initial reaction.

"I won't change poopy diapers!" Lovie insisted, grimacing.

"I don't think you have to worry. The baby should be well out of diapers by the time you're old enough to babysit," Shelby assured her, relieved the diversion worked.

"Good!" Lovie scooped up empty wrappers on the table and handed them to her aunt. "I'm going to tell Chase you're back and get our stuff packed for overnight and school tomorrow. I'll be back." Lovie headed toward the front door.

"When you get back, I'll give you what I brought home for you," Shelby called after her.

Alone in the kitchen, Shelby reflected: *"I am happy Mariana is going to have a baby; but sad I never will."*

Chapter Five

"What's up, homies?" Cal asked as he took the last seat in the living room for Thursday Meeting.

"Calcutta, have you been drinkin' pot liquor in the Garage Cave?" Elodie shot back at him, weirded out that Cal should express himself as a man of the streets.

"No! Can't a man inquire about his friends' activities without an accusation he's been tipping the spirits?" Cal's playful mood was replaced with a feigned pout.

"Not like that, you can't," Elodie laughed. "You're actin' more fool than cool. Someone should tell you."

"If Grant's 95-year-old mother can get away with being called by a gangsta name like 'G-Lu,' why can't I call you 'homies?'" Cal wanted to know.

"Because you can't," Elodie dug in. She rolled her eyes and looked to June for backup.

"I can't do anything with him. He's been in a mood all day," June smiled and raised her hands helplessly.

"Are we ready to start Tursday Meeting?" Marcus interrupted the bickering.

"We might be if El Camino is done beating down the man," Cal retorted.

Elodie shook her head as a grin spread across her face. She enjoyed sparring with Cal like a brother and sister perpetually annoyed with one another.

"Grant, you're coming into the office tomorrow to look at the church financial records, right?" Ava got down to business.

"Your wish is my command," Grant responded without looking up from scratching Mercy behind her ears, the dog sprawled across his feet.

"Well, if that's the case, when you're done reviewing the books, how about you paint my office, too? It still needs it. All the windows are filthy, too," Ava suggested.

"I amend my previous answer to a simple 'yes.' I'll be at the church tomorrow afternoon to see if Grace Fellowship Church is sinking or swimming financially," Grant corrected himself, still focused on the dog.

"Rats!" Ava muttered at the lost opportunity to get her office painted and windows washed.

"So, I was thinking we might invite the newlyweds to have dinner with us since Chase and Lovie are back home with Micah," Marie changed the subject.

"They'll have Sam and Silas every other weekend," June reminded. "But they'd be welcome, too, wouldn't they? We're kid-friendly."

"I wouldn't mind getting to know dos boys better," Marcus chimed in agreement.

"Has anyone seen Will and Shelby since they've been back?" Ava wondered.

"I waved to Will on his route yesterday, but we didn't get to speak," Cal offered.

"I didn't want to speak to anyone for a week after I got back from our honeymoon. Marcus, do you remember? We came home and found the countertop of our apartment kitchen crawling with brown ants. My sister, Rae Jean, set out a block of Limburger cheese and turned off our air conditioning. The stench was horrific, but those ants about did me in. Our countertop looked like it was alive! We spent an hour killing and cleaning up ant bodies. I was not amused by that practical joke," Ava declared, folding her arms across her chest.

"She was not!" Marcus confirmed, grimacing at the recollection of his wife's fury.

"But we didn't find out it was Rae Jean's doing until we saw her the next week. I was ready to kill whoever it was until she confessed," Ava remembered, then smiled.

"I know you suspected Marie and me, but we only short-sheeted your bed so you couldn't get in it," Elodie recalled and chuckled.

"Oh, the Limburger and ants sound awful," June commiserated.

"But it only took them an hour to clean up. We had to live with our prank for weeks," Cal reminded her.

June nodded and explained: "We got canned by my parents. We gave them the key to our apartment so they could take our wedding gifts to our place while we were away. While they were there, they ravaged cupboards and removed every label from every can we had stocked. Every time I tried to make supper, I'd have to guess what can I thought would have, say kidney beans, if I wanted to make chili. But I might open applesauce instead. It wasn't gross like your prank, Ava. But it was obnoxious and continued for weeks until we used all the cans."

"I got a lot of interesting meals in those early days," Cal recalled, shaking his head.

"Was that the only prank played on you?" Marie asked, leaning forward.

"It was enough, I assure you," Cal shook his head.

"Grant and I had a few, didn't we, Ava and El?" Marie looked directly at the responsible culprits.

"Did we? I guess I only remember the light bulbs," Grant furrowed his bushy brows, trying to remember.

"Well, your mother bore the brunt of them switching the sugar and the salt. Remember she came over to visit and put two teaspoons of salt in her coffee? She spat that mouthful out before digging into her plate of sugared eggs," Marie reminded.

"Oh, yeah," Grant laughed, recollecting his mother's pinched expressions.

"And the eggs were meant to be scrambled, but when I went to crack them in the frying pan, I discovered they'd been hard-boiled."

"That was Elodie's idea!" Ava tattled. "It was a good one, though."

Elodie looked at Ava and bobbed her head enthusiastically in agreement.

"What happened to your light bulbs, Grant?" Cal wondered.

"They didn't work – none of them. So, Marie had me go to the hardware store and buy replacements. When I returned, I discovered the light bulbs had only been loosened in their sockets and didn't need replacing. We didn't buy lightbulbs for years," Grant asserted and rubbed a hand over his bald head.

"You never thanked us for savin' you all that money as the price of lightbulbs increased. You got inventory at the cheaper rate," Elodie needled him with a grin.

"And I won't thank you now!" Grant insisted with a fake smile.

"I, for one, am glad that the pranking-the-newlywed fad seems to have died in the 80s," June confessed. "Lord knows, Shelby and Will had enough to come home to without all that nonsense."

"I guess you're right, June. At the same time, here we are 40-something years later, talking about them and laughing at ourselves," Marie observed.

"By God's grace," Ava smiled. "I still hate Limburger and ants, though."

Chapter Six

At five months pregnant, Mariana was rigorous about eating right and staying hydrated, but she craved gingersnaps like a precocious toddler craves attention. A single box lasted no more than four days in the house, even though Mariana was the only one who ate them. Since Big Mart was right down the street from the car lot, DeShawn made a lunch-break run to the store, dashing between raindrops into the store and making a beeline for the cookie section, his mind already on his next errand to the post office.

DeShawn hurried past several other shoppers in the snack food aisle and reached to grab a box of gingersnaps from the top shelf, over the shoulder of a senior woman reading the nutritional information on a box of vanilla wafers.

"Agggh!" Christine Williams let out an involuntary screech when she looked up and recognized the large man raising a muscular arm above her head.

Startled himself, DeShawn clutched the box of cookies to his chest at the sound of her shriek.

"The Felon!" Christine identified DeShawn with the dispersion, although she certainly knew his name. She took a step backward and continued with volume, grabbing the attention of the other customers in the aisle.

"Have I not made myself clear you are to keep your distance from me?

It's not enough that you threaten me in my neighborhood and church; now you accost me in the grocery store? I have witnesses!" she extended her arm and waved it toward the gawking customers.

"I apologize for frightening you, Mrs. Williams. I didn't see it was you because your head was bent down," DeShawn attempted to de-escalate the situation as he took several backward steps. "May God bless you with His grace and favor," he concluded and hurried away.

One of the on-lookers, a lanky, rumpled gentleman with a full head of wavy gray hair, noted the dramatic exchange with interest. He watched from a distance as the attractive but agitated senior woman recovered her nerves with a deep breath, added the box of vanilla wafers to the contents of her shopping cart, and walked to a checkout lane.

Curious, he positioned himself in the next checkout lane and strained to hear the old woman's conversation with the cashier. He was rewarded with Christine's diatribe regarding the events in the cookie aisle and the cause of her distress: the man was a murderer who now lived across the street from her.

Payment completed, Christine demanded and received assistance getting her groceries to her vehicle. She opened an umbrella and walked in front of the young woman pushing her grocery cart, leading the way to her Mercedes through the drizzling rain. With her sights set on her vehicle and not on the pavement, Christine landed a foot on a lost receipt adhered to the wet asphalt and slipped on it, falling to the ground in an awkward split.

"Are you alright, mam?" the store employee worried over Christine.

The breath knocked out of her, Christine didn't answer but wore a pained expression. The young woman looked around for help and, seeing none, said to Christine: "I'm going to call an ambulance. Be right back."

As she hurried back toward the store, a gust of wind took the umbrella Christine had dropped and flung it after the woman, nearly hitting her in the back. With the umbrella out of her reach, Christine sat miserably on the pavement, getting soaked as she waited for help.

The lanky older man saw Christine's fall from the shelter of the store's cart corral entrance and made no move to offer help. He did, however, wait and watch as the ambulance arrived and carried her away. And then a smile spread across his stubbled face.

Eric Hall, smartly dressed for court earlier that morning, helped his aunt maneuver from his car in the side driveway to her couch in the living room and considered his duty fulfilled. "I hope you heal quickly and feel better soon, Aunt Christine. I had better get back to the office. Dad and I will get your Mercedes from Big Mart and bring it back here either this evening or tomorrow," Eric dismissed himself, walking toward the door and speaking over his shoulder before his imperious aunt required further favors.

The emergency room papers stuffed in Christine's purse stated she had suffered a sprained ankle and strained groin muscle. Nothing broken. She came home with a walking boot, a cane for support, and a bottle of pain pills she would never ingest for fear of becoming addicted. Christine hadn't followed her mother's example of rigorous dietary discipline her entire life to succumb to pills this late in the game. Besides, she knew from her half-brothers' teenage weakness where that road led.

Christine listened as her nephew tromped through the kitchen and pulled the back door closed behind him harder than necessary, indicating his annoyance at the interruption to his day. After she heard him speed down Cedar Street in his Audi, she released the tension gathered in her shoulders and assessed her situation.

The clothes she wore were still damp, and she judged them ruined by the ignorance of the hospital staff, who balled them up in a bag after directing her to don a hospital gown for her x-rays. Christine had no choice but to put them back on when she was released.

As she sat on her couch in sticky slacks, Christine thought about the treasured laminated card in her sweater pocket and reached for it. Mishandling wrinkled it, and the damp warped it, but it was still completely legible.

I heard about the destruction of your flowers. I hope these poor substitutes will comfort you, not because they replace what you've lost, but because they come from someone who loves you and cares. With kind regards, LYE.

Christine did her best to press it smooth with her hands until she thought to wonder about the couch beneath her. She leaned on the cane and stood, aggravated to see a discolored spot on the white fabric. Her lips tightened, and she knew she'd have to change clothes. Upstairs. She turned and looked at the sweeping staircase and wanted to curse.

Afraid of falling backward, it took her six minutes to climb the staircase, which normally took less than a single minute. Once Christine made it to her bedroom, she sat on a chaise and grumbled as she unfastened the walking boot's Velcro straps, hoping she'd remember how to put it back on once she shed her soggy clothes. She dressed in the nightgown and robe draped at the bottom of her bed, sat back in the chaise as another round of rain beat on the roof, and felt her stomach growl with hunger. It was dinner time, and she'd missed lunch.

To eat, she'd have to put the boot on, maneuver down the staircase, and scavenge what she could since her groceries were in the trunk of her car at Big Mart. It was too much to undertake, she decided. Christine pulled a throw blanket from the back of the chaise across her legs and spent a miserable, fitful night in the chair meant for lounging, not sleeping.

Chapter Seven

The lanky gray-haired man, who had witnessed Christine Williams' Big Mart dramas two days previous, pulled his beater van in front of her house and gave himself an approving nod of encouragement in its rearview mirror.

"It's showtime, Big Boy!" he cheered himself out loud, exiting his vehicle and walking to the front door.

He pushed the doorbell and waited for the occupant to answer. He knew she would be slow with a gimpy leg. As he waited, he looked across the street at the house where he'd set up tables and chairs in a party tent for a wedding reception just a couple of weeks ago. He'd landed the job with Rental Scapes the very week he'd moved back to Faircourt. But he loathed the know-it-all punks he worked with and was relieved when they fired him two days ago. He felt it was a stroke of luck to be in the store instead of on the job when he discovered more about Christine Williams in 15 minutes than he'd been able to learn about her in the previous two weeks. And what he learned was that she needed him. He rang the doorbell a second time.

"What do you want?" Christine demanded, having made a great effort to get to her front door for what she was sure was some cold sales call.

"Actually," the man turned on both smile and charm, "I thought I might help you. I heard you'd had an accident and some distressing trouble with a neighbor. And, well, it's times like these that family should come together."

"Family?" Christine scoffed incredulously. "You're not…" she trailed off and studied the man's face. There was something familiar there.

"I'm Bradley. Bradley Hall," the man identified himself.

Christine felt the blood drain from her face, and she tightened her grip on her cane to steady herself. She'd only met her half-brother once, when her father, Edward, introduced her and Luther to his new wife and adolescent sons only weeks after their mother's death. Bradley was just a teenager then, and she was blinded by rage at her father. Could this really be one of the half-brothers whose ruin she'd orchestrated? The longer she looked at the man, the more apparent the resemblance to her father and Luther became, including the build, eyes that turned down and looked subtly sad, and the wavy Hall hairline.

"I'd heard you and your brother moved out of state," Christine spoke at last. She made no move to welcome him inside.

"California – not long after high school. But Brooks passed three years ago – heart attack," Bradley informed her.

"Oh," Christine responded to the latter information, sparing insincere condolences.

"I decided to come back home to Faircourt. I grew up here, like you, and since none of us are getting any younger, I'd like to end where I began," Bradley was trying desperately to connect and build sympathy. "Then I learned about your terrible accident and that you have a murderer living too close for comfort. So, I thought I'd come by and see if I could help my sister since you're all alone."

"What makes you believe I'm all alone?" Christine retorted, placing her cane between them.

"You're not? Well, that's certainly a relief to me. I'll be on my way then. I just wanted to make sure you had everything you needed and were safe," Bradley bluffed and turned to go.

"Wait!" Christine called out once he'd taken the first step off her porch. She wasn't used to anyone being concerned about her well-being and security. "Maybe we should talk a bit more. Would you care to come in?"

Bradley lifted his eyes to the sky as if he had to consider his answer. "Alright," he agreed and looked at his shoes to hide a satisfied smirk before crossing the threshold of Christine's grand home.

Christine caught a whiff of an ancient aftershave brand as he passed her. She glanced back at the shabby van her half-brother had parked in front of her house and wished she'd asked him to move it to the Tamarack Street side of the house before he had entered her home. Too late, she supposed.

"To the left," Christine directed Bradley into the living room as she hobbled behind him in her walking boot.

As she followed, Christine tried to assemble a strategy regarding this bolt from the blue appearance of a person she'd consigned to history. Perhaps Bradley's unexpected reentry into her life could benefit her now. After all these years, the timing seemed fortuitous, if not coincidental. On a practical level, it would be nice to have some help while she was handicapped with a sprained ankle and painful pelvis. She also recalled the night of her fall and how she'd slept, fearful that the rainstorm outside would grow fierce and she'd not be able to get quickly to the security of her basement cot. And then, of course, there was the matter of the felon across the street who seemed bent on terrifying her with sudden approaches.

The big question in Christine's mind was: could she trust Bradley? Her mind raced, trying to sort out any clues as to the extent of his knowledge regarding her patronage of his and his older brother Brooks' drug addiction and inevitable downward spiral. So far, he'd given no hint one way or the other.

They sat across from one another on the matching white sofas separated by a glass-topped coffee table.

"Whatever took you boys to California in the first place?" Christine quizzed.

"Stupidity. Looking for greener pastures than what we had, I guess. But mostly stupidity," Bradley was self-deprecating.

"And what did you do there?"

"Tried getting famous," Bradley laughed at himself. "Hung out with all the wrong people. Got married and divorced a few times and worked at various restaurants on and off. I did nothing to make Dad proud of me like he was of you and Luther. But we have no say about who our parents are, right?"

Christine flinched at the reference to Edward being proud of her, an admiration she did not return. But Bradley did have a point that it wasn't his fault Edward cheated on her mother. And he seemed to give a painfully honest account of his life without recrimination toward her.

"So, how do you imagine you might help me?" Christine inquired directly.

Bradley leaned his body forward. "As you no doubt have observed, my resources are slim. But I'm healthy and I'm family. Why don't you tell me what you need?" he suggested.

Because she thought her present circumstances made her vulnerable to various dangers, because her nephew showed no inclination to do more for her than the bare minimum, and because she wanted to believe this man was sincere, Christine made an uncharacteristically impulsive decision. She offered Bradley the occupancy of a spare bedroom in her house.

Chapter Eight

The tree leaves in Faircourt were just beginning to tinge with color from cooler evening temperatures. Elodie donned a lime green cotton knit sweater for an evening stroll with Bobby down Cedar Street. Since its Spring-time inception, their promenade had developed into a weekly occurrence.

"I don't think I'll ever get over that unlikely friendship," Marie confessed to Grant as they swayed on the porch glider, watching Bobby and El disappear down the street.

"It's not good for a man to be alone," Grant replied, squeezing his wife's hand.

"No. But you know, even though Elodie's not breathing fire in Bobby's face anymore, she won't be unequally yoked again."

"A position I wholeheartedly endorse. However, I understand why Bobby would appreciate female companionship from someone closer to his age than his daughter-in-law. And Bobby seems to have had some civilizing effect on El. She's nicer to him than she is to me," Grant complained.

Marie laughed. "After 45 years, you're like a brother to her. She doesn't have to be new-friend nice to you!"

"Well, she should treat her brother better than a new friend; that's all I'm saying," Grant griped.

"Excuse me. Didn't Elodie save you from choking to death last year?

She literally saved your life!"

"She busted my ribs, though. Remember?"

"See? You have your own mean streak when it comes to Elodie. It's rather petty to bring up two broken ribs when the alternative was death, don't you think? Why would you say that?" Marie challenged.

Grant let go of Marie's hand and scowled. "I tried to thank her for something recently and told her I could hug her for it. She walked away and said: 'Don't ever do that!'" Grant impersonated Elodie's voice unflatteringly.

"And it hurt your feelings?" Marie asked, though it was a statement. "So why didn't you tell her she hurt your feelings?"

"I wouldn't tell Elodie Ford she hurt my feelings for the same reason I wouldn't give an ax-murderer a blade sharpener. They'd just use it against you and finish you off," Grant scoffed.

"So, you're scared of her?" Marie summarized with a smirk.

"No! Well, maybe a little," Grant conceded.

"Elodie is not a hugger, if it makes you feel any better. She was probably just making sure you were aware. Really, dear, haven't you picked that up by now? I can make her run away just by threatening to hug her."

"Ha! You don't say? Apparently, I did that inadvertently. Now that I know its effect, I'll save this nugget of information for a rainy day," Grant chuckled.

"With knowledge comes responsibility. Use it wisely," Marie cautioned with a smile and reached to reclaim her husband's hand. "Speaking of knowledge and responsibility," she changed the subject, "how was your first-pass look at the church's financial records? Did ole Nelly Sullivan properly maintain them, or will you be auditing and overhauling?"

Grant lowered his head and shook it from side to side. "It's great for the church to have volunteer help when the volunteers have the appropriate level of ability. I'm afraid Mrs. Sullivan had more of a servant's heart than familiarity with 501c3 accounting procedures and controls.

It'll take some time, but I'll get it sorted out. That is, if I can get my hands on the invoices and receipts that I need to do a proper audit. Ava said they aren't in either Jonathan or her office, and she didn't know of any closet in the church building where they might be squirreled away. I'm guessing Mrs. Sullivan kept everything at her house. I'll ask her when I see her on Sunday. And speaking of Sunday," Grant took a turn changing the subject. "What's your lesson for the ladies' class this week?"

"First Samuel chapter 25 - Abigail and Nabal," Marie answered brightly.

"Hmm," Grant tried to recall the scene. "Is Nabal that fool who refused to feed David and the men who were guarding his flocks, and his wife bailed him out before David killed him?"

"The very same."

"Oh, boy! You ladies will have a real man-bashing session over that idiot," Grant snickered.

Marie released her husband's hand, pressed her foot against the porch floor to stop the glider, and turned toward Grant.

"Is that what you imagine we'll do? Man-bash? I hate to disappoint you, but the lesson focuses on Abigail, not Nabal. I intend to highlight creation order and complementarian roles in marriage. But I plan to guide our discussion toward acknowledging that there are instances where, in our role as "helper," we must not become an enabler of sin. There's at least one woman in our class – who shall be nameless – that, in the name of being a submissive wife, enables her husband to sin. What's more, she's following him into that sin."

"Oh," Grant responded.

"So, tell me your thoughts on the subject. Do you agree a husband is not the ultimate head of his wife but that Christ is her ultimate head? And if a man leads his wife into sin, she is right to resist him?" Marie pressed.

"Of course. I'm sorry, but I can't help that my mind is running through a mental list of the women in your class. They're all mature, godly women – every one of them. So why would a godly woman allow her husband to lead her into sin?"

Marie shifted her gaze from Grant to the rustling leaves of the magnolia tree in the yard. "I've thought about that question, too. The short answer is idolatry."

"Idolatry?" Grant raised his eyebrows.

"A timid and insecure woman's worst fear is that her husband would leave her. If that happens, she loses not only her financial support but also her reputation is tainted as a divorced woman. So, when it comes to choosing between being wholly obedient to God's commands or maintaining her security and image, she chooses the latter - which is idolatry. She'll justify it by telling herself she's being a submissive wife, but that spiritual smoke fools neither God nor anyone with an ounce of discernment. I'm hoping ole Abigail will be an example and an inspiration to this woman in my class, and she'll see that God can make wonderful things happen when we're willing to step up and stop enabling destructive behavior and sin."

"Do you think this woman will recognize herself in the discussion?" Grant wondered.

"That's above my pay grade. I can only present the Scripture and discuss applications. It's the Holy Spirit's job to open eyes and strengthen hearts to obey Him," Marie affirmed with conviction.

Chapter Nine

Attracted by the possibility he might pounce upon a dropped morsel of snack food, Rover scouted for Mercy before sauntering through the open overhead door of the Garage Cave. He'd been run off by the dog before and did not wish to make an embarrassing habit of it. The old cat, feeling secure, stretched out under Cal's workbench.

It was nearly a packed house at game night with Cal, Grant, Marcus, Bobby, Will, and Micah in attendance. Marcus had tried to round them up to two tables of four players by inviting DeShawn and Jonathan Jefferson to join them, but both declined, saying they couldn't commit to the weekly Friday evening men's gatherings because of family commitments. It was understandable, though regrettable. The senior and middle-aged men appreciated the spunk and hilarity of the "youth contingent," as they referred to DeShawn and Jonathan.

"What you got in that bag?" Bobby inquired of Will as he nodded toward the brown grocery sack Will had placed on Cal's stacked pile of scrap wood.

Will jumped from his seat to retrieve the bag and pulled out a red, white, and blue box with a yellow banner across its top that said "Family Pack."

"Ding Dongs!" Will exclaimed. "I had to hide these from Lovie. Your kid comes over to my house and goes right for the cupboard where she knows we keep these," Will chided Micah.

"That's because Ding Dongs are little girly food," Bobby sniffed and turned up his nose.

Micah laughed out loud and slapped Bobby on his shoulder. "Exactly right!" he agreed.

Will, embarrassed, returned the box to the bag.

"Wait a minute!" Grant interjected. "I'll take a few of those. Ding Dongs are only for men secure in their masculinity."

"I believe the wedding cake at the Marriage Supper of the Lamb will be a giant Ding Dong because there's nothing better than chocolate cake with a creamy filling covered in a delicate chocolate shell. It cannot be improved," Cal stated confidently. "Also, I happen to be secure in my masculinity." He chuckled and stretched out his arm to give Grant a fist bump.

Encouraged by the support of Grant and Cal, Will whipped the box from the bag with dramatic flair.

"Marcus, what's your position on Ding Dongs? We have three in favor and two opposed," Bobby was angling to split the opinion evenly.

Marcus cleared his throat. "All I'm going to say is dat I'm secure in my masculinity."

"Awwww," a chorus of complaints rang out from the other men who wanted a commitment one way or the other.

"Man-up and choose a side, Marcus!" Will admonished as he opened the box.

Marcus shook his head from side to side. "I won't be bullied."

Grant reached over to the open box in Will's hand and grabbed a cake.

"Fine," Grant said as he extended the treat to Marcus. "But would you eat one if it were offered to you?"

A smile spread across Marcus' face. He accepted the Ding Dong and began unwrapping it.

"Awwww," Bobby and Micah groaned again in unison.

"I didn't figure you for a girly food man," Bobby mocked, dismissively flinging a hand through the air.

"You never really know somebody till you find out their stance on Ding Dongs," Micah wagged his head, feigning dejection.

Will set the box on the card table, and Grant and Cal helped themselves, each grabbing two cakes.

"Who wants to hear my news?" Will wondered aloud.

"Shelby's pregnant!" Bobby guessed since he was, at present, preoccupied with Mariana's pregnancy.

"They've only been married a week," Cal scoffed.

"Nearly a month," Will corrected. "But no, it's not baby news. Well, maybe a baby of an entirely different sort."

His male audience raised their eyebrows in anticipation and invitation to divulge the information.

"Shelby and I have put in an offer to purchase Latte Da."

Jaws dropped around the table.

"You're quitting the post office?" Cal reacted.

"Oh, no! We need the health insurance. This will be mainly Shelby's project. Plus, she can still freelance her design work as time allows."

"Well, dat is news! None of us wanted to see dat place disappear from Main Street, including you two, I guess," Marcus offered.

"I'm not exaggerating when I say Shelby cried when I told her it was for sale. It's a very special place to us. So, we went for coffee and got the lowdown on the sale from our friend, Five, who works there and seems to manage the place. She said the business pays its bills, but just. The current owners are looking for something more lucrative and, if they don't find a buyer, plan to liquidate the assets to invest elsewhere," Will explained.

"That's what all of us feared," Micah acknowledged, noticing Grant open his second Ding Dong.

"Well, I've not been a patron of the establishment, but I did question why the owners didn't utilize that upstairs space where you had your rehearsal dinner. You could do better than just paying the bills if you promote that wasted space," Grant suggested before taking a bite.

"That's what we discussed with Five. She also strongly hinted she'd love to rent the upstairs apartment and continue to work for us if we bought the place. The prospect of having a trained barista/waitress would be an enormous asset in helping us along. Lord knows, we've never run a coffee shop, and there'd be a learning curve," Will admitted.

Micah absent-mindedly licked his lips as he watched Grant and Cal eat their pre-packaged cakes.

"I wish you every success in your endeavor, and Junie and I will make regular visits," Cal encouraged.

Will raked a hand through his short brown hair. "We only made the offer yesterday and haven't heard if it's been accepted. It could be they have more than one. But if it's the Lord's will for us to have it, we will."

His self-control drained, Micah lunged to grab a Ding Dong from the open box on the card table and, opening its wrapper, confessed: "Okay, so I like them as much as Lovie. I'm also secure with my masculinity."

The other guys laughed, except Bobby.

"Hmm. The cheese stands alone, then. You know, there's masculinity in protesting counterfeit cakes, too," Bobby defended himself with a smug grin.

Chapter Ten

"When you asked us to come with you to Eggleston's farm to pick up a few pumpkins, I imagined it would be three or four, not twenty-four," Elodie grumbled as she passed Marie on her fourth trip to retrieve a pumpkin from Ava's van, parked in the driveway for unloading.

Marie shrugged her shoulders and gave a sheepish grin.

"Pumpkins have gotten so expensive. I can understand Marie not wanting to pass on Edith's generous offer to take as many as she wanted. The cornstalk sheaves were a bonus, too," June offered to support Marie's efforts to adorn their front porch for the season.

"Our porch steps are going to look like a Fall festival!" Ava gushed.

Ava had over-wintered six crimson mums purchased for last year's Fall porch décor in a corner of the garden and repotted them in their original pots several weeks ago. They were nearly at their peak – lush and laden with popping blood-red buds.

"I'll be right back!" Marie shouted over her shoulder to the ladies still unloading pumpkins.

She went to the garage and returned with two large bags that taxed her ability not to drag them on the ground. One was white and printed with the Dollar Town logo; the other was a large black leaf bag.

"Finishing touches!" Marie exclaimed as she set the bags on the front walkway. "Now let's put three mums on each side of the steps and the cornstalks as a backdrop against the center pillars."

Elodie and Ava followed the directions and watched Marie pull six mini hay bales from the Dollar Town bag and arrange them to the side of each mum.

"Now, we fill in with the pumpkins!" Marie instructed.

"Any particular way you want that done?" Elodie asked, knowing Marie's nit-picky eye.

"Nope," Marie assured before adding, "Well, better mix up the sizes. Don't put all the largest ones on the bottom or all the smaller ones on the top. And, some go on the bales for height variation."

"Got it. Just random," Elodie noted as she picked up a pumpkin and placed it willy-nilly on a step.

Marie, biting her lip, joined her friends in scattering the pumpkins around the flowers. With that part of the task complete, she opened the black bag and produced several bouquets of silk leaves in fall color and a bag of pine cones she'd collected, with permission, from the backyard of Will and Shelby's rental house across the street. She tucked the silk leaves between pumpkins and instructed Ava, June, and Elodie to sprinkle the pine cones throughout the arrangement.

"Now, for the magic!" Marie declared as she reached back into the Dollar Town bag and produced six solar lights on stakes. "After these charge, they light up like flickering flames."

"Oooo," the ladies marveled together as Marie set three on each side of the arrangement.

"We should add gold glitter to the edges of the pinecones to catch the light," June suggested.

Marie bit her lip again and remained silent.

"That's a great idea!" Ava enthused. "I'll help you, June."

"I refuse to touch glitter," Elodie huffed. "When that mess gets on your skin, it takes weeks of showers to get it all off. People come up to you sayin' 'You got somethin' right there.' And they start pickin' at your body. No! I have nothin' to do with that demon-sparkle anymore."

"Tell us how you really feel about glitter, El," Ava laughed.

"I just told you," Elodie insisted with all seriousness.

"Don't look now," June began in a low voice, "but a man is standing on Christine Williams' porch and looking at us. I think he lives there now or something. That's his van, which is always parked on her side drive."

"Christine's got a boyfriend?" Ava wondered aloud.

At that seemingly impossible suggestion and in disregard of June's request that they not look, Ava, Elodie, and Marie immediately tossed their heads toward the man, who waved casually at the group.

Marie pushed her glasses up the bridge of her nose and focused her sight on the tall, smiling man with a full head of wavy gray hair while June timidly returned the man's gesture of greeting.

"I know him," Marie whispered. "Rather, I've seen him before. He was with the crew from Rental Scapes, who put up the tent for Shelby's reception. I talked to him."

"He's not walkin' over here to introduce himself, which is a great relief," Elodie muttered.

"We should get back to our own business," Ava advised and turned away.

Marie followed Ava's lead and took a few steps toward their porch, Elodie and June right behind her.

"I remember him because his younger co-workers were mean to him. It made me wonder why a guy around our age was doing such heavy manual labor. I think he was new on the job, as if he hadn't put up a tent before. That's why the other guys were mean." Marie was wringing out the details from her memory as the women stood, ostensibly admiring their decorating handiwork. "It's just strange that he's under Christine's roof – as a boyfriend or whatever. Hey!" Marie exclaimed as she recalled another fact. "He asked who lived in that house. And now he's living in it? Are we sure he's living there?"

"We're not sure of anything, just speculating," Ava conceded. "But you could ask Christine Williams since you're such buddies with her."

"Well...it's none...not my business..." Marie stammered.

"Tsk. That's never stopped you before," Elodie remarked.

"We don't know what we don't know. But I'm certain of this: our porch looks like a fall festival. Good job, ladies!" June congratulated them, then continued. "The guys will be looking for something to snack on this evening. Let's help them out and make old-time popcorn balls."

June and Elodie headed into the house while Ava returned her van to its regular parking spot in front of the Tamarack Street garage. Marie picked up the two empty bags from the walkway and checked left, right, and through the front door window to make sure the other ladies couldn't see her. Then, she hurriedly made several modifications to the arrangement of pumpkins on the steps to suit her taste.

"Glitter!" she muttered disdainfully, rolled her eyes, and wadded up the bags.

CHAPTER ELEVEN

"Good mornin' Miss Banana. How's little mama feeling today?" Bobby greeted Mariana as she shuffled into the kitchen.

"Tired," Mariana, dressed for work in navy maternity scrubs, responded and yawned. "I was always a belly sleeper, and I'm having trouble adjusting to sleeping on my side. How do people do that?"

DeShawn, pulling a fruit salad out of the refrigerator, looked at his wife and chuckled. "I love to sleep on my back, but then I snore, and you nudge me to roll over on my stomach. Your pregnancy will last only a few more months, and then you can go back to sleeping on your stomach. But I have to forfeit my preferred sleep position for the rest of our lives!"

Mariana patted her husband's back sympathetically. "Or, we could sleep in separate bedrooms like the European kings and queens used to," she suggested.

"Psssh. That's not going to happen," DeShawn assured and grinned.

Two slices of whole-wheat toast jumped from the toaster, and Bobby buttered them lightly before handing the plate to Mariana. "Here you go – still nice and warm," he beamed at her.

"Thank you, Dad. You spoil me," Mariana returned his smile and sat at the table.

"Today's the big day, right? You'll find out if our baby is a boy or girl at your doctor's appointment?" Bobby asked.

"You want to go with us to find out about 'our' baby?" DeShawn laughed.

"No! No! That's for a husband and wife to do. I'm just…interested or, er…" Bobby was tongue-tied.

"Interested," DeShawn repeated with a chuckle. "That's one way to put it! Dad, were you this crazy when Claire had her babies?"

Bobby pressed the lever on the toaster and tried to recall his daughter's pregnancies. He could not. His forehead furrowed as he realized Claire's pregnancies with Fendi and Prada were a complete blank in his memory.

"I'm having trouble remembering," Bobby said, a familiar anxiety rising.

"When did Claire move to Florida with her husband?" Mariana tried to help him.

"Ah! Before they had the girls! She wasn't here. I don't remember her pregnancies because she was in Florida," Bobby exhaled with relief.

"Okay. So, this is really your first time having a grandbaby up close," DeShawn acknowledged as he set three saucers of fruit salad on the table. "Continue being your crazy self about it then, and enjoy the journey with us!"

Bobby left his station at the toaster and sat with his son and daughter-in-law.

"Am I being crazy? I don't want to make you two crazy if I'm being crazy," Bobby was apologetic.

Mariana placed a hand on her father-in-law's and looked him in the eye. "All new parents should have someone in their corner like you've been in ours – sharing our joy and excitement - and giddy as I don't know what. Your delight delights us. It's just DeShawn's word for delight happens to be 'crazy.' Don't worry, Dad. You're fine. And this baby is already blessed because he or she has a grandfather who loves them so much."

Mariana had the table set and was heating the previous night's spaghetti and meatball leftovers when she heard Bobby's truck pull into the driveway after work.

"He's home! Go get the set we need," she instructed DeShawn, who flew up the stairs to retrieve what she'd requested.

They'd come home together after Mariana's late afternoon obstetrics appointment and agreed to be only slightly cagey about revealing their baby's gender when Bobby, who was sure to ask, did so.

However, unbeknownst to them, Bobby had lectured himself as he drove home from the car lot to be patient and let the kids tell him their news when they were ready.

Bobby walked in the kitchen door as DeShawn entered the kitchen from the hall, his hands stuffed in his pockets.

"Mmmm, smells good. I love spaghetti leftovers, and I know you've got garlic bread in the oven, too," Bobby inhaled the aroma.

"Everything's ready. Grab yourself a glass of water and have a seat. I'll have your plate for you in a minute," Mariana directed. "You too, DeShawn. I've got this."

The men seated themselves at the table, and Mariana placed steaming plates in front of them. Once she'd retrieved her plate, DeShawn gave thanks for their food.

"Lord, we acknowledge that every good and perfect gift comes from You, and we gratefully give thanks for this food before us. Amen."

The prayer was similar to what DeShawn said before other meals on ordinary days. However, this was no ordinary day, and Bobby expected there'd be some acknowledgment of either a son or a daughter. *"Patience!"* he reminded himself.

For their part, DeShawn and Mariana were perplexed that Bobby hadn't asked about his grandchild as soon as he walked through the door.

"You'll be glad to know I sold that Cadillac this afternoon. Got a real good price for her, too," Bobby made conversation.

"Credit application or cash?" DeShawn responded with a mouthful of meatball.

"Credit application. But their score was like 750," Bobby reassured.

DeShawn nodded and kept eating. Bobby and Mariana followed suit. After 15 minutes of conversational silence, dinner was consumed and done.

"Guess I'll start the dishes," DeShawn rose from his seat. "Right after I show you these!"

Unable to hold their news in, DeShawn pulled a pink bootie from each pant pocket and laid them on either side of his father's empty plate.

Bobby grinned with his entire face. "I was trying not to be 'crazy,'" he explained, and then he picked up each tiny knitted sock. "A little girl. We're having a baby girl," he said softly, marveling.

"Better lay it all on him now," DeShawn prodded his wife.

"And we've picked a name for our daughter," Mariana revealed.

Bobby turned his attention from the booties he held to his daughter-in-law.

"You should be the one," Mariana whispered to her husband.

"Her name is Julia," DeShawn said, his voice cracking as he spoke his mother's name.

Bobby's jaw fell, and he was speechless.

"Julia Elena McBride – for both of our mothers," Mariana confirmed.

Bobby pressed the pink socks to his cheeks and, still unable to speak, mouthed the words: "Thank you."

Chapter Twelve

"Hey, Calculator," Elodie greeted her breakfast buddy, fussing with the collar of her purple chenille bathrobe and heading for the coffeepot.

"Mornin' Elevator!" Cal retorted.

"What are you doin'?" Elodie stopped in her tracks, her expression stony.

"I'm going to start calling you random 'El' words," Cal stated, taking a bite of the buttered English muffin on the plate before him.

Elodie looked at him over the top of her glasses. "No, you're not, and I'll tell you why. Because one day you'll try calling me 'elephant,' and I'm gonna knock you out."

Cal smirked and rebutted: "You'll have to catch me first."

"Please. We both know you can't run on those knobby, arthritic knees," Elodie chided and proceeded around the kitchen island to get her coffee. Over the months, Cal's health had strengthened, and so had Elodie's puckish barbs.

The Van Zants and Rennigers paraded into the kitchen, all dressed for the day.

"Good morning, Cal and Elodie," Ava greeted them. "What's for breakfast?"

"Threats of violence," Cal mumbled.

"What's that?" Grant cocked his head to the side, unsure of what he'd heard.

"Ornery Elodie over there said if I called her 'elephant,' she'd knock me out," Cal elaborated in a mocking tone.

Grant and Marcus locked eyes, and both went for their wallets.

"I put $5 on Elodie." Marcus slapped the bill on the kitchen island.

"There's no doubt. My money's on El, too." He tossed a bill on top of Marcus'.

"What is wrong with you guys?" Marie was incredulous. "Why are you being so mean to Cal?"

"He disrespected a woman – called her 'Ornery Elodie.' We don't abide dat," Marcus was matter-of-fact.

"That's right. This is how we handle things in the manhood jungle. Cal understands that," Grant explained.

With a sheepish grin, Cal lowered his head and took his last bite of muffin.

"Oh, brother!" Marie rolled her eyes.

"Marie and I make it a rule never to entangle ourselves in the manhood jungle," Ava excused them from further conversation on the matter.

"You'd think after all these years, I'd learn not to fall into their nonsense traps," Marie lamented, turning toward Ava.

"You haven't had your coffee yet." Ava handed her an excuse and a mug from the counter.

"I'll get your honey, honey," Grant offered in an effort to assuage his wife's annoyance.

Marie accepted the honey bottle, squeezed a tablespoon into her coffee mug, and poured the remains of the coffeepot on top. Then she settled in a seat at the table next to Cal.

"What's everyone up to today?" Marcus asked, placing fresh grounds in the brewing basket.

Cal spoke up quickly. "Micah's got the day off work, so I'm going to show him how to snake his pipes - he's got a tub that won't drain. Since he knows I'll be checking in on him anyway, he's got me teaching him fix-it skills. No idea what my June-bug's up to. Sleepyhead is still in bed."

"After breakfast and gettin' dressed, I have to plan our dinner with Will and Shelby this weekend and make a grocery list for Marie. Then I'm goin' to get my braids re-done and look at baby strollers for Bobby," Elodie informed.

"His legs getting that bad?" Cal couldn't resist being deliberately obtuse.

"The stroller's not for Bobby, wise guy; it's for his new granddaughter. I just offered to do some scoutin' for him," Elodie informed.

"Granddaughter?" Ava and Marie asked in unison.

"Yup. Mariana's havin' a girl. They're gonna call her Julia after De-Shawn's momma," Elodie grinned, pleased to demonstrate her exclusive knowledge.

"Well, that's wonderful!" Marie gushed.

"What would you have said if they were having a boy?" Ava wondered aloud.

"The same. I think all babies are wonderful. I always wished Grant and I had had a daughter, though," Marie confessed.

Grant looked up from preparing his tea. "Should we keep trying?" he asked, eyebrows jumping on his forehead.

"People are trying to eat their breakfast, Grant," Marcus rebuked him.

"I have two daughters I'll sell you at a deep discount," Ava joked as she buttered her toasted English muffin halves. "They're scratch and dent models."

Marcus and Marie made eye contact, acknowledging Ava's progress in accepting the continuing estrangement from her daughters. She'd found a way to poke at it herself instead of merely reacting to accidental pokes from others.

"Ava has recruited me to help her pick tomatoes and green peppers from da garden," Marcus moved the conversation along. "But I have no idea what we're doing wit dem after dat."

"You will be released from your indenture once we get them in the kitchen. I'm just going to chop the peppers and peel and freeze the tomatoes for now. Those plants just won't quit producing – they're thriving on my neglect," Ava groaned.

"Hubby and I are driving out to Nelly Sullivan's place in LaGrange," Marie relayed their plans.

"She says she has a filing cabinet of 26 years of Grace Fellowship Church's financial records. We're relocating them back to the church, and I'll get rid of what I can after I take a look-see through what she's got," Grant explained with subtle lament.

"Do you need to go with Grant, Marie? You could have a ton of fun processing vegetables with your old friend, Ava, instead," Ava pasted on an artificial grin, trying to persuade her.

"You want me to send my hunky husband to another woman's home unchaperoned?" Marie rebutted.

"Ms. Sullivan's eyes aren't good. He's safe," Elodie assured. "But I'm beginnin' to wonder about your eyesight, Marie."

Cal snorted, trying to stifle a laugh.

"Or send California there with Grant," Elodie suggested.

"Nelly Sullivan is 90 years old!" Cal responded in defense of being recommended as a travel partner.

"84," Grant corrected. "But I'm pleased my wife is concerned she might present herself as a rival for my affections."

"In the interest of full disclosure, Nelly did promise to show me her quilt collection, which I hear is a marvel of handiwork. I can't pass that up. But I promise I'll keep one eye on her to make sure she's not preparing to fling herself on your neck," Marie grinned.

Marcus piped up: "Grant, you'll be back by tree o'clock, right? My television station changed dere schedule, and now dat's when Da Addams Family starts. Cal says dat's a good show."

"A capital idea!" Grant raised an index finger in the air like Gomez Addams.

Marcus looked confused.

"You'll get it after you've watched the show for a while," Cal laughed.

Chapter Thirteen

Mercy announced the guest's arrival on the front porch with three chipper barks and waddled to the front door to greet the visitors.

"Welcome, neighbors!" Marie beckoned them into the main hallway.

Shelby, wearing jean capris and a short-sleeved blouse with tiny blue flowers on a background of army green, and Will, in khaki shorts and a black golf shirt, stepped through the doorway.

"We'll never turn down a good meal with good friends," Will responded, then bent to give Mercy a scratch behind her ears. "This girl looks fat and happy," he noted.

"She's living her best life in this house. I'm afraid we all spoil her with treats," Marie admitted. "Come on back to the kitchen. Elodie and Ava are still putting the final touches on the main course, but we have an appetizer on the island to nibble on."

The couple followed Marie into the kitchen, where they were greeted by the rest of the household, who, aside from Elodie and Ava, were already digging into crackers, cream cheese, and spicy red pepper jelly.

"Will, you have to try dis jelly dat June made – guaranteed to change your life!" Marcus raved. He handed Will a cracker spread with whipped cream cheese, topped with a half teaspoon of the jelly.

Will took a bite and moaned. "My mouth is transported to paradise," he mumbled while chewing.

"See. Dat's what I'm talking about!" Marcus assembled another cracker and handed it to Shelby.

After swallowing the last bit, Shelby rendered her verdict: "I'm not usually one for spicy, but the cream cheese tempers the heat. I like it! Very flavorful."

"I'll take another." Will moved to prepare himself seconds. "Grant, Cal, don't you guys like this stuff?" he wondered aloud to the guys standing near the kitchen table.

"Oh, we do. We've each had four or five before you got here," Cal answered. "You're lucky there's any left."

"We're all set here. Let's shift into the dinin' room," Elodie instructed, leading the way with a large steaming bowl of beef tips and gravy, which she carried with quilted potholders.

Ava followed with a serving bowl of garlic mashed potatoes, June carried roasted asparagus, and Marie transported a platter of warm yeast rolls.

"Let's give thanks," Grant suggested when they gathered around the dining table.

"Lord God, we give You thanks and praise for the blessing of Will and Shelby – our friends, neighbors, and brother and sister in Christ. May our time together this evening be mutually edifying and encouraging, and may You be honored in our conversation. Thank You for the food before us and the senses You gave us to enjoy these and all Your good gifts. In Jesus' name we pray, amen."

Once everyone's plate was filled, Marie broached the subject she was eager to explore with their guests.

"We think we have a new neighbor at Christine Williams' house. Have you met him?" Marie looked to Will for a reply, supposing he'd be the more likely to know something since he delivered everyone's mail.

Shelby spoke up instead. "I met him the other day when he wandered over to our backyard. Friendly guy. Chatty, actually. His name is Bradley, and he recently moved here from California."

"Bradley," Marie repeated, committing it to memory. "A friend of hers?" Marie pushed, fishing for any available information.

"Brother. He said he was her brother," Shelby recalled.

"Really?" Marie's eyebrows elevated in reflex and then knit in confusion as she pieced this information with what she already knew about the familiar man. *"Why would Christine's brother have asked who lived in the house across the street if he knew the answer? Or, did he truly not know where his sister lived? Did he no longer need the job with Rental Scapes now that he'd moved in with her? He always seemed to be at home."* Something about the situation seemed odd to Marie, but she'd keep her suspicions to herself. Grant always said speculation was a cousin to gossip.

When her mind returned to the conversation around the table, Marie heard Will announce: "Our offer to purchase Latte Da was accepted. We're looking to close on it in three to four weeks if the building inspection goes well, and the loan goes through. It all happened so fast, we didn't have time for pre-approval."

"I understand the place is near and dear to your hearts, but will you enjoy the actual business end of it, Shelby? I hear this is to be primarily your project," Ava inquired.

"It's a little late now to ask that. If I'd known about this earlier, I could have put Shelby through my think-it-through paces," Elodie declared.

"Elodie, as helpful as your 'think-it-through paces' were for our household discussion about buying Latte Da, Will and Shelby are grown adults who don't need our interference," Grant admonished with a wink to blunt the edge.

"You guys considered buying it?" Shelby's eyes lit up with interest.

"For two entire minutes," Marie affirmed. "We couldn't help ourselves. We imagined what a fun project it would be and the opportunities for ministry. But then Elodie reminded us it costs money, time, and energy we don't have. It belongs in the hands of a younger generation if it's to last more than a few weeks."

"Well, if you still think it'll be a fun project after we own it, we could use any suggestions or help you're willing to offer!" Shelby was quick with the invitation.

"Will you be keeping the name Latte Da?" June wondered aloud.

"We will. After we made an offer, that was our next decision," Will responded as he buttered a roll.

"We'll do everyting we can to support you," Marcus encouraged.

"Will you be open on Sundays?" Cal asked pointedly.

"No," Shelby answered definitively. "7 AM to 4 PM, Monday through Saturday, and 6 PM through 9 PM added on Friday and Saturday evenings for date nights. We'll scuttle Sunday hours, but not date night hours. After all, our first date was at Latte Da."

Ava clapped her hands together. "I'm so excited for you! I'm going to pray the Lord makes your path straight until the day you close the deal. I'm sure you'll make it a success."

Will and Shelby beamed at one another, confirmed by believers they respected in this leap of faith.

CHAPTER FOURTEEN

"We got a headwind blowing this morning!" Grant shouted from mid-pack of the group walking to church against frequent cool gusts.

"October is coming in like it's running from the police," DeShawn shouted from the rear.

Grant, Marie, Elodie, Shelby, Will, Marcus, Ava, Mariana, and Chase turned their heads toward him.

"What? I'm not allowed to joke about the police?" DeShawn scanned the faces before him, stuffing his hands in his pockets.

"Oh, you're allowed to; we just didn't expect you to," Will admitted.

DeShawn stopped in his tracks, and the others followed suit, prepared to listen.

"I can understand that, but here's what I'd like you all to understand. My past will not be the elephant in the room I spend the rest of my life pretending is not there. I don't need to dwell on it, but I'm not going to avoid anything that might refer to it, either. I think that would rob God of the glory He's due for saving and sanctifying me through my years in prison. Jesus took my sin, and he took my shame, too. I don't have to carry either of them. And guess what? We're the same. You all have sin and shame in your past that you don't have to carry either. I may not be privy to exactly what that sin is, like you do mine, but I know you got it. So, anyway, I might mention the police or prison in some context or another in the future. Don't freak out on me."

Mariana squeezed her husband's hand and smiled up at him.

"I guess we can go home since we've had church on the sidewalk," Marie ventured in response.

DeShawn laughed. "Pastor Jonathan will suspect there's been a neighborhood plague if we all don't show up. Besides, you and Will have classes to teach. Better keep going on."

The group resumed their walk, and Chase nudged Mariana to walk next to DeShawn.

"What if our sin isn't all in our past?' Chase asked DeShawn in a low voice, his eyes focused on the sidewalk before him. "I mean, what if there's sin that's hard to let go of?"

DeShawn lowered his voice to the boy's identical level. "Is this a hypothetical question, or is there a sin you can't let go of?"

Chase opened his mouth in surprise at the directness of the question, but he gave no immediate reply.

"There are two things you need to remember. One, even the best Christian sins every day. I do, you do, Pastor Jonathan does because we all are still in the flesh and we won't be perfected until we reach heaven. The Bible says if we say we have no sin, we lie. But the Bible also says that God's mercies are new every morning. We just have to keep repenting of our sins to restore our fellowship with God. Second, if you're talking about a besetting sin – that's something that happens regularly – then the first thing you need to do is shine a light on it. Tell someone you trust. Satan loves for us to keep our sin in the dark because he can magnify it there and then accuse us about it. But if we shine a light on it, it takes away much of his power because it's no longer a secret. Let me ask you something: do you love this sin or hate it?"

"Hate it," Chase responded quickly.

"Good!" DeShawn answered. "When you're ready, shine that light."

"If you think I preached a sermon on the walk to church, y'all will be in for a real treat next month when you get to hear me preach a sermon for real," DeShawn announced to his neighbors as they headed to their homes. "Pastor Jefferson has asked me to fill in for him when his family goes to visit old seminary friends in Atlanta over Fall Break."

"Is dat so?" Marcus tried to hide hurt feelings that he'd not been asked.

"He should have asked you!" DeShawn thoughtfully consoled.

"Dat's right!" Marcus agreed but said instead, "Well, show us what you got, son!"

"I will!" DeShawn beamed, looking forward to the opportunity and challenge.

"How was the men's Sunday School class today?" Marie turned to make conversation with her husband.

"A little awkward if you want the truth," Grant scrunched his entire face to emphasize his feelings.

"Was Will not up to snuff? He's a newlywed, so cut him some slack."

"Had nothing to do with Will. It was Joe Jacobs. He's running for state representative in an election over a year away, but you'd think it was next month. We were treated to a campaign speech that took at least ten minutes of the class. Don't get me wrong, I'm glad he's getting involved. It just wasn't the time or the place. It made me uncomfortable and some of the other guys, too."

Marie's thoughts went back to the time a neighbor ran for elected office when she was a young teen. The candidate recruited and paid her and her sister to hang door tags printed with his name and platform positions on front doors in their district. It was only two Saturdays of work, but they made the girl, Marie, feel appreciated and valued for her contribution to the important effort. They were pleasant memories from a childhood with few of that type.

"Marie! Are you listening at all?" Grant asked, annoyed by her silence.

"I might like to help Joe Jacobs with his campaign," Marie answered at last.

"What?" Grant was startled by the perceived left-field response.

"I support Joe's conservative positions, and I think it would be exciting to be involved in helping him win a seat in the legislature."

"You've not shown any interest in politics before," Grant challenged.

"It's a new day! Maybe if I like it, I might run for office myself some time," Marie suggested for the shock value.

"You would not!" Grant called her bluff.

Marie smiled. Her husband knew her well. "Probably not. But I am serious about helping Joe Jacobs."

"How can you help him?" Grant asked, not meaning to be condescending or rude, just curious.

"I'm not sure. Sometimes, candidates just need a warm body to place door-hanger flyers on houses. There's no real expertise required for that."

"Yeah, I guess," Grant conceded. "You'd have to be conscious of your surroundings and safety. Faircourt is a safe town, but we don't know much about LaGrange."

"I will," Marie promised, smiling to herself that Grant was now picturing her doing the thing she wanted after she'd teased she might take it further. She knew her husband well, too.

CHAPTER FIFTEEN

Christine had missed two weeks at Grace Fellowship Church, constrained by sitting discomfort and the ungainly walking boot. She made her triumphal return to the front row pew, where she resumed casting disapproving scowls at Pastor Jefferson whenever a sermon point touched an exposed spiritual nerve.

For his part, Jonathan Jefferson saw his sermons as a sort of tomahawk reflex hammer and Mrs. William's glowering reactions as twinges of comprehension. They encouraged him, and the more she grimaced, the better he gauged his sermon.

After what she considered an especially tedious sermon on storing spiritual treasure in heaven, Christine returned home from church to a delightful surprise: an elegant lunch prepared by her half-brother.

Bradley had taken two place settings of china from the mahogany hutch and set them at the never-used dining room table. He'd filled crystal glasses with sparkling water and brought out the good silverware.

"What have we here?" Christine halted at the dining room entrance when she glimpsed Bradley standing next to the table.

"Croque monsieur toast points and tomato basil bisque. Your lunch is served," Bradley beamed.

"Heavens!" Christine exclaimed, pleased by the effort she assumed must have taken all morning to create. "Your restaurant experience must have been in Michelin-star establishments."

"I can neither confirm nor deny," Bradley evaded with a grin. "Have a seat, madam." He pulled out the chair at the head of the table to seat his sister.

Once she was settled, he offered an apology. "I'm sorry; there's no napkin. I didn't see any table linens in the hutch, and I didn't want to go rummaging through your house."

"Oh, they're in the butler's pantry – second drawer from the top on the right," Christine informed him.

"I'll be right back, then." Bradley went to retrieve the napkins. He returned momentarily with two white linen napkins, tinged amber at the folds from age and neglect.

"Oh, dear," Christine lamented in embarrassment. "I'm afraid these haven't seen the light of day in quite some time."

"A good soak in detergent, borax, and washing soda will take those stains out and get them looking brand new," Bradley assured.

"Really? I'll instruct the maid service to add that to this week's tasks."

"Oh, that's not necessary. I don't mind doing it. I know how, and I need to earn my keep. Besides, I'm here to help you, remember? Now, don't give the napkins another thought. Just enjoy your lunch while it's still hot."

Christine enjoyed the meal, especially the bisque. The toast points with their bechamel sauce and gruyere cheese were a bit rich for her, but she finished one and complimented the chef.

"You've outdone yourself!" Christine lauded, sitting back and placing her arms on the captain's chair armrests.

"I'm glad you enjoyed it. Now, why don't you relax while I clean up these few dishes?" Bradley suggested.

"I'll do as you say. Thank you." Christine rose and retreated to her bedroom.

Bradley expertly piled the china, crystal, silverware, and napkins in his arms to get them all to the kitchen in a single trip. His busboy experience had not been for nothing. Tossing the napkins to a side counter, he hand-washed the dishes and returned them to the dining room cabinet. And though it was only a third full, Bradley snatched the trash bag from the kitchen can and took it outside to the garbage bin. He didn't want his sister to see the box of pre-made tomato soup he'd spilled a bit of spice into and renamed "bisque," or the envelope of bechamel sauce mix that a child could make.

Bradley told Christine the truth when he said he'd worked in California restaurants, but not in the manner or establishments which his sister assumed. He had, however, seen a few tricks in the places he'd been. It took two long weeks before his sister would leave the house so he could perform those tricks – leading her to believe he'd been laboring long in the kitchen instead of doing the very thing he claimed he was loath to do: rummaging through her house.

Upstairs, Christine kicked off her crocodile loafers and removed a heavy gold bangle bracelet, placing it in the jewelry box on top of the chest of drawers that long ago held her Clarkson's clothing. Sated and sleepy from the filling lunch, she stretched out on the chaise lounge and pulled a light throw blanket to her chest.

"This is working out well," Christine mused to herself regarding the short time her half-brother had been under her roof and subsidy. She still made her own breakfasts of toast and hard-boiled egg because Bradley slept in until around 10 am most mornings. But he fixed her preferred lunch salad with lean protein daily and brought her tea and two short-bread cookies each evening.

One afternoon, early on, Bradley suggested they play Scrabble after recalling an ancient memory of their father boasting to Margie, his mother, what a champ his daughter was at the game. Christine couldn't remember the last time she'd played a game with anyone and found she enjoyed it, especially since her skills had not suffered from disuse. She beat Bradley handily, and they developed the habit of playing two or three times a week. Christine was pleased with the consistency of her victories in these meaningless contests and thought the mental stimulation was a benefit.

Christine noticed she was sleeping better and sounder. The creaking sounds the old house sometimes made didn't unsettle her with suspicions of an intruder – perhaps the felon right across the street. And though there'd been no storms in the past few weeks to chase her to the basement for security, she felt that if one came, she might not need to flee to that miserable cot since there was a man in the house.

After recalling the advantages of welcoming her brother into her home, she wondered how different his life might have turned out if she hadn't been responsible for derailing it early on with access to free drugs. Would he, like her brother Luther, have become a respected and financially stable member of Faircourt society? Might he have been a successful restaurateur?

She brushed the intrusive speculations away like a bothersome gnat, resolving to thank God someday that Bradley did not know how she'd orchestrated the demise of his family life in Faircourt. Christine resettled herself on the chaise, feeling her eyes growing heavy. She was about to close them when she noticed something odd about the nightstand directly across the room from where she lay. The drawer wasn't flush, protruding a careless inch from the face boards. She was sure she hadn't left it that way. Or had she?

Chapter Sixteen

"Ava," Grant spoke from the doorway of her church office. "Does Pastor Jefferson have a moment to spare?"

"No appointment?" Ava responded as more of a mild scold than a question since she knew the answer.

"No, but it's important," Grant responded, clutching a folder tightly against his leg.

"Just knock on his door and pop your head in then."

Grant did as Ava instructed, was invited inside Jonathan's office, and closed the door behind him.

"What's up, Grant? Have a seat," Jonathan offered with a welcoming smile, noting his visitor shifting from foot to foot as he stood.

Grant remained standing. "You're aware I've taken over the church accounting from Nelly Sullivan," Grant stated as a fact to introduce the topic of his visit. "Grace Fellowship has a problem. For the past 17 years, we've been paying a company to clean the church's windows."

"What? No one's ever come to clean the windows since I've been the pastor. Just had my 17th-anniversary last month," Jonathan confirmed as the coincidence dawned on him.

"That's the problem. The church has been paying for services we've not received. The annual invoices were for $3,500. Times 17 years, and that's $59,500 we've been ripped off."

Jonathan dropped his head, closed his eyes, and let out a long sigh.

"There's more," Grant added, sitting across from his pastor so he could lower the volume of his voice. "The invoices were paid to Farmer Services. Tom Farmer has been collecting the payments and cashing the checks."

Jonathan stretched back in his chair, lacing his fingers behind his head at the mention of the church's part-time maintenance man.

"In 17 years, the invoice amount never changed. That's what first caught my attention. Nothing costs the same as it did 17 years ago," Grant explained. "In recent years, the invoices didn't even detail the services. I had to dig back to find it was for window cleaning, and I realized something was amiss because the church secretary," he nodded toward Ava's office, "mentioned once or twice that the church windows are filthy. Not something I would have noticed, but it bothers her, and I remembered it."

"He's not only an employee, he's a member," Jonathan said, biting the corner of his lip. "You got the invoices?"

"Right here. Copies of the cashed checks are there, too." Grant slid the folder across the large desk.

"Well, this is going to be messy," Jonathan said as he opened the folder. As he made the statement, Grant understood he wasn't talking about the folder's contents.

"Will you call the police?" Grant wondered.

"I think that depends on how Tom responds. If he's repentant and the deacons agree, we can deal with it ourselves. But as soon as we call the police, given the amount of money involved, it may be out of our hands even if we don't want to press charges."

Grant furrowed his eyebrows. "Aren't you mad?" he challenged his pastor.

"I'm always mad at sin. But it took us 17 years to figure out we've been scammed, so I'm also mad at myself for that. Does Marcus know about this?" Jonathan asked.

"No. Just you and me."

"Hmm. I thought that with all his years in ministry, he might have dealt with something like this. I'd like to ask him."

"That's your call. Will Tom be fired at least?" Grant couldn't hide his contempt for the crime, if not the criminal as well.

"Without a doubt. There must be consequences for theft, not only for Tom's good but as an example to the congregation. They're the ones who were sinned against. However, as Christ's under-shepherd, I bear a responsibility for his soul. In a biblical scenario, Tom would be confronted, and then he'd confess, repent, and accept the consequences of his actions. He would also remain a member of this body, disciplined, but loved as a forgiven child of God."

Grant emitted a reflexive snort. "Never seen it happen. Probably never will."

"Oh, I get it," Jonathan conceded. "To tell you the truth, I've never seen it happen either. I've only been involved in two cases of church discipline since I've been a pastor, and both times, the disciplined person left the church. Broke my heart. In one instance, I think the man's pride was the big factor. He had no desire to hang around with us. The time before that, to our own shame as a church, the person was prayed out the door. Wasn't that spiritual? Too many of us just wanted them gone so we wouldn't have to pick up the pieces. It's much easier to sweep the pieces under the rug of their next church – if they went back to church, that is."

Grant sank in his chair. He knew the latter example was his own in-clination toward Tom and felt convicted by his pastor's godlier, humbler attitude.

"I'm guilty of that," Grant confessed. "Too quick with the tar and feathers. Although if I'm frank, there are still some sins a brother might commit – especially sins against children – where I don't want to hear their confession and repentance. They can tell it to God and be on their way to get help somewhere else. I wouldn't want them anywhere near my kids or grandkids."

"Grant, we should focus on the situation and brother before us and not take a hypothetical rabbit trail. Fair enough?"

Grant pursed his lips and nodded his agreement. "You see what I did there, right? I justified the guilt I had just confessed to by reaching for a straw man to blame. I'm reeking of self-righteousness."

"I saw it," Jonathan chuckled. "Everybody does it, but not everybody has the self-awareness to see it in themselves. That's something you have going for you, Grant, so don't be too hard on yourself. And thank you for taking on the thankless, unpaid task of reviewing and managing the church's financials. I know that discovering this theft was an unpleasant surprise. Let's pray God shows us that biblical church discipline can result in a brother being restored and a church matured for His glory."

"Agreed," Grant affirmed and rose from his seat. "You still want to talk to Marcus about this? I can ask him to call you when I get home."

"Marcus has a wealth of wisdom and experience. I might as well avail myself of it if I want the best possible outcome for Tom and our church body. Tell him I'll be here till five o'clock." Jonathan stood and extended his hand to Grant.

The men shook hands, and Grant departed, stopping in Ava's office to look at the large window she'd complained about.

"I see what you mean. This window is filthy now that I'm looking at it," he remarked.

CHAPTER SEVENTEEN

The sweet melody of *Softly and Tenderly* wafted through the house as June played her mid-morning piano devotions. She'd completed three verses when her reverie was interrupted by Elodie shrieking from the study across the hall.

"This is not happenin'! This is not happenin'! Rennigers! Van Zants! Shermans! Come to the study to see what's happenin'!"

Drawn by the cries of their friend, the summoned couples rushed from their scattered locations in the house. As each arrived, they formed a tight semicircle inside the study doorway, jaws agape at the sight before them.

"Do we do anything?" Ava asked, her hand to her mouth.

"We are not prepared for this!" Marie gasped.

"How did this happen?" Grant, rubbing a hand over his bald head, was stunned.

"Oh, boy!" laughed Cal.

"I just came in here to read," Elodie whined, disappointed her plans were scuttled.

In front of one of the crewelwork rocking chairs, Mercy had given birth to two wriggling puppies and was delivering another.

"Good ting da rug is brown," Marcus stated pragmatically.

"I'm going to get an old towel. She should have that at least," June marched off.

"I feel like we should have known this was coming. How did we not realize?" Ava was genuinely puzzled.

"How did this happen?" Grant repeated himself.

"Well, first you have a girl dog, then you add a boy dog..." Cal attempted an explanation but was cut off by Grant's sharp swat on the arm.

"I mean, *when* did this happen, numbskull?" Grant clarified.

"She ran off that one day. Remember, we had to go pick her up?" Marie reminded.

Grant sighed, loud and long, and rubbed his temples. He understood these puppies would be his responsibility to care for and eventually find homes.

"Dis is da chance you take when you bring home a stray. You don't know if dey've been fixed or not," Marcus reflected.

"Um, um, um. We know this one wasn't," Elodie shook her head and stated the obvious.

June returned with a large blue towel, unfolded it, and carefully put one end under Mercy's hind parts. Then she placed now three tiny puppies on the other end while momma continued to labor.

"Wonder how many she'll have," Marie asked, biting a fingernail.

"Tell me when it's over. I'm goin' to my room to read. This is enough trauma for one day – and I'm talkin' 'bout mine, not Mercy's." Elodie turned and headed upstairs.

"I'm going back to the piano. Maybe Mercy liked the music, and it helped her," June hypothesized, and was gone.

"Don't think there's anything Marcus and I can do here. Good luck, Grant!" Ava grinned and took her husband's arm as they walked back toward the kitchen.

"What if something goes wrong?" Marie fretted. "We don't know anything about puppies."

"I'll stay with you," Cal offered, sitting in the chair behind the desk.

"I don't claim to be an expert, but we had a few litters when I was a kid. As best as I can recall, the mom pretty much takes care of everything. It'll be fine."

"Thanks, buddy." Grant was reassured by Cal's words and the resumption of June's gentle hymn on the piano.

"There's number four!" Marie observed. "Say, we'd better figure out where we'll put them. They can't stay here."

"How about a corner of the basement? We can block off a section for them and give them an old blanket and newspaper to do their business on," Grant suggested.

"It's pretty cool down there," Marie reminded. "Wait! When they gave us the chickens, the Brewers also threw in some equipment. There's a heat lamp for warming chicks in that stuff in the Garage Cave. It should work for puppies. We could hang it on the wall above them."

"Sounds like a plan to me," Grant agreed.

After dinner, June brought Lovie down to the basement to see Mercy and her puppies.

"Oh, they're so tiny," Lovie cooed and began counting. "One, two, three, four, five, six, seven. There's seven! Only two of them look like Mercy – tan and white. The other five are all black. Do they look like the dad?"

June cleared her throat. "Ah, well, probably. We're not really sure of dad's identity. Mercy kept it a secret from us," she joked to distract the child from serious inquiry.

Lovie shrugged. "How come they all have their eyes closed?"

"Mrs. Renniger looked that up today. Puppies keep their eyes closed for a week or two because the nerves in their eyes need to develop a bit more," June answered confidently.

"People babies aren't like that," Lovie noted, visually examining the seven newborns. "How come that one over there is a lot smaller than the others?" She pointed to a black puppy lying still, away from its siblings.

"That poor one is the runt of the litter. I think it might need more rest than the others. It's not quite as strong."

"You're not going to keep them all, are you?"

"Heaven's no! The dogs would outnumber the people in our house! Mr. Renniger will ensure the puppies go to good homes once they no longer need Mercy."

Lovie took a step closer to the sleeping runt. After a moment, she said, "I don't think it's alive."

"What?" June moved to Lovie's side and noted the puppy's side was not rising and falling. "Okay, time to go! June put her hands on Lovie's shoulders. "It's a school night, and I'd better get you home."

"Remember the dead chicken Uncle Will had to carry out of your coop? He put it in a plastic garbage bag," Lovie recalled bluntly, trying to be helpful.

"Well, let's not think about that. Come on, up the stairs!" June guided her young neighbor.

"Bye, Mercy! Sorry about your puppy," Lovie called over her shoulder with tenderness.

June was distraught as she walked Lovie to her back door by the light of the garage floodlamp. She contemplated how to tell Micah what happened when Lovie patted her arm as they reached the back porch and said: "It's sad about the puppy, but sometimes kids lose their moms, and sometimes moms lose their kids. It just happens. Goodnight, Miss June."

June walked back to her house, tears spilling down her cheeks. The puppy forgotten, she cried about Lovie's tragic loss of her mother and how the child managed her pain without Jesus and without the comfort of reuniting hope. *"It just happens."*

CHAPTER EIGHTEEN

The mood was somber around the office conference table as deacons Earl Eggleston, Lefty Schneider, and Joe Fowler sat with Pastor Jefferson, waiting for Tom Farmer to arrive for their meeting. They'd come half an hour earlier than the agreed-upon 7 PM meeting in order to have time to pray and ask God for humility, discernment, and faithfulness to biblical instruction regarding church discipline. Now, the group noted it was three minutes before seven o'clock.

"Anyone got any TUMS?" Lefty requested, making a sick face.

"Actually, I do." Jonathan jumped up and retrieved a plastic bottle from his desk.

"Pass 'em around," Earl, the group's eldest member, instructed.

The men sat chewing the antacids when Tom walked through the open office door. He didn't know the exact nature of the meeting but assumed it had something to do with his responsibility for the church building.

"Hey, guys!" Tom greeted them jovially, wearing navy shorts and a rumpled gray t-shirt the same shade as his crew cut.

"Hey, Tom! Have a seat," Jonathan directed him to the empty chair at the other end of the table while stealthily setting the container of antacids on the floor and out of sight.

"Tom, what can you tell us about these?" Earl wasted no time. He slid the folder of invoices from Farmer Services in front of Tom.

Tom opened the folder and looked only at the top sheet of paper. His formerly bright expression sagged, and he cast a glance at the doorway he'd just entered as if he'd like to run the other way through it. "I don't know," he answered weakly.

"Your signature on the checks you cashed suggests you do know something about them," Jonathan countered with a steady voice.

Tom's hands began to tremble. "The church kept sending the money!" he responded without thought.

"Oh, you're saying it's our responsibility?" Lefty, sitting up straighter, was indignant.

Jonathan raised his hand to Lefty in silent admonition to remain calm. "The checks were sent in response to the invoices," Jonathan reminded Tom. "The one on top is dated six weeks ago."

Tom nodded once, staring blankly somewhere past his pastor's head.

"Did Nelly Sullivan realize the work wasn't being done? Was she part of this?" Joe Fowler asked, the thought just occurring to him that Tom might not be in it alone.

Tom shook his head. "I guess she wasn't paying attention. I actually cleaned the windows for a couple of years, and Nelly paid those bills – she knew I did the work. But then things changed. I hurt my shoulder and couldn't work much, and we got you for a new pastor and you hired a part-time secretary. Nelly handed over the task of paying the invoices, and your secretary paid them every year, not knowing anything about them. She paid them because Nelly had. When Ava came on, she did the same. By that time, though, the invoices weren't very specific," he admitted, at last looking Jonathan in the eye.

"Yeah, we finally picked up on that," Jonathan agreed.

"Patty doesn't need to know about this, does she? It'll hurt her bad," Tom begged, suddenly animated.

Jonathan surveyed his deacons' faces before responding. He weighed the fact that Tom had confessed, albeit not instantly, against the need for just consequences.

"We won't add insult to injury with any pretense. We expect you'll explain to your wife truthfully why you've lost your position here. It's impossible for you to continue. You've defrauded Grace Fellowship Church of nearly $60,000. But I'm sure Patty will be glad we're handling this matter privately and not involving the police," Jonathan was firm.

Tom looked stricken. "I don't have the money to pay it back. Our Social Security and Patty's job at the florist is all we have to live on now!"

Earl, Lefty, Joe, and Jonathan exchanged glances, unsure where to go from here.

"Give us some time to think about that. You be thinking about it, too. Instead of focusing on what you can't do to repay the congregation you stole from, I'm asking you to consider what you can do," Jonathan began. "I will say this, and I believe the other gentlemen around this table will agree with me. Grace Fellowship bears a significant part of the responsibility for lacking proper financial controls that allowed this to continue for so long. And when I say 'Grace Fellowship,' I mean the deacons and me. I'm not sure what percentage we bear, but it's significant."

The deacons nodded in somber agreement.

"I need to ask one thing." Joe sat forward in his chair and looked Tom in the eye. "Why didn't you just clean the windows? You were here 20 hours a week. You could have done it."

Tom looked away to the spot beyond Jonathan's head. "I was afraid everyone would expect it was part of my job," he muttered.

"Then Farmer Services wouldn't be able to bill us the extra $3,500 for it," Earl completed his explanation.

"Yeah," Tom whispered, lowering his head.

"Tom, we appreciate that you've been fairly upfront with us this evening. I guess we've gotten everything out in the open and can make a plan that prioritizes honoring God and obedience to His word as we move forward. Thank you for coming," Jonathan concluded the meeting.

Tom said nothing and left the church building.

"That went about as well as it could have," Joe reflected, looking to Jonathan and expecting confirmation.

"Did it?" Jonathan asked, finally relaxing and lacing his hands behind his head. "I should have said something to let him know we expected to see him here on Sunday. I meant to."

"We do?" Lefty questioned. "Wouldn't it be better if he were gone altogether?"

"How does that prioritize honoring God and His word?" Jonathan brought his arms down, resting them on the table.

"Brothers, if anyone is caught in any transgression, you who are spiritual should restore him in a spirit of gentleness. Keep watch on yourself, lest you too be tempted. Galatians 6:1" Earl quoted.

"Exactly," Jonathan agreed. "Would it be easier to send the man packing? Yes, it would. But it's our responsibility to faithfully obey God's word, not look for the easy way out. Our goal is Tom's restoration, not his excommunication. I think the best place for that to happen is with people who've known and loved him for years. Strangers won't care like we do."

"In a spirit of *gentleness*," Joe repeated, emphasizing the tough part.

"Spirit of gentleness," Lefty echoed. "That's going to be the challenging part."

Jonathan smiled and summarized: "If it's going to challenge us to be obedient, then we should develop some spiritual muscle in the process. Restoration will benefit Tom, the challenge will promote growth in us and our membership, and both will honor God."

Chapter Nineteen

"I know you're missing your guy's night with the neighbors, so thanks for taking me out instead, Dad," Chase expressed his appreciation to his father from the van's front passenger seat.

"We've been talking about driving to LaGrange to try Dos Loros long enough. It was time we did it," Micah responded with a quick smile in Chase's direction before turning his eyes back to the highway. "Besides, I'm still having a guy's night – with you."

Since that terrible day when Child Protective Services took him from their home, Micah worked hard to maintain his sobriety and regain his son's trust and respect. Steadily, he was making progress. This was their first solo outing, and Micah was pleased Chase jumped at the offer when he presented it. He noticed Chase had dressed up a bit for the occasion, donning his best blue jeans, a fresh light green t-shirt, and swapping his everyday sneakers for his trendy lace-less ones.

"Who's your favorite?" Chase quizzed.

"Sorry? Favorite who?" Micah was puzzled. He flicked on the wipers as a light rain peppered the windshield.

"Your favorite neighbor from your other guy's nights. Who do you like the best?" Chase clarified.

"Oh, wow. That's a tough one. Wait! Is this a trick question? Am I supposed to say Will because he's family now and lives across the street?"

Chase laughed. "No! Not Uncle Will. I mean, of the old guys."

"Okay. Back to 'tough one,' then. They're all different. Marcus is smart and takes charge. Grant is a nut, but yet, sensible – a combination of opposites. He's funny even though he rarely means to be. Cal is kind, even when he gets in my face."

"He gets in your face?" Chase was astounded and turned his body toward his dad.

"He has. I'm sure he would again if he thought he needed to," Micah admitted.

Chase turned to face forward again, mulling this information. "I never thought of someone getting in your face since you're an adult and everything."

"Oh, believe me, adults still get yelled at. Sometimes, it happens because people are just cranky and rude. But other times, someone will fuss at you because you need to hear something you don't want to hear. You know that saying, 'The truth hurts?' That's a common saying because, a lot of times, the truth does hurt to hear. But people who truly care about you will risk telling you the truth even if it makes you mad. We need people like that in our lives – but they're rare. Most people won't speak truth to us because it's more important to them to keep the peace. So, if you have a friend who says hard but true things to you, keep them around because they care more about your good than their peace. I guess that helps me answer your question. I like them all, but if I have to have a favorite, I guess it's Cal."

"What about Mr. McBride?" Chase wanted to include him.

"Bobby? He's fine. Says what's on his mind. He's happiest when he's talking about his son or that new grandbaby on the way," Micah fired off his impressions. "What about you? Do you have a favorite?"

"Mr. Van Zant," Chase answered immediately. "He pays the most attention to me and asks me what I think about things. I like him."

"See, Marcus? This is why nobody likes you," Grant grumbled upon spying the bag of honey-mustard pretzel pieces Marcus had concealed on the Garage Cave floor between himself and Bobby.

"The jig is up," Bobby laughed, handing the bag to Grant. "Here you go, buddy."

Grant snatched the bag from Bobby. "Don't 'buddy' me! The two of you in cahoots over there – conspiring against me."

"Dat's what it was – a snack conspiracy," Marcus agreed mockingly, licking his fingers.

"How'd we get honey-mustard pretzel pieces? I thought Will always brought them," Cal wondered.

"I brought 'em this time since neither Will nor Micah would be here," Bobby confessed.

"It's just the four original Garage Cavers tonight," Grant observed, calmed with a fistful of his favorite man snack.

"You know what this place needs?" Bobby asked, his head surveying the perimeter of the garage. "A fridge for our drinks!"

Marcus, Grant, and Cal looked around and shook their heads in agreement.

"It just so happens. I have one in my garage that I'm not using. It's yours if you want to haul it across the street," Bobby offered.

Marcus stood and raised an index finger. "A capital idea! Let's go get it!" He'd caught on to Gomez Addams' expression since watching several episodes of the classic TV show and adopted it as his own.

"Just one problem with that – no Micah or Will. We need the young bucks and their strong backs," Cal objected with a frown.

"Do you also happen to have a dolly, Bobby?" Grant asked hopefully.

"Negatory on the dolly. But I've got a giant piece of cardboard from the box baby Julia's crib came in. I knew that would come in handy, so I kept it. We can walk the fridge onto the cardboard and just slide it over. The young guys use strong backs and legs, but we use common sense and experience," Bobby grinned, tapping his temple with an index finger.

"Okay, let's do it," Marcus urged them.

The men traipsed across the street to Bobby's garage, where Grant, Marcus, and Bobby heaved the refrigerator, inch by inch, onto the cardboard sheet.

"This is a pretty good-sized fridge – bigger than I imagined," Grant said through ragged breaths.

"Let's keep going. Inertia is our enemy," Marcus prodded.

Grant and Bobby pulled the three feet of excess cardboard in front of the part the fridge sat on. Marcus pushed from behind while Cal provided moral support and encouragement. The appliance slid easily across the smooth concrete floor of the garage but met some resistance when it reached Bobby's rough, unpaved driveway. The men added more physical effort to move it along.

No one had noticed the light rain that fell before they began the endeavor. When the men pulled the cardboard across the driveway and into the street, the cardboard under the load absorbed too much moisture and disintegrated. The fridge stood in the middle of Tamarack Street with no means of moving it.

"Oh, boy. Now what do we do?" Marcus worried.

"I recall saying we needed the young bucks. But, noooo. We have 'common sense and experience,'" Cal tapped his temple with an index finger.

"Thank you for that helpful reminder, Cal," Bobby replied sarcastically.

"Focus, guys!" Grant interjected. "We've got a problem here – we can't have a refrigerator in the middle of the street. It's a hazard. Suggestions, anyone?"

"I could get DeShawn. And Will's at home – we could ask them to help us," Bobby offered.

"No!" came the chorus from Marcus, Grant, and Cal. "Anyone but dem. We'd never hear da end of it. Micah would be the only one who wouldn't give us any grief," Marcus added.

"Jonathan?" Cal suggested their pastor.

"Pastors get a lot of urgent after-hours calls. Moving a refrigerator from da middle of a street should not be one of dem," Marcus insisted.

"Then who's left? The police?" Grant was growing frustrated.

"Well, it is a public safety issue at the moment," Cal seemed agreeable to Grant's half-serious suggestion.

Bobby took his cell phone from his pocket, dialed 911, and explained the situation to the dispatcher while Marcus and Grant looked on in disbelief.

"You might need to send two cars if the first one doesn't have a partner with him. The fridge is pretty big," Bobby suggested. "And we'd appreciate it if the patrol cars rolled up silent-like. We have wives and adult children who would give us endless grief over this. Thanks!"

After an agonizing thirteen-minute wait in the middle of the street, ready to wave off any oncoming vehicles, the men welcomed two police cruisers, which pulled silently over on the side of Tamarack Street. Before the officers exited their cars to assess the situation, they inexplicably turned on the light bars with rotating beacons of red and blue and flashes of white and let their sirens make a single, ear-piercing 'whoop.' Curious neighbors drew aside window curtains to view the spectacle – including the two houses with the best views: their own.

Chapter Twenty

"Last one to church is a rotten egg!" Chase challenged Silas to a race instead of their usual walk with the other neighbors.

"I can smell you already," Silas agreed with a taunt. "Dad, say 'on your mark.'"

Will laughed at the teen boys, delighted the new cousins were already best friends. "Okay. On your mark, get set, go!"

The boys shot down Cedar Street from the walkway in front of the Norman's blue-green Craftsman house.

"Run like the wind, son!" Micah yelled encouragement to Chase from their front porch, Lovie at his elbow.

"Good morning, Micah, Lovie. Enjoy your pancakes!" Marie greeted her neighbors, who didn't attend church, with a chipper salutation and a wave.

"We've got blueberries!" Lovie gushed.

"They'll be extra yummy then!" Marie tossed the words over her shoulder as she passed with the other walkers.

When the group was a little further down the street, Shelby exclaimed: "This time next year! I'm praying that by this time next year, my brother and Lovie will be joining us regularly at Grace Fellowship Church because God has saved them both."

"Why next year?" Marcus wondered, genuinely curious.

Shelby turned to face him, holding Will's arm to keep her balance as she continued to walk. "I don't know. I wasn't expecting anyone to ask," she responded, adding a nervous laugh. "It's not that God has to wait a year. He could save them this afternoon, and I'd be overjoyed. And it's not a deadline either – like I'm giving Him just a year to do what I ask. I'll pray for them as long as it takes, even if that's the rest of my life. But honestly, I just want them to be saved by at least this time next year, so that's what I'm asking for. Is that wrong?" Shelby was suddenly concerned. "Am I testing God or provoking Him?"

"I wonder if God hears my non-specific prayers as weak and faithless," Ava reflected.

"Yes! I mean, I wonder the same thing about mine," Marie confessed.

"James 4:2 says, 'You do not have because you do not ask,'" DeShawn piped up.

"When I was a kid, I prayed for a red Columbia three-speed bike with a banana seat and a chrome headlight," Grant recalled. "Now, that was a prayer loaded with specifics! God didn't miraculously make one appear in our garage, but He gave me a paper route so I could buy it. It had everything I wanted, and I was no less grateful to God that I got to pick it out at the store. Would I have been satisfied with a blue Schwinn? Probably. But I was over the moon for that red Columbia bike, and I think it delighted God to hear my request and fulfill it to the letter. That's how I felt when my boys were young and asked something of me."

"So, do you apply dat level of detail to your prayers today, Grant?" Marcus challenged.

"I don't," Grant admitted, lowering his head.

"Do any of us? We could think of asking for something within a year as either presumptuous or as pushing the boundaries of our faith to expand them," Will noted, spinning his head to look back at Marcus. "Thank God, He sees our hearts to know which it is, right?"

"Children aren't afraid to ask for what they want!" Mariana interjected. "Somewhere along the way to adulthood, we stop asking with child-like faith – no demands, how-to instructions, and no lines in the sand - just sharing with our Heavenly Father our heart's deep desire and asking Him for it. Maybe we need more of that in our prayers."

"Shelby has it down," Will observed proudly, patting his wife's hand, which still rested on his arm. "Do you all see how she challenges so much about my entrenched spiritual habits?"

"I tink spiritual babes are God's gift to da church to remind weathered saints of tings we've lost," Marcus suggested.

With one block before they reached the church, the group walked in silence, considering how child-like requests to their Father might invigorate their prayer lives.

Jonathan Jefferson sat on the dais in a blue wingback chair as Beth Ann Sharp played the piano prelude and Christine Williams marched to her favored front row pew. But as the pastor surveyed the congregation, he furrowed his brows over the two members he did not see: Tom and Patty Farmer.

Jonathan chastised himself for failing to ask Tom to continue coming to Sunday services. In the stressful meeting where he acted as Tom's employer, he lost sight of the fact that he was also Tom's pastor. Jonathan wanted Tom to grow in character and grace by navigating the painful process of church discipline instead of walking away as most did. Tom's absence today didn't make the prospect seem promising.

As the last chord of the prelude faded, Jonathan approached the pulpit and set his Bible on it.

"Good morning, congregation. I have a few announcements before we open God's Word. First, my family and I will be away this week as the schools are on fall break. The church offices will be closed, and DeShawn McBride will preach next Sunday's sermon."

An audible gasp escaped Christine Williams' speechless, O-shaped mouth.

"Next, it's that time of year again. The women's ministry is beginning its Christmas collection for needy children in Eastern Kentucky. There are two ways to give. You can either bring an unwrapped toy you've purchased and place it in the giant box in the foyer next week. Or, you can contribute monetarily, and the women's ministry will purchase the toys for you. Checks can be put in the offering plate with a designation in the memo line. Just write 'toys,' and we'll know what it's for."

Jonathan shuffled back and forth on his feet and wiped sweaty hands on his navy trousers before continuing.

"The third announcement I have to make is of utmost importance: I'm not a perfect pastor, and I'm grateful you don't require that of me," he began, avoiding eye contact with Christine Williams lest she challenge his assumption. "But I want you to know that I love you all as imperfectly as I might show it. I realize I've never said this from behind this pulpit before, and that's a failing I wanted to remedy. I love you.

Now, a Pastor can't be all talk and no action. But he shouldn't be all action with no talk, either. The Body of Christ is to love one another in word and deed, right? And the truth is, you make it easy to love you. You're growing in grace. You're patient with me and with one another. And you're all so kind to my wife and rambunctious boys. For these things and more, I love you all. I just wanted to make sure I've said it, and you've heard it."

He deliberately looked Christine Williams right in the eye and gave her half a smile.

"Now, let's open our Bibles to the love chapter, I Corinthians 13," Jonathan instructed.

CHAPTER TWENTY-ONE

B radley had never considered that his sister might be religious. Still, it was a boon to his efforts to discover, after sufficient recovery from her injuries, that Christine was a regular church attender.

He'd had a narrow escape from religion himself during a three-year marriage to his second wife, Candy. Raised in a strict Plymouth Brethren home, she rebelled and quit high school in her senior year. At age 47, after two months of marriage to Bradley – her fourth husband - she was inclined to return to the faith of her upbringing and pestered her new husband to join her in Bible reading and prayer. At first, he thought it was a joke, but as she persisted, Bradley spent less time at their tiny apartment and more time at a friend's dilapidated fishing cabin. When he was a no-show for their third anniversary, Candy sent divorce papers to the cabin, which Bradley signed lickety-split.

Relieved that his sister's religion was something she kept strictly to herself, Bradley supported her church attendance without overdoing it. During the week, he researched on his phone quick recipes he could tinker with to appear time-consuming. He might also get a head start on something and hide it in the fridge or pantry on Saturday evening after Christine went to bed. The more time he had to snoop during her absence from the house, the better.

Bradley didn't search for valuables; they were scattered liberally throughout the house like hotdogs in a baseball stadium. Each room had walls displaying original oil paintings and watercolors by nationally renowned artists. Pricy antiques were mixed among upscale contemporary furnishings, and objets d'art, vases, and collectibles adorned open shelves and glass-fronted cabinets. Bradley hadn't even bothered to peruse the jewelry box on top of Christine's dresser - too obvious if something vanished. He preferred to focus on what wasn't openly displayed.

Bradley hoped to discover the hidden spot for financial records, stock certificates, and a Last Will and Testament. Then he'd know the extent of his sister's assets and who would benefit. He had no illusions Christine would have named him in the existing will, but at least he'd understand who he had to work his angle against for a future version. Luther Hall, his sister's full biological brother, would be the logical recipient. But Bradley realized, perhaps better than most, that families were complicated, and the primary beneficiary could be a surprise to everyone.

Once he heard his sister drive away in her Mercedes, Bradley retrieved the pre-made marinade for Korean Bulgogi from the pantry. All he had to do was let the bite-sized short rib chunks soak for 30 minutes, stir-fry them for 3 minutes, spoon them over microwaved pre-packaged jasmine rice, and toss on a few scallions for color and presentation. Christine would assume he spent the morning on it, an impression he'd reinforce with mild complaints about standing on his feet.

As the meat marinated, Bradley pulled on a pair of rubber dishwashing gloves discarded under the kitchen sink in order to scrutinize Christine's office without leaving fingerprints. His primary preoccupation centered around the fancy, feminine old desk that his sister warily protected when the cleaning service came. Even though there weren't likely to be anything significant in the open pigeonhole nooks, he still examined the contents of the few envelopes in them. These contained inconsequential handwritten lists and reminders. One nook held a small address book, yellowed with age, that Bradley guessed was long outdated.

Next, he opened each drawer by its silver pull. The top drawer held a checkbook with unused checks and no register. The faux-leather cover was embossed with the words: "Petty Cash." He surmised Christine didn't need to keep track of the amounts written from this account or someone else did it for her. The other two drawers contained unused monogrammed stationery and old gardening magazines.

Mindful of the time, Bradley surveyed the rest of the room. He moved pictures to scout for a hidden wall safe. He lifted the rug at each corner to look for a concealed floor safe and found none. Removing the cushions from the jacquard settee, Bradley inspected the foundation, top and bottom, and repeated the process with Christine's tapestry upholstered desk chair. Finally, and most time-consuming of all, he removed over 200 books from the bookcase, flipping through each for hollowed compartments or loose papers. He found nothing and concluded that wherever his sister's personal papers were, it was definitely not in this room.

It was time to throw lunch together.

Christine entered the kitchen through the back door and inhaled deeply.

"I detect spice!" she declared warily. "I try to avoid much spice."

"I created an Asian fusion luncheon with your delicate palate in mind," Bradley assured her. "Sit at the dining table, and I'll serve your plate momentarily."

When he heard his sister adjusting herself in the captain's chair, Bradley rinsed a scoop of Bulgogi under a stream of hot water from the faucet and ladled it over the steaming rice.

"That ought to be bland enough for the baby," he thought.

"Here you are! I trust you'll find the flavor more delicate than the initial aroma," Bradley set the dish before Christine with a flourish of his arm.

Christine took a small forkful and a tentative bite of the entrée. After swallowing, she declared, "It's perfect! Why don't you make a plate for yourself and join me?"

"To be honest," Bradley lied, "I've already had some. The legs aren't what they used to be, and they're a little tired from standing at the stove. I think I'll just relax in my room and watch the golf tournament. I'll clean up the dishes after a while."

"Suit yourself," Christine agreed and continued her lunch. She was used to eating alone.

When she finished, Christine thought she'd take a Sunday afternoon rest in her own room. But first, she'd write a check for the Toys For Needy Children fund Pastor Jefferson mentioned at church that morning before she forgot about it.

As soon as she entered her office, Christine sensed something amiss. Everything was in its place, but the early afternoon light streaming in the windows highlighted random polka dots everywhere. They covered every piece of furniture and picture. She tugged at her glasses and scrutinized one. The spot appeared oily and textured. *"Dirty dish gloves!"* she concluded.

Christine pulled her petty-cash checkbook from a pigeonhole in the desk, spied several residue marks on it, and sank onto the settee. It had to be Bradley's doing. The cleaning service had been there earlier in the week, and she was one hundred percent certain these spots weren't left under her nose as she sat sentry at her desk, checkbook in hand. She recalled the previous Sunday when she had noticed her nightstand drawer ajar and now came to the only conclusion available: Bradley was going through her things while she attended church. Christine could feel her blood pressure rising with anger. Or was it fear?

Chapter Twenty-Two

The knock at the front door startled Ava, who was reading in the study with her husband before they turned in for the night.

"Who on earth would that be at nearly 10 PM?" she wondered aloud, her shoulders tense.

"Why don't you answer da door and find out?"

Ava scowled at the suggestion. "Answering the door late at night is a blue job, not a pink job – unless you're trying to cash in on my life insurance policy by sending me to greet a maniacal intruder. Is that what you're doing?"

Marcus chuckled. "I'll go wit you den," he offered, rising from his chair behind the desk.

"You'll go alone!" Ava countered, cemented to the crewelwork rocking chair.

Marcus answered the front door out of Ava's sight, putting a finger to his lips to silence the guests as he bid them entrance.

"Marley! Ethan!" Ava squealed, jumping from her chair to embrace her daughter and grandson as soon as she caught sight of them.

"Sorry, we're so late. There was a wreck on Interstate 65, and we sat for two hours while they cleaned it up," Marley apologized.

"You can't be late if we didn't expect you in the first place!" Ava laughed.

"Ethan is out of school for Fall Break and wanted to visit Grandma and Grandpa for a few days. He's never been here. Once Dad reserved your guest room, I asked him to keep it a secret so Ethan could surprise you."

"Are ya surprised, Grandma?" Ethan's face beamed.

"Delightfully surprised!" Ava assured, squeezing the dark-haired, blue-eyed, 8-year-old boy to her side. "Are you guys hungry? Would you like a snack before bed? June made a Boston Cream Cake, and there are leftovers."

Marley and Ethan looked at each other, their expressions melting.

"We were bored while waiting on the interstate. Packed snacks for three days and ate every one. So thanks, Mom, but we're bloated and tired," Marley confessed.

"Why don't you ladies head upstairs, and I'll give Etan a quick tour down here? Den, we'll be upstairs," Marcus suggested.

"Everyone else gone to bed?" Marley inquired as she trudged up the staircase with a suitcase.

"Yeah. Your Dad and I are the nighthawks."

"Okay, we'll be quiet as church mice then," Marley promised in a whisper.

Just then, Ethan's excited voice rang through the registers from the basement to the second-floor bedrooms. "You got puppies!"

"Marley Marie! So good to see you again, sweetie," Marie gushed as she entered the kitchen and spotted her namesake seated at the kitchen table. "And hello to you, too, Ethan! Stand up and let me see if you're taller than your Grandpa yet," she teased at Marcus' expense.

"He probably is," Elodie agreed, a mischievous grin displacing the deadpan expression she intended.

Marcus rolled his eyes at the women. "He's got a way to go. I'm not dat short."

"Hey, Ethan. I heard you discovered we have a litter of puppies in the basement," Grant addressed the boy while making his way around the kitchen island to prepare a mug of tea.

"Yeah! Grandma said I could go down to see them again after breakfast," Ethan informed.

"Well, we have a neighbor – also on Fall Break - who's your same age and has been invited to visit the puppies again. Should be here soon. Then you'll have a new friend to visit with, too," Grant replied.

"Grant is arranging play-dates? Didn't have that on my bingo card today," Ava snickered.

"Um, that was Marie's effort," Grant clarified. "Where's the leftover cake?"

"Well, whoever arranged it, it was very thoughtful. Thank you," Marley responded gratefully.

"I didn't know there was leftover cake!" Cal interjected. "I wouldn't have wasted my insulin on cereal carbs."

"It's news to me you pay attention to your insulin, Calcutta. I thought June did all that for you and cut up the meat on your plate, too," Elodie was back to taunting Cal full bore.

"The leftovers were promised to our guests. Thank you for not eating the cake for breakfast, Cal," Ava soothed, ignoring Elodie's jab.

Cal nodded his head amenably toward Ava and took another bite of cereal.

"That'll be our young neighbor!" Marie reacted to the gentle knock on the kitchen door.

"Come in, Lovie. Have you had your breakfast?" Marcus asked, opening the door.

"French toast sticks. Microwaved them myself!" Lovie bragged as she entered the kitchen. "Are the puppies awake?" she asked, making a beeline toward the basement door.

"You'll be the first one to find out. But we have a visitor who'll join you to check on them," Ava answered.

Lovie stopped in her tracks; eyebrows knit together at this unwelcome news. She assumed she'd have the puppies all to herself and be in charge of them for a while.

Ethan stood up and wiped his mouth on the sleeve of his long-sleeved t-shirt. He'd only gotten a peek at the puppies the night before and was eager to get acquainted.

"Lovie, this is my grandson, Ethan. He's eight, just like you, and is visiting from Bloomington. Ethan, this is our next-door neighbor, Lovie," Ava made the introductions.

The children eyed one another. They said nothing and proceeded down the basement stairs.

"*Girl* neighbor," Marley stated her observation. "Bet that surprised Ethan."

"Lovie won't mind dat her new companion is a boy. She's got an older broder," Marcus assured his daughter.

Down in the basement, Ethan patted Mercy's head before picking up one of her babies and cuddling it under his chin. He spoke softly to the puppy in his hands: "You're a good little guy. I like you. I think you're the best of the bunch. Hmmm. What would I name you if you were mine? Maybe Thor. Or maybe Smokey since you're black. No, Thor is a good name for you."

As Ethan continued to fawn over the tiny black puppy, Lovie sat nearby, combing fingers through her tangled hair, and watching. Her interest in the puppies evaporated like a mist. She could not take her eyes off the gentle, dark-haired, blue-eyed boy who had come to visit her neighbors.

CHAPTER TWENTY-THREE

"Excuse me. Sorry for interrupting. I'll just get my lunch out of the fridge and be out of your way," Bobby apologized, ducking in and out of the breakroom at McBride Motor Mart as quickly as he could.

"You're fine, Dad," DeShawn reassured him as he popped the top of a soda can.

DeShawn was sitting at the table with Shorty, the most senior employee of the detail shop who'd had to place his father in a memory-care facility, and James Daniels, the 18-year-old rookie who'd lost his mom to heart disease. The two employees worked together and shared a two-bedroom apartment close to the job, which neither of them could afford on their own. Once a week, as the three of them ate their lunch, DeShawn led a brief discussion based on chapters from a book he'd read in prison: *Objections To Christianity*. Neither Shorty nor James was a believer, but they had questions DeShawn was eager to answer.

Bobby left the door to his office open to eavesdrop on the conversations he'd been invited to participate in but declined. "Somebody has to mind the lot for customers during lunch," he'd excused himself. So, Bobby ate his roast beef sandwich and cookies at his desk, looking out the window occasionally to scan the property for a potential buyer but listening intently to the voices in the breakroom.

"Let's talk about hell!" DeShawn began.

"I'm probably going to hell when I die," Shorty blurted and took a bite of cold fried chicken.

"Probably," DeShawn agreed, catching Shorty, who was expecting consolation, off-guard.

Bobby's eyebrows flew upward as he listened. He did not expect his son to say that.

DeShawn let his comment hang in the air like a noxious fume for a few seconds before continuing. "Hell is everybody's default destination. All people face that fate because their sin warrants judgment. And sin against a Holy God deserves eternal punishment."

"But sending people to an eternal hell...isn't God supposed to be loving and forgiving?" James wondered.

"He is both of those to those who seek His love and forgiveness. But He is not only those things as if He had no other qualities. He is also just because He loves justice. Think about it: If there's no hell, there can't be any justice," DeShawn asserted. He watched the men's faces as they pondered this proposition.

"I can think of half a dozen people off the top of my head who need to be in hell for what they've done on earth. I guess there'd be no place for the worst of the worst of humanity if there weren't any hell. I never thought about that," Shorty mused, putting his fork in a container of leftover mac & cheese he'd warmed.

"You said hell is everyone's default destination. What about those who aren't the worst of the worst - those who only mess up a little? Shouldn't the punishment fit the crime?" James asked.

"Who are those people?" DeShawn challenged this hypothetical group.

"I'm not sure exactly. People who don't live long lives or people who work so much they don't have time for sin," James was thinking on the fly.

"Like you?" Shorty asked. "You're only 18, and you just work and watch TV. Basically, that's your life, right?"

James lowered his mop of shaggy dark hair and shuffled his feet underneath his chair. "I, uh, I didn't mean me, necessarily," he admitted.

"Wouldn't have been me either. At 18, I was starting a 25-year prison sentence. But even before that...way before that...I was a seasoned sinner," DeShawn reminded the guys who were aware of his history.

"By 18, I'd gotten two different girls pregnant in my high school. My parents sent me to Wisconsin to live with my mom's folks on their dairy farm. It wasn't prison, but I didn't imagine it was much different," Shorty confessed. "My grandfather worked me so hard I was too tired to look at a girl. What about you, James? What'd you do?"

DeShawn protested the question. "If he wanted us to know something, we'd know it. What we share here is voluntary, not compelled. The takeaway is that we should focus our discussion on what applies to us and not theoretical people to cover for us. Can we agree to that?"

"Yup," James answered gratefully while Shorty nodded and continued to eat.

"James, I am going to circle back to your comment about the punishment not seeming to fit the crime because, from a human perspective, it can seem that way. And I can tell you from experience that when I'd see guys get significantly lighter prison sentences than I did for basically the same crime, it seemed like the justice system was messed up. I wanted the punishment for a particular crime to be administered in the same way, no matter who the offender was. But God's justice is not messed up because He knows about the sins we commit that nobody else does. And He can't be bought off and corrupted like some earthly judges. When judgment day comes, no one will get away with even one sin, and every sentence God hands down will be perfectly just."

"Whew," Shorty exhaled and pushed his food aside.

"It's heavy, right?" DeShawn sympathized with Shorty's deflated energy.

Listening in his office, Bobby rubbed the back of his neck.

"Well, that's all I got to say about hell today. Maybe next week we'll talk about whether God created the entire universe in six days," De-Shawn concluded.

"How 'bout we talk about heaven?" Shorty offered a counterproposal.

"Yeah, we gave hell a turn. We should talk about heaven!" James agreed.

DeShawn smiled. He'd resolved to be patient with these guys and give them one or two things to ponder during the week instead of turning a theological firehose on them. If he doled out biblical concepts slowly, like valuable pearls, perhaps the guys would appreciate their value. A discussion of heaven didn't fit the topic of objections to Christianity, but that's what the guys yearned for. DeShawn could see an igniting a hunger, and he was pleased.

"Okay, heaven's our topic next week. I want to let you know, in case you're interested, I'll be preaching this Sunday at Grace Fellowship Church. Service starts at 10:45 if you want to come. It's the old brick church on Sycamore Street. No pressure," DeShawn invited.

"You're a preacher?" James was stunned.

DeShawn chuckled in self-deprecation. "Only when my pastor is desperate."

Bobby heard the men gather their lunch trash and slide their chairs on the linoleum floor. He pushed his own lunch bag into the trashcan under his desk and pulled up a spreadsheet file on his computer in order to look busy, if not engrossed. It was useless. The numbers on the screen seemed to taunt Bobby to make sense of them. His mind focused on the fact that DeShawn hadn't told him he was preaching for Jonathan this Sunday. He wanted to be invited. He wanted to go.

CHAPTER TWENTY-FOUR

"Ethan! How would you like to go to Breakfast Barn with Grandma since it's your last day here? There's one in Crestwood, which isn't far, and it would be like the breakfast dates we used to have in Bloomington," Ava enticed her young grandson as he sauntered into the study where his mom and grandparents had gathered as the sun rose.

"Can I go with Grandpa instead?" Ethan countered, beaming at Marcus, sitting behind the study desk sipping coffee.

His response, forthright and without malice, hit Ava like a sucker punch. She drew a breath in sharply to replace the one knocked out of her. Her chin quivered, and she willed it to stop by pressing the nails of her right hand into the flesh of her left foot, which was tucked under her bottom.

Marcus and Marley exchanged quick, troubled glances.

"Grandpa did not invite you; Grandma did," Marley corrected her son.

"No! No! It's okay," Ava insisted. "Whatever he wants. Marcus, you'd love to take Ethan to the Breakfast Barn, wouldn't you? It'll be a men's outing."

"See, Grandma says it's okay. Do you want to take me, Grandpa?" Ethen smiled at Marcus, showing a top row of adult teeth.

Marcus hesitated, knowing the rejection wounded his wife. He looked at her and asked, "Are you sure?"

"Go!" Ava forced a smile. "Have fun!"

Marcus set his mug on the desk, stood, and raised an index finger in the air. "A capital idea! We're off to da Breakfast Barn!" he agreed.

On his way around the desk, Marcus stopped to kiss the top of his wife's head and whispered: "It's not personal. He wants to be wit men now."

Marley sat with her mother as Marcus and Ethan closed the front door behind them.

"I'm so sorry, Mom," Marley began. "Kids don't think before they speak. He didn't mean to hurt you; he just..."

Ava raised a palm and cut her off. "I know. It's okay. Kids are kids, and they speak their minds. I just wasn't prepared."

The women sat silently for a minute, Marley rocking in the crewel-work chair beside her mother.

"I'm not the same person, am I?" Ava sought confirmation of what she already knew. "Three years ago, if Ethan had said he preferred Grand-pa, I'd have gotten in his face and asked what was so great about Grandpa. Or, I might say to him it's too bad his grandfather doesn't think of taking him to breakfast as I do. I'd have made him regret his choice – with love, of course."

Marley laughed, picturing how her mom used to approach superficial conflict with teasing. But Ava was right; she was different now. The stranglehold of a years-long family estrangement had left its constricting marks on her psyche.

Marley wasn't sure if her mom's question was hypothetical or if she was expecting a genuine answer. She sighed in relief as Ava continued.

"I know it's God's plan to grow His children, and growth means change. And since we should never stop growing, we should never stop changing. That's comforting to me, Marley. God willing, another layer of growth and change will be laid over this one. It won't always be this way – my being sensitive and unprepared for the unexpected. Isn't that hopeful? God builds us up with layers - like rings underneath a tree's bark. The outside might look the same or even a little worse for wear, but inside, we're being built up. I'm being built up," Ava concluded, a smile overtaking her countenance and crinkling the corners of her blue eyes.

Since he was at the Breakfast Barn, Marcus decided he might as well indulge in the Farmer's Feast: three eggs, two links of sausage, two slices of bacon, a serving of hash brown potatoes with onions and ham, and two pancakes.

"I'll get that, too. And a glass of orange juice!" Ethan informed the waitress.

Marcus' eyes grew wide. "Tink you can eat all dat, little man?" he doubtfully questioned.

"Watch me, Grandpa," Ethan boasted.

"I will!" Marcus assured, making plans to ask for a to-go box when the waitress brought the check. He'd eat what Ethan didn't for lunch.

Ethan sat back against the booth. "Does that neighbor girl of yours come over to your house every day? I'm glad we've come here, and I don't have to play with the puppies with her again."

"She doesn't come over every day. We tought you might like someone your own age to visit wit. You don't like her?" Marcus responded.

"Aw, she's alright, I guess. It'd be better if she were a boy. Boys are more fun!" Ethan was emphatic in his assertion.

"Do you have boys you have fun with at home?"

"I used to." Ethan grew somber and looked at something invisible in his lap.

"What happened? You still go to da same school. Did your friends move away?"

"Grandpaaaa," Ethan whined, astounded he could forget his other grandchildren so easily. "Jordan and Luke," he named the cousins – sons of his Aunt Mia – whom he was not allowed to see for mysterious reasons.

Marcus closed his eyes and shook his head from side to side. After taking a deep breath, he responded to the pain evident on his grandson's face.

"Of course, you miss dem. I miss dem, too."

"Do you think they miss us?" Ethan wondered.

"I would tink so."

"We had so much fun the last time I saw them. The leaves were falling off the trees in the backyard. We shot squirt guns at the leaves and earned points for shooting down different colors. Red and brown were one point, yellow was two points, and a leaf that was still green was three points, but nobody got one of those," Ethan reminisced with detailed clarity, picturing the day. "I'd like to do that again. The leaves are just right now!"

Marcus ached for all Ethan was missing with his cousins – the leaf game and other made-up amusements, birthday parties, extended family vacations, and holidays. He grieved these boys would never get these childhood years back.

His face growing hot, Marcus looked away to a television set mounted in the restaurant's corner. He saw a scene from some faraway war where newly homeless families wandered bombed-out streets. It seemed an apt metaphor for the bewilderment his grandsons must be experiencing – all victims of the war raging in the hearts of adults who devastated their family's children and flew away in their bomber ignorant of the casualty of innocents.

"It won't be like dis in Heaven," was all Marcus could say.

CHAPTER TWENTY-FIVE

It wasn't a spontaneous reaction. The minute DeShawn McBride stepped behind the pulpit, Christine Williams stood from her front-row seat at Grace Fellowship Church and marched out in protest, just as she'd planned all week. She thought she might have company, given that others had also voted against the convict's membership. But this time, she was the lone protester.

Christine didn't care. In her mind, a murderous felon had no business behind the pulpit of any church, and if she had to be the one to make that clear by setting an example, so be it.

"Eagles fly solo," she muttered in self-encouragement as the large church door closed behind her.

From his seat in the back row, trying to be as inconspicuous as possible, Bobby McBride seethed at the disrespect his long-time neighbor showed his son. He wished her an excruciatingly slow, painful, and humiliating death and hoped the process would commence immediately. Bobby was proud of his son. And even if he'd not been informed or invited to hear him preach for the first time, he'd come to bask in his son's public redemption.

"Open your Bibles to the Gospel of Luke, chapter six. We're going to look at verses 27 through 36 and see what God has to say about loving our enemies. My prayer is that by the time we've concluded today, we'll not only understand this commandment from our Lord, but the Holy Spirit will also empower us to obey it so that God is glorified in our frames of dust."

As the congregation turned the pages of their Bibles to find the passage, DeShawn surveyed the congregation. Mariana was beaming at him from a second-row pew. His neighbors and friends were all in attendance, but he noted the absence of the Farmers for the second week in a row. Even Shorty and James were there, cleaned up and smiling in a middle row. But most significantly, DeShawn spied the top of a familiar gray-haired head in the back row.

He'd deliberately not invited his father, preferring to be fussed at after the fact by a man forced to hear himself admit a desire to be in God's house. Taking the same tact as with Shorty and James, DeShawn wasn't tossing around theological pearls or inclusion in worship gatherings without observing a prior spiritual hunger. He'd seen that done by various ministries that came to Kentucky State Reformatory with a miserable rate of falling away and outright apostasy.

Emboldened by the example of Jesus and the Syrophoenician woman, DeShawn vowed he'd do it differently if the Lord allowed him to minister outside the prison someday.

"And he [Jesus] said to her, 'Let the children be fed first, for it is not right to take the children's bread and throw it to the dogs. But she answered. Him, "Yes, Lord; yet even the dogs under the table eat the children's crumbs." Mark 7:27-28

A smile crept into the corners of DeShawn's mouth as he realized his father must have learned about his preaching opportunity by overhearing him tell the guys at work. And if he overheard that, he was also privy to the weeks of conversations answering Objections To Christianity. Perhaps his father was drawn to the discussions. The possibility ignited gratitude and reverence for God's mysterious work and ways, and fueled by His power, DeShawn preached a barn burner on loving one's enemies.

For the second week in a row, Patty Farmer dressed for church but didn't attend. Last week, she was shocked by her husband's last-minute, tearful revelation that he'd been fired from Grace Fellowship for theft. Instead of attending church, she sat with Tom at the kitchen table as he tried to justify cashing checks for work he had not done. She listened as he recounted meeting with Pastor Jefferson and the deacons, a meeting he characterized as an 'ambush.' Tom told her that, to his knowledge, only the church leadership was aware of the specific sin involved. But since he'd been fired, people were bound to ask questions about his absence, and word would leak out.

This week, Patty expected to stand supportively by her husband as he faced the church he'd wronged. Following her usual Sunday morning routine, Patty cleaned the breakfast dishes while she supposed Tom was getting dressed for church. When she'd finished handwashing the dishes and frying pan, and he hadn't come to the kitchen, Patty climbed the stairs to their bedroom to check on him.

"We're going to be late!" she admonished when she saw him gazing out the window, still in his pajamas.

"We're not going," Tom stated as a matter of fact.

"You're not serious," Patty responded. Though from her husband's expression, she could tell he was.

"We can find another church; start over. We could go to LaGrange or Crestwood," Tom suggested, his countenance brightening as he tried to sell the idea to his wife.

"You can't ask me to do that! My parents were members of Grace Fellowship and are buried in the cemetery. I was raised at that church. It's the only church I've ever attended, and now you want me to walk away from the only spiritual home I've ever known or want to know? I didn't do anything wrong!" Patty was indignant, fists clenched at her sides. "Besides, we have plots next to my parents, remember?" she thought to add to her objection.

"I can't go back," Tom said evenly, brushing a hand over his crew cut and turning away from his wife to look out the window again.

Patty lowered herself onto the edge of their bed, frustrated by the impasse. She prayed: *"Lord, help me help him."*

"Come sit next to me, Tom. Let's talk it through and see if you still want to leave Grace. Can we do that?" Patty invited, softening the tone of her voice.

Tom turned and joined her on the edge of their bed; his gaze focused on Patty's right hand and the antique garnet ring inherited from her grandmother. It gave him something to look at besides his wife's expectant face.

"I've been thinking this past week about DeShawn McBride and how he's made our church his family after two decades in prison. I realize our situations are different, but our roads will be challenging in many of the same ways. We'll find out who our genuine friends are. It couldn't have been easy for DeShawn and Mariana to see petty people vote against their membership. But those folks told on themselves, and at least the McBrides know who they are. And so do we.

As for the rest of the congregation, you know they love and respect DeShawn for being humble, and an example of repentance and victory. In fact, he's preaching today in Pastor Jefferson's absence! His sin is not his identity. His identity is a beloved child of God. And that's our identity, too, Tom. Our lifelong friends at Grace Fellowship love us, and they'll forgive our sin because they understand they're also forgiven sinners.

Please, Tom. We can do this together. We don't have to run. I'll be right by your side. Yes, this is going to be hard. So what? We can do something hard if it makes us more Christ-like and honors Him, right?"

Patty concluded her rationale and plea.

Tom made eye contact with his wife and responded noncommittally: "I'll think about it."

Chapter Twenty-Six

"Blast it!" Bradley slammed the palm of his hand against the steering wheel of his beater van as smoke leaked from the seams of the hood. He followed this invective with a stream of cursing and eased the sputtering van into the handy parking lot of Big Mart. Parking in the nearest spot available, Bradley turned off the ignition and leaned back into his seat.

"Just great," he muttered. He knew the engine was gone, and he had no money to replace it. He had no money, period. Bradly went to Big Mart to spend the last twenty dollars on cigarettes and melatonin gummies.

It wasn't even his van. It belonged to Brooks, his deceased older brother, and then to Brooks' widow, Joan, who Bradley never got along with. When he left California and return to Faircourt, Bradley needed a means of transportation. He figured Brooks owed him repayment for various favors – some real, some imagined - and decided taking the van would square up the dead brother. Technically, the van was stolen.

Bradley sorted through the trash-filled van and scooped the glove compartment's contents onto the passenger seat for inspection. He filled a discarded Big Mart plastic bag with anything he deemed valuable or incriminating, including two pay stubs from his brief local employment with Rental Scapes, a faded Polaroid of Brooks and Joan wrapped around one another at a party, a fluorescent-orange thermal carafe with no dents, a lost half-pack of cigarettes which were sure to be stale, three bungee cords, and an entire roll of duct tape with the labeling wrap intact.

"Planning to abduct someone, Brooks?" Bradley chuckled as he tossed the last item into the bag.

Since he was already there, Bradley decided to make his purchases in the store, unsure when he could return since he no longer had transportation. He left the bag of collected goods on the passenger seat and walked across the entire parking lot to reach the Big Mart entrance.

"Hello. Bradley, isn't it?" Marie greeted her neighbor's brother as she exited the store with Grant.

Bradley nodded and smiled his acknowledgment but kept walking. His disposition wasn't sociable at the moment.

"It appears we've lost that certain je ne sais quoi that makes people want to greet us and be friendly," Grant remarked, brushing off the social slight.

"His loss," Marie remarked casually.

Ten minutes later, Bradley returned to the van with his cigarettes and melatonin, grabbed the bag on the passenger seat, and slammed the door shut.

"Goodbye, traveling partner!" he bid farewell to the vehicle and tossed the keys in a cluster of plum yews before starting the 4-mile walk home in ill-fitting shoes not made for walking in excess of half a mile.

As he began walking, a bag in each hand, Bradley mentally kicked himself for not asking his neighbors for a ride home. It hadn't occurred to him when he had the opportunity. At the pace he made, Bradley figured he'd reach home in time to throw something on a plate for Christine's dinner, which, he was grateful, was more of a snack. However, each plodding step grew more painful than the last.

"There you are!" Christine greeted her half-brother when he walked through the kitchen door, his feet agonizingly blistered. "I was just about to fix my own tea and cookie tray. Now that you're here..." Christine left her sentence unfinished, but her expectation was clear.

"Can you give me a minute, or do you have to pounce on me for your tray the second I walk in the door?" Bradley snapped, his composure decimated by his painful feet. He kicked off his shoes, carelessly letting them hit the wall and leaving scuff marks.

Christine drew a breath in sharply and exhaled: "I'll thank you not to throw shoes against my walls. Remove those marks at once! I will not tolerate this incivility in my home."

"Incivility?" Bradley repeated the word with a growl in his throat while stepping toward his sister until he towered over her, a few inches between them, still holding a bag in each hand. Neither civility nor composure would return until he'd vented his anger.

"My van is totaled and sitting in a parking lot across town. I walked miles to get home, and my feet are covered in blisters that are burst and torn. I don't care if those blasted shoes put holes in your wall, got it?" he peered down, his eyes mere slits and mouth tight at first, but softening as he remembered to be sympathetic.

"I, um, I didn't realize," Christine stammered and stepped backward.

"That's right. You don't realize that you don't know everything, and you're the one treating me with incivility," Bradley reinforced Christine's admission of ignorance and used it against her.

While Christine considered whether the accusation was valid, Bradley smelled an opportunity and continued his manipulation.

"Why do you accuse others of what you're guilty of yourself?" he challenged her.

"I'm sorry," Christine heard herself apologize in an unsteady voice.

"Are you?" Bradley retreated a few steps and set his bags on the kitchen table. Tempering his voice, he added: "If you're truly sorry and not just throwing words around, you'll get me a new vehicle. I'm not saying it has to be a Mercedes, like yours. But I need a nice one - I mean, a reliable one, if I'm going to be able to keep helping you here."

"A new vehicle?" Christine questioned from the other side of the kitchen table, stunned by the presumptive request.

"Don't you think you owe it to me, sister?" Bradley sneered, his eyes returning to slits.

Christine shivered involuntarily. *"He must know!"* she was convinced. *"He knows I set him up to be a drug addict – him and his brother. But how did he find out? There was no trail to Clarkson or me."*

Without time to figure it out, Christine did the only thing she could do to resolve the tension without answering the question, which was still hanging in the air.

"We'll find something for you tomorrow," Christine agreed to Bradley's terms and retreated from the kitchen without a tea tray or the expectation of one to follow.

Bradley punched his fist above his head and snickered silently when he heard his sister climbing the staircase. He enjoyed the victory and determined it would be the first of many.

Chapter Twenty-Seven

"El Camino! There you are. Come here and help a brother and a mother out," Cal requested, spotting her exiting the powder room after conducting a brief search downstairs.

"Assumin' you're the brother; who's the mother?" Elodie was weighing her interest in being distracted from the mystery novel she intended to read.

"Mercy. She needs a break from those pups climbing over her 24/7. How about you go to the basement and carry them upstairs for me? I'll watch them after that. You know I just can't do those stairs with these knees."

Elodie noticed an unusual softness around Cal's eyes. "This has nothin' to do with Mercy. You just want to see those pups!" she insisted, putting hands on hips.

"Well, I do. But it would also give Mercy a chance to nap, right? Besides, all the rest of you have been visiting those pups in the basement at least once a day. I haven't seen them since they were born. Their eyes are open now, I'll bet," Cal bolstered his case with pleading puppy eyes of his own.

"Where do you want them?" Elodie relented.

"The kitchen is probably the best place. There's room for them to stretch their legs and no carpet for them to tinkle on."

"Alright. Be right back with 'em," Elodie headed for the basement door.

A few minutes later, Elodie appeared in the kitchen with six puppies nestled in a hammock made from a corner of her skirt. Cal, seated in a kitchen chair pulled away from the table, instructed her to place the puppies at his feet.

"Give me that last fella. I'll hold that one first and see what he's about," Cal was giddy.

"All right, you good here? I've got a new mystery novel waitin' on me to turn some pages," Elodie excused herself after setting the puppies down.

"I'm good. Thanks, El," Cal replied, snuggling a tiny tan and white pup.

"I'll be in the study. Just holler when you want 'em go back to their mother, and I'll bring 'em back," Elodie offered, then was gone.

Cal turned his attention to the wriggling pup in his lap. "You're a handsome guy. The ladies are going to love those blue eyes of yours. My June-bug says my blue eyes were the ticket for her. Although now that I think about it, yours will likely turn brown like your momma's. That's okay. Some women like brown eyes. Apparently, Marcus and Grant's brown eyes weren't enough of a deterrent to their wives. I guess those guys had to rely on other redeeming qualities. Anyway, you have got a nice fur jacket going for you. Yes, you do. Such a handsome guy!"

Cal continued cuddling and cooing to the little nameless pup for a few minutes before he thought to move on to another. When he looked down at his feet where Elodie had deposited them, there were none. Cal swiveled his head back and forth and caught sight of a black one scampering around the corner of the kitchen island.

"Hey! Get back here!" Cal barked at it.

He stood, tucking the puppy in his possession inside his bib overalls, and went after the wandering pup while keeping an eye out for the others. He didn't see any others, at least not in the kitchen. Cal chased the black puppy around the island as quickly as his knees allowed before reversing course and meeting him head-on to scoop him up.

"Ha! Out-smarted ya, little feller!" he boasted. "Now, where did your brothers and sisters run off?

"Eeeww!" Marie groaned in the front hall. After the few seconds it took her to identify what she'd encountered, she followed with: "Puppy piddle! I stepped in it in stocking feet!"

Elodie, seated just a few feet away in the study, burst out laughing.

Sitting next to Elodie, Ava wondered aloud: "How did a puppy get upstairs?"

"Oh, they're all up here. Cal asked me to bring 'em up for him. He's watchin' 'em. Or, he was supposed to be," Elodie answered, still chuckling at Marie's unfortunate run-in.

"Sorry about that, Marie," Cal apologized with a grimace. "They kind of got away from me – four of them, anyway. Got two right here," he patted the bulging bib of his overalls.

"What's the commotion?" June asked, exiting her bedroom.

"Your husband lost some puppies," Marie informed, pulling off her wet sock. "And I found their trail."

"Oh no, I'm sorry," June said before breaking out in a titter.

"Guess we'd better find them," Ava suggested, rising from her chair.

"Puppies, come forth!" Marie commanded.

"Oh, for heaven's sake!" Elodie rolled her eyes and rose to help look for the tiny critters. "I don't believe they know that instruction yet, Marie."

"There's one!" Ava shouted and bolted into the living room. "Oh, it's gone under the couch. Someone help me!"

Marie darted into action, laying on the floor beside the couch to shoo it toward Ava while the Shermans encouraged the pup to emerge.

"What's happening here?" Marcus asked as he and Grant entered the front door and saw everyone gathered in the living room, talking to the sofa.

"Puppies running amok," Ava answered, still focused on the errant pup.

"What?!" Grant, who took responsibility for the puppies, yelped. He dropped the car-cleaning rags he'd brought in from the Garage Cave and joined the recapture effort.

"Hey! Dere's anoder one going into da study. I'll get it," Marcus chased after it and scooped a black puppy up.

Marie swept her bare foot under the couch and flushed out the puppy hiding there. Ava picked it up and handed it to Grant.

"That's two!" Grant counted.

"No, that's four. Got two more in here," Cal patted his chest.

"Here's the last two." Elodie held a black pup in one hand and a tan and white one in the other. "Found these runaways in the dining room."

"El, you're an ace tracker – maybe you're part bloodhound yourself," Grant congratulated her.

"Maybe you should keep better track of your responsibilities," Elodie scoffed at him, irked by the bloodhound comparison.

Grant looked at Marie, and she knew mischief was imminent.

"You're right, El. Part of my responsibility in this situation is to thank you for your efforts properly," Grant responded, passing the puppy he held to his wife.

"Let's start with a hug!" he threatened with a sly grin.

"Oh, no!" Elodie pushed her puppies into Ava's hands, bolted from the room, and up the staircase.

"You were right, dear. A hug to Elodie is like sunshine to a vampire," Grant laughed.

Chapter Twenty-Eight

Weeks before Halloween, Chase stated emphatically he would not accompany Lovie on her trick-or-treating rounds this year. He would be neither begged nor bribed. Chase urged his dad to step up to his parental responsibility, suppressing a snicker, confident Lovie would insist they have coordinating costumes.

With suggestions and plenty of help from Aunt Shelby, father and daughter were ready for the big night. Micah dressed as a large gray wolf in a ready-made costume purchased online. Shelby sewed her niece a black and white gingham dress with a red hooded cape to wear over it. She also thrifted a nice-sized wicker basket for Lovie to carry on her arm for candy collection. To everyone except Chase, who howled in ridicule, they were an adorable Big Bad Wolf and Little Red Riding Hood.

From Silas' darkened second-floor bedroom window at his dad's house, Silas and Chase sat on beanbag chairs and watched the trick-or-treaters parade up and down Cedar Street.

"When was the last time you trick-or-treated?" Silas asked his friend, now cousin, who was spending the night.

"Aunt Shelby paid me to take Lovie last year and wear an embarrassing royal guard costume with a ginormous fur hat. Technically, I wasn't trick or treating, but a few people felt sorry for me and passed me some candy. But the last time I put on a costume and participated willingly was the Halloween before my mom died, so two years ago. How about you?" Chase answered.

Silas wrinkled his nose. "I went last year by myself. Sam was too old, and you were..." his voice dropped off.

"I was being a jerk with my so-called basketball friends," Chase admitted.

"I wasn't going to say it like that," Silas assured.

"It's okay. I said it." Chase shifted in his chair to face his friend. "Hey! Let me make it up to you. Let's have some fun this year – maybe a little harmless mischief! What do you think? What could we do?" Chase grew animated.

A slow grin crept across Silas' face. "Sam and his friends toilet-papered a tree in someone's yard last year. He hardly got in trouble, and it doesn't hurt anyone!" he suggested.

"I like it! Let me sneak home while Dad and Lovie are still out, and I'll grab three rolls. You find three rolls here. That should be enough, right? I'll be right back," Chase stood.

"Wait! Whose tree are we going to hit?" Silas asked excitedly.

Chase stopped to consider. "I don't know. But I know whose tree we won't hit – Christine Williams. There's no way that old lady can take a joke. She'd find a way to send us to juvenile prison. Let's think about it after we gather our supplies. Since your Dad and Aunt Shelby are giving out candy at the front door, I'll sneak out the back door. Be back soon!"

At 11 PM, the boys were ready to execute their Halloween 'trick.' Will and Shelby had gone to bed an hour previously, leaving the boys downstairs in the living room watching an old black and white Alfred Hitchcock movie.

"Ready?" Silas asked, nervous now that the moment was upon them.

"Ready!" Chase answered confidently. "This won't take long. Leave the TV on, and let's go out the kitchen door so they don't hear us, just in case they're awake."

"Rats! I forgot about the streetlights. We'd better be quick!" Chase whispered as they crossed the street.

In less than 15 minutes, the boys completed their mission to wrap the old maple tree in Bobby McBride's front yard in a toilet paper cocoon.

Shelby and Will crept around the kitchen as they made French toast and sausage for breakfast, not wanting to wake Silas and Chase, who were still asleep in the living room.

"Hello?" Will grabbed the cell phone from his bathrobe pocket, answering before it rang a second time.

Standing over the griddle, Shelby listened to only her husband's half of the conversation.

"No, I haven't. Oh, really? Every street needs pregnant women to be its Neighborhood Watch. Is he mad? I'm open to suggestions, my friend. I like it! Will you call Micah? Thirty minutes. They'll be there."

"What's going on?" Shelby asked, unable to make out the situation.

"It seems the boys were up to some tricks last night. They toilet-papered the tree in front of DeShawn's house. Mariana got up to go to the bathroom and heard something. She saw the tree and Silas and Chase running back to our house," Will informed her.

"Oh, no! Is Bobby angry?" Shelby groaned.

"Not a bit. DeShawn says his father laughed and is perversely proud to have been selected for such attention. He's still outside taking pictures of it," Will chuckled.

"What will you do?" Shelby asked, filling a plate for Will.

"There's a plan, actually. We're going to teach the boys the laws of the manhood jungle."

Shelby's eyebrows stretched upward. "What? That's not a real thing."

"Allow me to have my morning meal, then watch and learn the process," Will answered.

Thirty minutes later, Will had eaten, dressed, and convincingly scolded his son and nephew as he marched them across the street to the McBride's house.

"You gentlemen aren't as stealthy as you think you are. You were seen and identified as the culprits," Will acted sternly. "This is vandalism, you know. Now you're going to face the consequences!" His breath was visible in the chilly morning air.

Standing on the porch, Bobby, Micah, and DeShawn wore mean-mug faces as Will and the boys approached, Rover threading a lazy path amongst their legs.

"I can't! I'm gonna laugh. Micah, you do the talkin'" Bobby whispered as the boys approached his porch still wearing their nightclothes.

"The first thing you guys are going to do is apologize to Mr. McBride," Micah fairly growled at the stricken young men.

"It was a dumb idea," Silas began, embarrassed and shivering in his pajamas.

"We're sor, sorry, Mr. McBride," Chase added, teeth chattering. "We weren't thinking."

Not trusting himself to speak, Bobby nodded.

"The second thing you guys are going to do is take it all down. Mr. McBride is graciously lending you his hose. One can spray, and the other can put what falls to the ground in this trash bag," Micah handed Chase the hose and the bag to Silas.

Shelby looked from her front porch as the boys set about their task.

Chase and Silas soon focused on targeting strands and clumps. So focused they didn't notice Grant running a hose from the side of his house across Tamarack Street and handing the nozzle to Micah or when DeShawn brought a hose from around the back of the McBride house and handed it to Will. At Will's signal, Bobby turned off the spigot to the hose Chase aimed at the tree. And then, the law of the manhood jungle was administered to the boys in stinging showers of cold water as their dads, who had tricks of their own, roared with laughter.

CHAPTER TWENTY-NINE

arl Eggleston, Lefty Schneider, and Joe Fowler looked uneasily amongst themselves as Tom Farmer walked into the Men's Sunday School Class a few minutes late, his eyes fastened on the floor as he took his seat. After missing two weeks in a row, the deacons assumed Tom would not be returning to Grace Fellowship Church. And they felt terrible, knowing that not only had word leaked throughout the congregation about Tom's firing, but the reason for it.

Joe Fowler's 19-year-old daughter, Emma, who had competed with Ava for the part-time secretarial position, overheard him discussing the matter further with Pastor Jefferson on the phone. She gossiped the news to younger friends in the youth group, who took it home to their parents, who told their friends. The story version Pastor Jefferson heard was that a quantity of illicit drugs was found in Tom's janitorial closet in the church basement. Pastor intended to address the issue from the pulpit before his sermon today to quell the whispering.

Feigning a coughing fit, Earl Eggleston excused himself from the class to inform Pastor that Tom Farmer was in attendance. Grant followed to offer assistance, unaware Earl's fit was a pretense and not actual distress. In the hall, Earl explained his mission to Grant.

"Might as well go with you since I'm out here," Grant supposed as they walked to the office.

Jonathan hadn't seen the Farmers, who were deliberately tardy, enter the building, and the news Earl relayed surprised and delighted him.

"Praise God! I appreciate the head's up. It changes my plans. I think I need to put away the scalpel I intended to use and take out the bone saw," Jonathan rose from the chair behind his desk, taking a few steps toward a filing cabinet. "If you gentlemen will excuse me, I need to shift on the fly and review an old sermon."

Earl and Grant retreated to the foyer where Earl suggested they pray for their Pastor, Tom Farmer, and the congregation. After Earl prayed, they headed back to the Men's Class.

"I'm not proud of it, but my first response when I discovered the theft was vengeance. I wanted to see Tom punished and banished," Grant confessed to the older man.

"After the deacons confronted Tom, we discussed Galatians 6:1, where Paul instructs those who are spiritual to restore anyone caught in sin in a spirit of gentleness. We agreed that gentleness was our challenge, too. It shouldn't be, though, right? After all, gentleness is a fruit of the Spirit. I've been asking myself if the reason 'those who are spiritual' are singled out as the ones to restore the sinner is because they're the only ones capable of being gentle." Earl stopped in his tracks before continuing, prompting Grant to follow suit.

"I've been reading a lot about that passage," Earl continued. "Several commentators say that verse talks about people who have sin sneak up on them. They didn't plan to sin; they just fell into it accidentally-like. They say it's those kinds of sinners we need to restore with gentleness, not those who premeditate their sin or are habitual like Tom. So, I was wondering how we're supposed to deal with that class of sinners. Grant! Why are you making that face?" Earl interrupted himself.

"Sorry. I was just trying to think of a time I accidentally fell into sin. Is that even possible? And if it's accidental, is it a sin or a mistake?" Grant puzzled.

Earl scratched his white-haired head. "I feel confident saying accidental sin, if possible, is the rare exception and not the rule for man's behavior. Most of the time, we throw ourselves at it."

"True," Grant sadly agreed.

"And if Galatians 6:1 only applies to that rare sinner – only he is to be restored with gentleness – then what are we to do with men like Tom after we impose reasonable consequences? I mean, we fired him and asked him to think about restitution. Now what? He's back today, and Pastor thinks that's a good thing. I have to agree. I remember when his wife was brought into the nursery by her parents. It would break my heart to see Patty leave – probably hers, too."

"Did you ask him for a public apology?" Grant wondered.

"We didn't. Probably should have," Earl admitted and resumed walking toward the classroom. "It's hard to imagine a man doing that – not in this day and age. People would rather pick up stakes and move to another church, or worse, give up on church altogether."

"And Pharisees like me make that the attractive option," Grant closed his eyes for a step. "But not this time! I will be on the gentle restoration team if it kills me. There's no reason Tom can't be held accountable for his sin and restored with gentleness, right? Why does it have to be a choice between one or the other?"

"It doesn't," Earl confirmed and opened the classroom door.

The two men were just in time to hear the tail end of what Tom Farmer, standing in front of his chair, had to say to his Sunday School class.

"I'm as ashamed of what I've done as a man can be, and I ask your forgiveness," Tom concluded his speech, raising his eyes from the floor to look each man present in the eye.

"That's the gutsiest thing I've ever seen," Cal blurted.

Earl and Grant exchanged grins and took their seats.

"Thank you, Tom. You have my forgiveness." Will took charge of his class.

Each man took his turn expressing gratitude for Tom's repentance and granting forgiveness as Tom struggled to maintain his composure. When everyone had spoken, Marcus made a random confession about his own struggle with sin. It opened a floodgate of similar stories among the class members, and Will abandoned his meticulously prepared lesson as the Spirit moved the men to encourage one another.

Pastor Jefferson caught Tom and Patty Farmer in the vestibule before the service began and whispered his intention to them. The couple nodded in agreement, focused on their Pastor and oblivious to the side-eyed looks of several congregation members who passed the couple on their way into the sanctuary for worship.

When the worship in song and the announcements, given by Lefty Schneider, were complete, Pastor Jefferson stepped up to the pulpit.

"There's been gossip and rumors buzzing these past two weeks about a fellow member of this church. I'm going to set the record straight with the facts. For many years, Tom Farmer billed our church as an outside contractor for services he did not perform. The deacons confronted him, and he was fired from his position. He has repented, and we will discuss restitution. Tom, will you please stand?"

Tom Farmer stood, and every eye in the church was riveted on him.

"Is what I have said accurate?" Pastor Jefferson asked.

"It...it is," Tom agreed in a shaky voice, sensing the attention upon himself. "Except I'd like to add my sincere apology to everyone. I'm so ashamed."

"I want you all to turn your eyes up here and look at me. Thank you, Tom. You may be seated. Deacons, will you please stand?" Pastor continued.

All seated in a front row, Earl Eggleston, Lefty Schneider, and Joe Fowler stood to their feet.

"A factor in what happened is that the leadership of this church failed to ensure proper financial controls were in place. We were not careful stewards of the money you gave to the Lord, and for that, the deacons and I are also ashamed and ask your forgiveness for our sin of omission. Grant Renniger, with his expertise as the former manager of a large CPA firm, has volunteered to help us make the necessary corrections."

Pastor Jefferson paused to let the congregation process this additional admission.

"Deacons, you may sit," he instructed before continuing. "Now that we've looked at Tom, we've looked at Earl, Lefty, Joe, and myself, we're going to look to the word of God and see some pertinent instruction that should cause us all to evaluate ourselves. Why is that necessary, you may ask? Because in the same breath, Paul exhorts us in Galatians 6:1 to restore the brother caught in sin in a spirit of gentleness; he tells us to keep watch on ourselves lest we also be tempted. So, turn in your Bibles to James, chapter 3."

Above the sound of rustling pages, Pastor Jefferson's voice reverberated in the old sanctuary as he read aloud verses five and six.

"So also the tongue is a small member, yet it boasts of great things. How great a forest is set ablaze by such a small fire! And the tongue is a fire, a world of unrighteousness. The tongue is set among our members, staining the whole body, setting on fire the entire course of life, and set on fire by hell."

As he preached the sermon he'd delivered years ago and resurrected from his files, Emma Fowler and half the congregation with her squirmed uncomfortably in their pews.

CHAPTER THIRTY

"I can't believe it's ours!" Shelby squealed as Will turned the key in the front door of Latte Da and opened it for Shelby and Five to pass through ahead of himself.

Shelby and Will had closed on the property late that afternoon and then drove to the apartment Five shared with three other girls to help load several packed boxes in the van borrowed from Micah. They were astounded at how little Five had and that she owned no furniture, not even a bed. The twin bed she'd been using was part of a set belonging to a roommate, she told them.

Closing the door of the cafe behind him, Will muttered: "I hope the lights work. I just transferred them this morning. But knowing where the switches are located would also be helpful."

"I gotcha," Five piped up and took just a few steps toward the back wall, tripping a motion-activated floodlight mounted in a ceiling corner.

Seeing her way easily now, Five flipped two switches on the back wall, which turned on the bright overhead lighting behind the serving counter and the dimmer ambient lighting of the dining space.

"That's better. Okay. Light switches are on the back wall. Check!" Shelby instructed her memory. "Let me just have a minute to soak in this space, and then we can move your things upstairs, Five."

"You take all the minutes you want. You too, Will. I've had three years of soaking in this space, so I'm just going to take things up myself. I need a key, though," Five reminded.

"Yeah, that would make it easier for you," Will chuckled and handed Five the key marked for the door on the side street side of the building.

Five was off like a flash, her petite frame and bright pink hair aiding the effect. She could hardly stand the excitement of having a place of her own for the first time. Her old soul craved solitude and space, but the chaotic living situations she had endured since she arrived in the world 26 years ago never accommodated it.

She climbed the stairs to her second-floor one-bedroom apartment with a lamp rescued from a sidewalk heap in one hand and a bucket filled with cleaning supplies in the other. The apartment door lacked a deadbolt lock, which Will had promised to remedy as soon as possible. Five pushed through it, set her bucket and lamp on the floor, turned on the overhead living room light, and grinned like a love-struck teenage girl.

There were only three rooms besides the bathroom – living room, eat-in kitchen, and bedroom. But the space retained every bit of its original 1920s charm, with high ceilings, radiators, wide wooden base-boards, a cast iron soaking tub on a black and white penny tile floor, a white-enameled cast iron kitchen sink with a built-in drainboard, and vintage glass door knobs on two five-panel interior doors. Two massive arched windows in the living room overlooked the intersection of Chest-nut and Main Street, and soft light from the streetlamps poured through the uncovered windows.

From a single spot in the middle of the living room, Five surveyed her 850-square-foot apartment, filled with years of neglect and dust. How-ever, she easily imagined it as a bohemian oasis filled with cozy, thrifted furniture, rugs, and lush green plants against a backdrop of creamy-white walls. She pictured a bookcase between the living room windows filled with vintage books with ornate, foil-stamped spines – books she'd read on rainy evenings with a cup of hot tea. Maybe she'd have a purring cat to sit next to her or a fish tank with a school of iridescent red and blue striped neons, at the very least.

"Knock-knock. Can we come in? Say 'yes' because these boxes are heavy," Will announced from outside the apartment door Five had left open.

"Are you weak, Will?" Five teased.

"He's only weak-Willed when it comes to me," Shelby retorted with a pun and a wink toward her husband.

Five lowered her chin and gave Shelby a dead look. "I just threw up a little in my mouth right now," she joked.

"Haha. Get over it. We're still newlyweds," Shelby chuckled.

"She looked at you, and I swear I saw Elodie standing there!" Will exclaimed to his wife. "They couldn't be any more opposite-looking than they are, but that look Five gave you was a dead ringer for Elodie."

"Who's Elodie?" Five asked, intrigued.

"She's our neighbor, and we love her. We're a little scared of her like everyone else, but we love her," Will answered honestly.

"You're bound to meet her now that we own Latte Da," Shelby assured.

"I've been described as lovable and frightening occasionally, or some version of those terms. I hope I meet her," Five responded brightly.

Will began walking around the apartment, taking in the condition and lack of furnishings. He continued his survey to the open space across the hall, where he and Shelby had their rehearsal dinner.

Returning to the women in the apartment, Will remarked: "I wonder why they never used this space. Such a waste of income potential."

"They couldn't use it. Not according to the Fire Marshall. If you roast coffee beans, you're not supposed to have rental space above without a firewall – or, in this case, a fire ceiling," Five explained, realizing in her haste to be helpful she'd let the cat out of the bag.

Will was stunned by this revelation. "You knew this, yet you still asked us for this apartment."

"It's not technically rental space if I'm not paying you rent. You said I'd get the first year rent-free in addition to my regular pay," Five justified.

Will looked at Shelby and took a deep breath before returning his attention to Five.

"Five, that's not how we're going to do business. We won't play the angles or stick it to the man. We want God to bless our business, and He won't if we operate like that."

"So, you're God-fearing folk?" Five added a little Eastern Kentucky twang to her voice before remembering these were her employers. Correcting herself, she said softly, "Jesus people?"

"Jesus people through and through," Will affirmed, adding a smile.

"Oh, Lord!" Five uttered before her hand flew to cover her mouth.

Shelby focused on solving their immediate problem. "I guess we could take the roaster home and roast the beans there temporarily until we can install a fire ceiling," she suggested.

"That's a good fix to keep us legal with the Fire Marshall," Will agreed, relaxing the shoulders he'd tensed.

"Five, would you like to spend the night at our house tonight? We have a room the boys aren't using," Shelby offered.

"No, thanks. I'm home," Five beamed. "I want to clean. I'll have to make myself go to sleep tonight!"

"But...there's nothing here," Shelby tried to say the obvious gently.

Five shook her head defiantly. "I see a worn rug in the middle of this floor and an old couch covered in linen slipcovers looking shabby chic right here," she placed the imaginary piece in the room. "I should actually get rid of some pillows because it's too much! The windows there have massive spider plants hanging from hooks and a mother-in-law's tongue at least three feet tall in that corner. I have books and quirky treasures from thrift stores on the bookcase between the windows. Do you smell that? That's spicy beef stew cooking on my stove and cornbread in the oven. I'll serve it in my mismatched floral-patterned dishes and then soak in the tub and dry off with Turkish towels. All that is here!" Five was animated and adamant.

"I see it now," Shelby connected with Five, placing her hands on each side of the younger woman's face. "I see what you have here, and it's beautiful. We'll go home now and leave you to enjoy it. Don't forget to lock the door downstairs after we leave."

Shelby nudged a bewildered Will out the door and down the steps to the sidewalk.

"What was that?" Will asked as they walked to the van.

"That was learning about each other. We told Five we're Jesus people, and she told us everything her heart ever hoped for was wrapped up in that bare, dusty apartment."

"I didn't hear that," Will confessed.

"It's okay. I did," Shelby smiled.

Chapter Thirty-One

I t was a mild shock for Marie to receive the mid-morning phone call from Christine Williams inviting her over that afternoon for "tea and chat." Marie couldn't decide which part was more startling, the invitation to her neighbor's home or the notion of Christine feeling chatty. At 3 PM, Marie donned a red cardigan over her white button-down blouse and wide-leg camel slacks and made the short walk across the street at the corner. She noted that Bradley's old white van, usually parked in the side driveway, had been replaced with a late model silver SUV.

"Hmm, must have been a gift from Sister. Good for him," Marie mused as she proceeded up the walkway toward the porch steps.

"Good afternoon, Marie. I'm glad you were able to come," Christine welcomed her as the front door swung open before Marie had reached it.

"So am I," Marie responded genuinely, following her host into the foyer and then into Christine's home office, which was traditionally decorated but less imposing than the grand living room.

"That desk is stunning," Marie remarked of the ornate yet delicate centerpiece of the functional room.

"Thank you. This escritoire has been in my family for generations," Christine corrected Marie's terminology.

"Ah, the fancy desk has a fancy name," Marie responded, refusing to conform to Christine's upper-class standards.

Christine stifled a smile. Marie's gentle resistance to her imposing personality was the very thing that made Christine like her. She wasn't intimidated, unlike everyone else. And it was this quality, Christine believed, that could help her make an objective assessment of Bradley, of whom she was growing more wary of each week that passed.

Christine directed her guest to the settee. "Sit here," she ushered with an outstretched arm.

A sparkling silver tray set with a Royal Albert tea service rested on the coffee table before the settee. In its midst, a plate of delicate macaroons recognizable as a signature item from the Faircourt bakery, Flour & Flake, caught Marie's eye.

"Of course, your china pattern is Autumn Rose. Tell me, was this a good year for your garden roses?" Marie inquired.

"The State Fair judges seemed to think so," Christine beamed proudly. "I added another blue ribbon to my collection. I would have had a record-breaking unbroken streak if not for that wicked vandalism last year."

Christine shook her head to dislodge rising anger at the recollection of the crime against her that was never solved.

"A grave disappointment, I'm sure," Marie commiserated. "I'd love a tenth of your success with my quilting. Then again, winning blue ribbons is difficult if you don't enter your projects."

"You've got it all figured out," Christine chortled. "So, you quilt?"

"It keeps me from roaming the streets and honky-tonking," Marie joked. She lifted the saucer and teacup from the tray and inspected them.

"Let me fill that for you," Christine offered, reaching for the teapot.

"I was just thinking what a lovely inspiration this china pattern would be for a quilt. The colors are marvelous," Marie noted, extending the cup for her host to fill.

"Hello there!" Bradley greeted the ladies, stopping outside the office entrance.

"Hello," Christine responded. "Bradley, come here. I'd like to introduce you to our neighbor across the street. This is Marie Renniger."

Bradley crossed the room and extended his hand to Marie. "I'm glad to meet you. I'm Christine's little brother, Bradley."

"Well, we do keep running into one another – lately, at Big Mart, and before that, when you set up the reception in our yard. But it's good to be formally introduced at last," Marie smiled.

A furrow creased Bradley's brow. "I'm sorry, you must be mistaking me for someone else. I don't recall ever having had an encounter, and certainly not in your yard. What did you say? Setting up a reception? I don't think so," Bradley claimed with polite insistence.

"As you say," Marie answered cooly.

"Well, it's nice to meet you for the first time," Bradley forced a smile. "I'll excuse myself and let you ladies enjoy your tea." And he was gone.

"You seem at odds with your recollections," Christine commented.

"So it seems. Say, you wouldn't happen to be in need of a four-legged companion, would you?" Marie was eager to change the subject before she spouted an unfavorable opinion of her host's brother.

"Pardon?" Christine cocked her head, more surprised than uncomprehending of the unexpected question.

"We took in a stray dog last summer – Mercy is her name – and she's presented us with a litter of puppies. We'll be looking for homes for them," Marie explained.

"Don't look here!" Christine was succinct, eyebrows raised on her forehead.

"Okay, then," Marie chuckled. "Do you play rummy by any chance?"

Christine's face lit up like a Christmas tree. "Why yes! I haven't played in ages, but my Clark and I used to play almost every evening."

"If you have a deck of cards, we could play while we chat," Marie suggested.

"Let me look. It has been ages, as I said." Christine fairly leaped from her seat and departed to search for playing cards.

While she was gone, Marie sampled a macaroon and contemplated Bradley's denial of ever interacting with her. It was mind-boggling. Bradley either suffered dementia, or he was deliberately deceitful.

Christine returned, raising a sealed deck of cards in the air triumphantly.

"I'll give you fair warning: I'm competitive," Christine advised, smiling as she unwrapped the deck.

"Duly noted," Marie acknowledged. "Best of five rounds?"

"Agreed!" Christine shuffled and dealt the cards expertly, losing little of her dexterity in the years she'd been away from playing.

Christine took the first round in short order, forcing Marie to sit straighter and focus harder.

"Can anyone join?" Bradley requested, passing by the office entrance again and enticed by the activity. He was bored with weeks of nothing but television viewing and the Scrabble games he felt obligated to let Christine win.

"Sorry. Ladies table only," Marie demurred, answering for herself and Christine.

"So much for friendly neighbors," Bradley growled and stomped away.

"So much for dementia," Marie concluded, eliminating that possibility.

Christine shrugged her shoulders to Marie instead of defending her sibling and dealt the next round. After a few plays, Christine discarded a card and, realizing an error, attempted to reclaim it.

"Oh, no you don't! You put it down and withdrew your hand. Put it back," Marie insisted.

Christine frowned, grudgingly followed the order, and lost the hand. And then she lost the next three rounds, whipped by her neighbor, four to one.

"So, what's your assessment of my half-brother?" Christine consoled herself that she could still achieve the objective for which she'd invited Marie.

Marie attempted to tamp down her reverie from her decisive victory and weigh the response she should give. After several moments, she sighed and answered bluntly: "He's a gaslighting narcissist."

"I appreciate your directness," Christine responded, her shoulders sagging.

"Most people don't. I tried to find kinder words, honestly. I'm not good at that."

Christine waved away Marie's admission, focusing on her problem at hand. "I just have to figure out what to do about him," she mused in a whisper.

"I'm sure you will. Thank you for inviting me over this afternoon," Marie said as she stood to leave.

"And I thank you for coming and for your reliable candor."

"We should play rummy again!" Marie suggested with eagerness.

"Marie, playing with you is not much fun," Christine pronounced.

Marie smirked. "That's what people tell me."

Chapter Thirty-Two

Shelby and Five sat at the cafe table nearest to the LED lights of the prep area, pouring over inventory and payroll accounts. Five patiently explained the order levels, wage ranges, and taxes, repeating herself at least twice, sometimes three times, until Shelby claimed to understand.

"I hope you won't respect me less for being dense about numbers. They make my head swim. I'm more artsy-brained and word-oriented," Shelby apologized.

"Well, if you trust me, it's fine for now that I understand how to manage it. You'll catch on once you live in Latte Da for a while," Five reassured.

Shelby sat back in her chair. "I have no choice but to trust you."

Five frowned as she processed the comment and then relaxed. "I get it. People should earn our trust. But we don't always have the luxury of the time that takes." She seemed to speak from experience.

"That's exactly it, Five. You get it," Shelby confirmed the young woman's interpretation.

Five smiled shyly, turning her head and displaying the tattooed music notes running down her neck.

A light rapping on the cafe's front door made both women look toward the sound. Ava, Elodie, June, Marie, and Mariana bunched their faces together near the glass. Shelby sprang to the door to let them in.

"I'm so glad you all came!" Shelby gushed as she welcomed the group inside.

"We couldn't turn down the invite!" Ava replied, her head swiveling to view various areas of the shop, trying to take in the place as if for the first time.

"I always thought this was a marvelous old building. I'm so glad you and Will bought it," June commented, meandering toward the prep area.

"Five, I want you to meet my neighbors," Shelby beckoned her employee to join her. "Ladies, this is Five. She's the lifeblood of our operation, and we couldn't do this without her. Five, these are my neighbors, friends, and fellow members of Grace Fellowship Church: Ava, Marie, Elodie, Mariana, and June."

"Ah, Jesus people," Five categorized the women, trying not to sound judgy. She pasted on a smile.

"To the bone," Elodie emphasized, reading the young woman's fiery tone and throwing gasoline on it.

"Elodie, right?" Five recalled. "Will said I have an expression that reminds him of you."

"That was a straight-up compliment, girl!" Elodie laughed and turned to take a self-guided tour of the prep area and restrooms.

"Ladies, look around. I need your suggestions for improvements. I don't want to turn the place upside down, but I want to put a fresh stamp on it," Shelby instructed as the women dispersed.

"Mariana, are you alright?" Marie asked, concern written on her face.

Five, Shelby, and June, all nearby to hear the question, looked at the visibly pregnant woman and noted what Marie noted on Mariana - a sign of distress.

"The wave is coming. I can feel it," Mariana lost her composure and sobbed.

"What's wrong?!" Shelby, unfamiliar with mid-stage pregnancy, was frightened and stepped forward to embrace her friend.

"That's the problem. There's absolutely nothing wrong. I just have to cry sometimes. Hormones, I guess," Mariana wailed.

"I cried through my pregnancy, too," Marie consoled, patting Mariana's back.

From the prep area, Elodie noticed the women huddled around Mariana, Shelby hugging her. Curiosity compelled her to investigate the problem.

"Hormones," Five leaned to whisper when Elodie reached her side.

Shelby released Mariana, and Elodie stepped forward to offer sympathy.

"Are you cryin' because your skin's gettin' patchy?" Elodie asked with sincerity.

"I wasn't!" Mariana, horrified by this new information, wailed louder than before.

Five turned away to hide her laughter and then leaned to whisper in Shelby's ear. "Elodie and I are more alike than Will knows. I like her."

"You're going to like her and the other ladies even more when you see what they have for you outside," Shelby informed her.

Five was thrown. "For me? They don't even know me."

"My friends want to be your friends. I shared your vision for your apartment, and they have a few things to bring it along. Come see!" Shelby led Five outside to where she knew Cal's F150 would be parked around the corner.

"Hi," Will waved, standing beside the truck with DeShawn. Cal grinned from the driver's seat in the rearview mirror.

The ladies inside came outside to witness Five's reaction to their effort on her behalf.

Five's hazel eyes grew wide, and her jaw dropped when she recognized the outlines of a double mattress, bed frame, a couch, and a small wooden table and chair.

"The ladies also scavenged kitchen essentials, bath towels, and bed-ding. It's not much. Nothing is fancy or matches, but it's a start," Shelby explained.

Five's eyes filled, and she was lost for words.

DeShawn held up a decorative hook in one hand and a drill in the other, which he revved to draw Shelby's attention.

"Oh, there's one more thing in the cab. A little housewarming gift from Will and me." Shelby opened the truck's passenger door and presented Five with a gift she knew would be perfect – a massive spider plant in a macrame sling.

"No one has ever…" Five began and could not finish as tears spilled onto her cheeks.

Shelby smiled and began issuing commands. "Let's get this furniture upstairs, guys! Five, show them where you want things placed. Ladies, grab a box you can manage."

"Grab a box, Fiver," Elodie encouraged, initiating the girl to her association with a new moniker.

Five chuckled, brushed the tears from her cheeks, and hoisted a hefty box of kitchenware from the truck bed. "No one has ever…" she repeated joyfully.

CHAPTER THIRTY-THREE

"What time is it?" Grant asked sleepily, aware his wife was awake by her unsettled movements.

"3:20. Sorry if I woke you," Marie apologized.

"I got to go to the bathroom, anyway. Be right back." Grant rose and trudged away, navigating by the moonlight peeking around the window blinds.

Soon, he climbed back into the bed and propped himself on his left side to face Marie.

"Bad dream?" he guessed at the reason for her sleeplessness.

"No. There's just a lot on my mind, I guess. Christine Williams has her hands full with that leeching brother of hers – correction: half-brother. And I've been wondering about our brothers, David and Daniel. You haven't heard from the boys, have you?"

"Not recently," Grant admitted without concern.

"Me either, and it bothers me. Sometimes I think I could change my phone number and they wouldn't realize it for months."

"They're grown men, Marie. They have responsibilities and lives of their own."

"Well, so did you. But did you let that stop you from calling your mom regularly to check in on her?" Marie spoke to the ceiling, lying on her back.

"That's different. My mom's been alone since Dad died. Who was going to check on her if Gerard and I didn't? Our boys know you've got me."

"Do you suppose Ava has forgotten Mia and Marit because she still has Marcus and Marley Marie?" Marie snapped.

Grant sighed and rearranged the pillow under his elbow for lack of anything else to do. He'd wanted to console his wife and seemed to stir her up instead. Deciding her question was hypothetical, he remained silent.

"I hoped our family would be the close family I didn't have growing up," Marie began, turning her body on its right side to face Grant and propped up on her elbow. Her eyes acclimated to the low light, and she observed his expressions. "And we were close when we were raising the boys. But sometime after their college graduations, it was like trying to hold a fistful of sand. They slid through my fingers until there was hardly anything left anymore. How is a mother supposed to be happy with that? Tell me you're happy with it."

"I don't think 'happy' is how I'd describe it, Babydoll. 'Resigned' is more accurate – but not miserably so. I simply hold different expectations than you. Unmet expectations make people miserable."

Marie let her elbow drop, and her head hit the pillow. "So, you just take what you get?" she asked, knowing the answer.

"Basically. What's the alternative? Stomp my foot and stir up drama? I've done that before, and you don't like it so much, remember?"

"I know," Marie sighed. "But they still expect us to be the Fire Department. When there's trouble, they remember us, and we're supposed to run to them with sirens blazing and water cannons ready to extinguish the blaze. Once the fire's out, we go home and wait for the next one. That's aggravating," Marie complained.

"I don't mind being a fireman. Say, lady, you got a fire you need me to put out?" Grant twitched his eyebrows at his wife, trying to make her smile.

"Oh, good grief! I don't possess a single hormone at this hour," Marie exclaimed, turning over. "Go back to sleep!"

"How's it going, guys?" Grant, killing two birds with one stone, spoke to David and Daniel on an evening three-way call.

"Good, good," the men responded in twin unison.

"Who needs a puppy?" Grant asked, getting their attention. Renniger men loved dogs.

David, the attorney, laughed and chided his father. "Nobody needs a puppy, Dad. They make life pure hell until they're grown, and everyone guts it out till then. Whose puppies are you trying to pawn off?"

"Mine," Grant answered matter-of-factly.

"What? Is this a new hobby? Are you breeding dogs? What kind?" Daniel, the insurance agency owner, fired his questions in succession.

"It wasn't intentional. We took in a stray last summer and, voila, puppies. We've got six doodle-lab mixes ready for homes in early December."

"Fester is all we can manage in our high-rise condo. But thanks, Dad," David answered, referencing the 6-year-old French bulldog he and Liza already owned.

"I knew you were a long shot," Grant chuckled. "How about you, Daniel?"

"I'm sure Grant and Georgia would love one, but high school activities have them stretched thin. Andie would kill me if she had one more thing to look after. I wouldn't mind having a dog myself, but I'm positive it won't fly with Andie," Daniel lamented.

"I understand," Grant reassured.

And he understood. Everyone understood that Andie called the shots in Daniel's household and that her decisions were based on what was optimal for Andie above all else. In the back of his mind, Grant half expected the "Fire Department," as Marie had put it, to be called in someday to deal with the emotional inferno of a second failed marriage for Daniel, but he prayed not.

"How's Liza doing?" Daniel asked his brother, wanting to change the subject to his sister-in-law's health.

"She's feeling great, and we're hopeful she's beaten the cancer. I don't think I could go through what we went through again," David answered.

"Hey man, I want to let you know how bad I feel I wasn't there for you and Liza like I should have been when she was going through her treatments," Daniel admitted, attempting transparency and vulnerability with the twin from whom he'd grown distant.

David didn't respond for several seconds. Finally, he replied: "You're telling me you felt bad, not that you're sorry, and you'll try to do better, God forbid, there's a next time. Do I have that right?"

"No! You know what I mean," Daniel grew defensive.

"Why don't you say what you mean instead of making me supply the nobler spin to what you do say?" David shot back.

Grant could sense the tension in the airwaves between the brothers and subconsciously tensed his upper body, bracing for an explosive impact.

"Okay. That's fair, man," Daniel exhaled in admission.

Father and brothers relaxed and spent the next 15 minutes in more friendly conversation, catching up on the latest news each had to share. After their goodbyes, Grant set his cell phone on the armrest of the cream-colored rocker recliner where he sat. He wondered if and how the trajectory of the conversation might have been different if David hadn't risked challenging his brother about the impact of his words. He thought for a long while about it.

Chapter Thirty-Four

"This isn't in your job description, Ava, but I appreciate your help. You're a real trooper," Jonathan commended his part-time office assistant as they cleaned the church bathrooms.

"I'm sure you didn't go to seminary to do this either," Ava responded, brushing a stray lock of hair that had fallen in front of her eyes with a swipe of her forearm.

"As a matter of fact, there was a one-credit course in toilet scrubbing and disinfecting," Jonathan asserted.

"Really?"

"No."

"I didn't think so, but you never know. You did go to Southern," Ava teased the young man, who was her eldest daughter, Marley's age.

"Touche!" Jonathan chuckled. "So, I gather the calls aren't pouring in with responses to our ad for a part-time custodian to take Tom's place?"

"Not a single one," Ava lamented. "Perhaps we have to advertise it differently to attract a wider pool of candidates.

"Such as..." Jonathan invited her suggestion and placed the toilet bowl scrubber in its holder on the utility cart.

"Well, Tom did the job part time during the day. That pretty much eliminates anyone who has a full-time day job. What if this position worked evening hours so someone might work it as a second job?

"Hmm. I don't know..." Jonathan was reluctant.

"Or, we could just keep doing it ourselves," Ava offered with feigned enthusiasm. She sprayed the mirror with cleaner, wiping it off with a dust-free rag in circular motions.

"Hmm. I'll consider it. Are you ready to tackle the sanctuary?" Jonathan asked.

"Ready or not, here it comes!" Ava responded and held the bathroom door open to enable Jonathan to wheel the cart into the hall.

Inside the sanctuary, Ava and Jonathan each took a garbage bag and, starting on opposite sides of the room, canvassed the rows of pews for candy wrappers, discarded tissues, and other assorted trash.

"Hey! I got a paper airplane here!" Jonathan announced and launched the folded bulletin in Ava's direction.

"Nice!" Ava laughed. "All I know is we'd better find someone for Tom's job before Vacation Bible School, when the kids are in here with popcorn."

"That's what? Six or seven months from now? Yeah, we better find someone way before that!" Jonathan agreed.

"Way before that! Christmas Candlelight Service is less than six weeks away. Every church that has them gets wax on the pews and floors." Ava reminded.

The two employees of Grace Fellowship Church zig-zagged through the rows, filling their trash bags quietly for a few minutes.

"Do you know if Tom Farmer has a new job yet?" Jonathan's voice broke the silence.

Ava dropped her bag at her side and turned to face the pastor. "Why? You don't want to rehire him, do you? I've heard he's still looking for something and having difficulty."

"No, no. I can't do that. But a thought occurred. I understand he needs income from another job. But he also needs to make restitution to this church, and he knows what needs to be done here. Maybe your idea of cleaning the church in the evening hours would work for both of us!

I might also know someone who'd give him a job that paid something to compensate for the lost income he and Patty need."

"A capital idea!" Ava encouraged spontaneously and then laughed at herself. "Sorry. Marcus has discovered The Addams Family. He loves that phrase and has all of us saying it."

Jonathan smiled and shook his head. But soon, an intruding notion furrowed his brows.

"Do you suppose people would throw a fit if word got out that Tom was working off his restitution back here? Word always seems to get out."

"How else is the man supposed to pay his debt?" Ava's tone was exasperated at the thought of adverse reactions from church members. As a former pastor's wife, she'd seen her share from the good seats.

"As much as I'd love to spare Tom more grief, we'd have to inform the congregation of our intention beforehand. When you try to keep something on the down low to spare someone, people seem to assign the worst intentions to it – like we're trying to be sneaky," Jonathan lamented and sat sideways in the last pew.

"That's our sinful human nature," Ava agreed, leaning against the pew Jonathan sat on. "It's also our nature to be curious, and I'm curious about something that's none of my business. I'm going to ask it anyway, and you'll probably tell me so. How much does Tom have to pay back? Like, would he work it off in a year or ten? He's a Boomer like me – not a spring chicken."

"For the record, it's none of your business, Ava," Jonathan confirmed. Then he smiled and added: "Off the record, it's still to be decided. But since you came up with the good idea of someone working off hours, do you have any thoughts on this subject?"

Ava laughed. "One good idea per day might be my limit." Then she put a finger to her mouth and bit a nail as she considered an answer. "You told the congregation that you and the deacons bore some responsibility for the billing going on so long without appropriate controls. Might that be 50% responsibility? Then he'd have his debt paid in, let's see, two and a half to three years. That's doable."

In a burst of energy, Jonathan jumped up from his seat. "I feel like some things got sorted here. Thank you, Ava. I'll present this plan to the deacons and see what they have to say. Ready to tackle the Sunday School room trash cans?"

"Oh, sure. After we finish Tom's job, maybe we can do our own," Ava suggested.

Jonathan snickered, raised an index finger, and recited: "A capital idea!"

Chapter Thirty-Five

Per his established habit, Luther Hall waited a day to return his sister's telephone message. Though her message was oddly cryptic rather than her usual direct demand, she clearly needed his help to solve another interpersonal crisis of her own making, and he wasn't eager for the task.

"Hold on a moment, Luther," were the first words out of Christine's mouth after picking up her brother's call on the second ring.

Christine locked her bedroom door, entered her ensuite bathroom, and closed that door; then, she pulled a monogrammed towel from the linen closet and placed it over the floor register. She was taking no chances of Bradley overhearing her conversation with Luther.

"Okay, I'm back. I'm just going to come out and tell you: Bradley has returned to Faircourt," Christine informed.

It took Luther a minute to process the information, having not heard that name in decades.

"Bradley Hall?" Luther, surprised, sought clarification.

"None other. Showed up on my doorstep several weeks ago offering help just after I'd had my fall."

"Convenient timing. Very convenient, as a matter of fact," Luther mused. "Where's he living?"

"Under my roof," Christine sighed, brushing wrinkles from her pink satin pajama pants.

"What?! You let him move in - a total stranger?" Luther asked in disbelief.

"As you said, his timing was good. I needed help, what with the staircase in this house and all. I can't tell you how difficult it was to navigate up and down on my own, although you'd have known if you'd even called to check on me. Besides, you know I don't like to be alone in this house when it storms. And I still have that murderer living across the street whose fault it was that I injured myself in the first place," Christine defended her decision-making, playing loosely with the facts of what happened.

"Why didn't you call me and tell me our half-brother had come back?" Luther's question sounded like a cross-examination to Christine.

"Well, I'm telling you now. And the truth is, I'm regretting my decision, which, I'll admit, was made impulsively."

"Did he pressure you?" Luther asked, beginning to think more calmly.

"Not exactly, no. I'm not sure. He turned to go – who knows where, I wonder now – and I saw an opportunity slipping away. I thought it might work out. I was vulnerable, Luther!" Christine was exasperated with herself, an unfamiliar feeling.

"Has he asked about me? Does he realize I still live in Faircourt?"

Christine wrinkled her brow as she tried to recall Bradley's interest in Luther. "He hasn't asked about you, now that you mention it. That does seem strange."

Luther frowned unseen into the phone. "Tell me everything you've learned about him since he's been with you," he directed, hoping his voice did not betray his growing suspicion.

"He mentioned he's been married more than once. He worked as a chef. Wait, he didn't say chef; he said he worked in restaurants. He can cook decently, though. He told me Brooks, the other brother, passed away a few years ago. And he arrived in a white van in disgraceful condition with California license plates. That's it. That's all I've learned. He prepares my meals and does errands, but aside from that, he watches television in his room."

"Is he financially independent?" Luther wondered.

"Apparently, he is my dependent now. I had to replace that old van of his already."

"That's it!" Luther concluded to himself. He knew little of Christine and Clarkson's efforts to ruin Edward Hall, his new wife, and these half-brothers. Though he remembered his sister was ecstatic when the brothers left Faircourt for California, followed a few months later by their father, Edward, and Margie.

As he assessed the current situation, Luther found it too coincidental and fortuitous that Bradley had so quickly wormed his way into Christine's patronage, a patronage which was already paying off for him. Since his sister was a widow of obvious means, Luther was sure Bradley would be after more significant prizes. When he thought about Christine's will, of which Luther himself was the primary beneficiary, he grew alarmed.

"Tell me what happened to make you regret your decision," Luther asked.

"He's going through my things. When I go to church, he goes through my things."

"Christine! He's got to go!" Luther exploded.

"Relax. Nothing's missing. He hasn't taken anything; I've checked. He's just nosey." Christine defended Bradley and wasn't sure why.

"He hasn't taken anything because he hasn't found what he's looking for. Sister, don't be so naïve!"

Christine did not appreciate being called naïve by her younger brother, even if he was one of the most intelligent people she knew. She decided she would not tell him about Marie's visit and her appraisal of Bradley.

"Look, Luther! I made an impulsive decision to take Bradley in, and I'm not looking to make another to throw him out. He's useful to me,"

Christine snapped.

"So, what is it you want me to do for you?" Luther demanded; his patience evaporated.

"I want you to use your resources to learn more about him. Has he told me the truth about his years in California? I need more information. Is he simply moody, or does his past suggest he has deeper issues?"

"He's moody?" Luther repeated her description.

"At times, though, aren't we all?"

"Okay, I'll see what I can find out. In the meantime, remind me, your copy of your Last Will and Testament is in your safe deposit box at the bank, right?"

"Yes, it's at the bank," Christine answered and ended the call.

It had not occurred to her that Bradley might try to manipulate her to change her will until that moment.

CHAPTER THIRTY-SIX

"Here you go, Calisthenics," Elodie handed Cal a sleepy black puppy to cuddle while the household conducted Thursday Meeting.

"Thanks, El," Cal carefully received the puppy he'd requested.

A contented grin spread across Cal's face as he laid the puppy on his chest and began stroking the top of its silky head with an index finger.

"Now dat everyone's here, including our canine guest, we can begin our meeting. Tanksgiving is just two weeks away. Do we have a plan?" Marcus kicked things off.

"Shelby wants to host Thanksgiving this year. She called this afternoon and invited all of us to the upper room at Latte Da. I told her I would get back to her after we meet this evening." June informed.

"I'm happy to let someone else have a turn at hostin'," Elodie answered quickly.

"What about the Cowboys game? Will there be a television?" Grant wanted to know.

"I doubt there will be a television, Grant. Can you survive?" Ava looked at him side-eyed.

"I guess we'll find out," Grant mumbled.

"Is she inviting anyone else? Surely her brother and the kiddoes, right?" Marie asked.

"Yes, Shelby's planning for a big crew. Besides herself and Will, she's inviting her brother's family, the McBrides, two guys who work at the car lot, Tom and Patty Farmer, and Five. Oh, and Sam and Silas, of course. If we accept, there will be 22 altogether," June informed.

"Dat's a lot of people for her first Tanksgiving," Marcus remarked.

"That's what I said. But it's sign-up potluck except for the turkeys that they're providing. And she insisted 22 was a harmonious round number, and if we didn't come, there'd only be 15, and that number was odd and awful," June recounted with a chuckle.

"Impeccable logic!" Grant scoffed, shaking his head.

"Her math is off. That would be 26 people," Cal corrected.

June squinted her face as she calculated in her head. "No. 22 is correct."

"You said Shelby and Will and their two boys, three Normans, three McBrides, two guys from the car lot, two Farmers, five others, and seven of us. That makes 26," Cal insisted.

"There's no 'five others.' There's Five. That's just one," Ava explained.

"Five is one? Since when? That makes no sense," Cal puzzled, scratching his thin white beard.

The ladies began to chuckle.

"Five is one person. Shelby and Will have an employee whose name is Five," Marie took a crack at explaining it to Cal.

"His name is Five? That's different. Who gives their child a number instead of a name?" Cal wondered aloud. The sleeping puppy on his chest stirred and looked up at him.

"Sweetie, the furniture you delivered to Latte Da last week was for Five's apartment," June reminded, hoping another health issue wasn't brewing for her husband.

"Nobody told me who it was for – just where it was going," Cal responded defensively.

"And 'he' is actually a 'her,'" Elodie supplemented the information regarding Five.

Cal cocked his head, trying to process what he'd been told.

"And Five is her given name?" he questioned, disbelieving.

"Well, we don't know about that. But she seems like a nice girl, a little shy, maybe, but very appreciative of our help, including yours, I'm sure, dear," June soothed.

"If you don't like her name, call her somethin' else," Elodie suggested mischievously. "How about Six or Seven? Personally, I'm callin' her Fiver, but not 'cause I don't like her name. It's my way of bein' friendly."

"Stripping a person of their identity and replacing it with something of your own liking might be considered being as friendly as a badger with a baby. Just putting that out there for your consideration, El," Marie suggested to her friend.

"Nope. It makes folks tougher, right, Calcutta? Go ahead and testify how I've been good for you," Elodie chuckled, rejecting the hypothesis.

Cal obliged and raised a hand in silent testimony.

"No one's ever going to change Elodie. Dat mold is fixed!" Marcus declared.

"Why would anyone want to change this masterpiece of God's handiwork?" Elodie challenged.

June ducked as if a lightning bolt were imminent. "Ut oh!"

"Pride goes before destruction," Ava began quoting.

"And a haughty spirit before a fall," Marie finished Proverbs 16:18

"Well, if the Lord takes me home to sanctify my pride, at least I'll be surrounded by all you old people as I take my dyin' breath," Elodie reflected, shrugging off the rebuke.

"Dat's a strange consolation," Marcus observed.

Grant shifted uncomfortably in his chair. "Please don't dig into her psyche, Marcus," he begged. "Everything about her is strange. We've all accepted it, so let's move on. Can we get back to the Thanksgiving food?"

"What do you want us to sign up for, Grant?" June asked after a moment of awkward silence.

"Stuffing!" Marie and Ava answered in unison for Grant, who smirked, acknowledging their correct response.

"Really? Not pies?" June questioned.

Marie recited her husband's strict definition of stuffing: "Stuffing shall consist of white bread cubes, onion, celery, and spices. Period."

"Breadcrumbs are not a suitable substitute for cubes," Elodie added, rolling her eyes.

Ava completed the rant she'd heard every year from Grant's lips for 30 years. "There shall be no foreign substances added, including, but not limited to, sausage, chestnuts, cranberries, or apricot jam. Gizzards render stuffing inedible and fit for the trash can."

"Don't forget: 'Dressing is what goes on a salad. Don't call it dat,'" Marcus sighed. "Grant has powerful feelings about stuffing, June."

"I see," June acknowledged. "Since Shelby's planning on such a large group, why don't we make Grant's recipe and another that's a little more...more..." she searched for the right word.

"Appetizing? Creative?" Elodie tried to help.

Sensing Thursday Meeting was devolving into culinary chaos and there was nothing else to discuss, Grant rose from his chair, flapped an arm in June's direction for her wild suggestion of compromise, and dismissed himself to his room.

"I'll tell Shelby we accept her invitation and will bring two different kinds of stuffing," June advised those who remained.

"A capital idea!" Marcus agreed, index finger raised.

"Agh!" Cal shrieked, followed by a sheepish grin. He lifted the puppy from his chest, where a sizeable wet spot was visible. "Puppy piddle strikes again," he groaned.

Chapter Thirty-Seven

"Do you know what Mariana has signed up to bring to Will and Shelby's Thanksgiving?" Grant interrogated Bobby, who had just stepped foot inside the Garage Cave.

"You mean what DeShawn signed up for? He's the better cook," Bobby corrected.

"Fine. Whoever. What's coming from your house? Does that cover it?" Grant huffed.

"Sweet potato casserole and green bean almandine," Bobby announced, satisfied with his household's contribution.

"Ugh! Vegetables," Grant hung his head and turned away.

"What did vegetables ever do to him?" Bobby asked, looking at Marcus.

"Existed. Dat is dere crime," Marcus explained flatly.

"How's your daughter-in-law feeling these days?" Grant changed the subject and sat at the card table.

"She's doing great, and little Julia is growing like she should, according to the doctor," Bobby beamed. "Appreciate your asking."

"I heard Mariana has crying spells," Cal blurted.

Bobby raised his eyebrows, taken aback by the public revelation of information he considered private.

"The girl just has more hormones flying around her head than she's used to, that's all. She's alright," Bobby defended.

Grant laughed out loud. "My Marie cried for the last six months of her pregnancy. Then, our twins were born, and they cried for the next six months. Don't know why I'm laughing. I could have used a turn at crying and never got it."

"Go ahead, Grant. Maybe repressing it all dese years is what's wrong wit you," Marcus mocked.

"Thanks. I'm good," Grant retorted testily.

Acclimating to the transparency of his neighbors, Bobby relaxed and admitted: "I told the kids that when the baby is born, and she cries, I might just cry from pity right along with her. They think I'm kidding, but I might not be. It'll break my heart to hear it."

"From one grandfader to anoder, never forget who da parents are. You'll have to let dem discipline Julia and make her cry," Marcus warned. "I mean, when she's older den a baby."

"I know," Bobby sighed. "But I might have to retreat to your house when that happens, and you might have to tie me to a chair. I realize I'm being over the top. And I wasn't like this when my own kids were little. I'm not sure what's happened. Gone soft in my old age, I guess."

"Something happens between old men and babies," Grant mused.

"Something happened between an old man and puppies, in my case," Cal admitted.

"It's great of you ladies to come to help us get ready for our grand re-opening Monday," Shelby thanked her 306 Cedar Street neighbors.

"We're happy to do it," Ava answered, wiping baseboards on her hands and knees.

"We are," June echoed. "Besides, it's Garage Cave night for the guys, so they're not missing us."

Five chuckled at the implication. "So, your husbands would miss you if you were away any other night?" she challenged, disbelieving.

Ava popped her head up to exchange glances and wordless consultations with June and Marie.

"Yeah, they would," Ava answered with a shrug and returned to her work.

"Oh, there's no 'probably' about it," Elodie chimed in, rinsing the rag she was using to clean the dairy fridge shelves. "Last time we went shopping together, Marie and June got phone calls asking when we thought we'd be home. Ava got a text. Those men are practically helpless without their wives."

"They're not helpless," Marie defended. "They just get a little at loose ends with themselves." She and June sat at a table painting new "Men" and "Women" signs for the restrooms.

"Cal says the house isn't a home when we're not there," June smiled at recalling the compliment as she painted.

"Aww, that's sweet," Shelby reacted. She and Five were cleaning the upholstered couch with a spray foam stain remover and sponges.

"A little too sweet," Five blurted. Realizing her impulsive comment had sounded mean, she softened. "My father was the exact opposite. The longer my mother stayed out of the house, the gladder he was." Five stopped herself from further confession. She reminded herself that these women weren't in her peer therapy group.

June looked at her and consoled sincerely: "I'm sorry to hear that, Five."

"It's no big deal," Five brushed her words away and focused on her task.

"My family put another spin on being glad when someone was out of the house. My parents were happiest when it was me who wasn't home," Marie stated this – common knowledge to her childhood friends – for

Five's benefit. Thinking perhaps that her misery might like company.

Indeed, it did. Five looked over at Marie. "Eventually, I was happiest when it was me who was out of the house. I've never looked back," she admitted, connecting with Marie.

"But look at me now!" Marie reversed course. "Now I'm missed at home, and I wouldn't have it any other way. God's been good to me."

"Good? But wasn't it God who gave you parents who didn't like you?" Five puzzled without a trace of meanness.

"Everybody has sinful parents to some degree or another – including my children, who were affected by my sinful failings as a parent. I try to remember that. But I've also learned that what I think of as bad or evil isn't necessarily so in God's view. Pain, for example. What's good about pain? Well, it's a signal that something's wrong so that we can do something about the underlying cause. I'm not only talking about physical pain. Emotional pain tells us something's wrong – this isn't how it should be. Then, we'll understand to do something differently or look for our answers in a different place than where we've been trying to find them. My parents helped me see I wanted to be different as a parent. And by God's goodness and grace, I was. Not perfect by any means, but better. So, I give Him all the credit," Marie explained in a steady, soothing voice.

From her vantage point, working shoulder to shoulder with Five, Shelby could see Five's eyes filling before she turned her head to hide them.

Chapter Thirty-Eight

"Does it look like we're hosting a baby shower rather than a grand opening?" Will asked, standing in front of Latte Da in the predawn darkness with a grocery bag in each hand. He tried to be gentle in his critique of the pink, silver, and white balloon arch framing the front door of the cafe, illuminated by an overhead floodlight.

"No!" Shelby objected. "It ties in with our pink and white awnings. But if you don't like it, I'm afraid you'll hate what's happening inside."

She turned the key in the lock and threw open the door, tripping the light on a motion sensor. Half a dozen giant bouquets of pink, silver, and white helium balloons graced the interior, giving it a girl-party vibe. Will's eyes widened, but he said nothing.

"It's just for a few days until they sag. Five loves it, and so do I," Shelby demurred.

Will chuckled. "You both have hair that's some shade of pink! Of course, you both love it."

Shelby entered the cafe and inspected a strand of strawberry blonde hair. She dismissed her husband's declaration that it was a shade of pink.

"Thank you so much for taking the day off to get us through Day One. I'm so nervous!" Shelby bubbled.

"This town hasn't been properly caffeinated for a week while this place was closed. I'm sure you'll have a very successful first day. What can I do to be of help?" Will offered.

"Five and I can handle the counter service. I need you to be the Mayor of Latte Da. Welcome our customers, chat them up if they're morning people, and keep the seating areas picked up. You're friendly, and most everyone will know you from your day job," Shelby directed.

"Can do!" Will affirmed, then checked his watch. "T minus 45 minutes."

"Good morning, bosses!" Five greeted Shelby and Will as she entered the back door. "Got my roasted beans?" she asked as she pulled scone dough, which she had premade the day before, out of the fridge.

"Right here!" Will set the grocery bags on a prep table. "We roasted these on our back porch last evening and made the whole block have the aroma of coffee heaven."

Five inspected the contents of the bags and handed one off to Shelby. "Perfect! Shelby, grind a quarter of the beans in this bag for the drip coffee maker, if you would. I'll put the other varieties in their containers by the espresso machine while the oven preheats.

For the next 40 minutes, scones were baked and arranged in the display case, drip coffee was brewed, cream carafes filled, and surfaces that had already been cleaned were cleaned again. At precisely 7 AM, Will unlocked the front door and was surprised to find half a dozen people waiting to enter and evaluate the cafe, now under new management.

"Hey, Jonathan!" Will greeted his Pastor, the first customer in the door.

"Is the coffee any good here?" Jonathan joked, lightly punched Will's arm, and made his way to the counter to place his order.

"Hello, Mr. and Mrs. Grimes! Welcome to the new and improved Latte Da," Will shook hands with the senior couple on his mail route.

"Joe Jacobs! Thank you for coming," Will welcomed his newest Sunday School class member.

"Hiya, Sarah! Sure appreciate your support. I'll be back on my route tomorrow," Will ushered in a coworker.

"I was sent to bring coffee back for everyone at the post office. All of us hope your new business makes you a fortune," Sarah informed him with a smile.

"Bradley, right?" Will guessed as he held the door for his next-door neighbor.

"You got it! Thought I'd come on over and support the new kids on the block," Bradley slapped Will on the back. "Had my window open last evening while watching television in my room. A coffee commercial came on, and I wondered if there was some new smell-a-vision technology because I actually smelled roasted coffee beans. Finally, I got up, looked out the window, and saw you roasting on your back porch. Took a minute to get over the disappointment there wasn't any smell-a-vision, but now I'm here hoping the product I smelled last night tastes as good this morning."

"You let me know if it doesn't," Will requested. "Thanks so much for coming!"

No sooner had Will closed the door after the initial group of patrons entered than the door opened again, and Tom and Patty Farmer walked in.

"Hey! It's the Farmers!" Will exclaimed enthusiastically. "How sweet of you to help us celebrate our grand opening."

"I hear the help here is pretty friendly," Tom shrugged shoulders that perpetually hung low since his return to Grace Fellowship Church.

"Better stake our place in line," Patty nudged her husband forward.

As Tom approached the order counter, Patty whispered to Will: "We wouldn't have missed this for the world. I can't tell you how much it meant to both of us for you and Shelby to invite us to your Thanksgiving dinner. People we thought were friends have all dropped us like a bad habit. Socially, we're starting from scratch, you could say. I just want to thank you for blessing us with forgiveness and kindness."

"It was only a few years ago that I started from scratch after my divorce. I've been where you are – if not exactly, at least in the same painful neighborhood. So, you're welcome. We're looking forward to having you and Tom join us. Even when so much is gone, there's much to be thankful for. We'll focus on that, won't we?" Will answered in a low voice, patting the shoulder of his older sister in Christ.

Patty Farmer grabbed Will's hand, giving it a grateful squeeze before joining her husband in the growing customer line.

"You haven't bought all da coffee, have you?" Marcus asked as he opened the cafe door and stepped aside to let a woman in a USPS jacket carrying a cardboard carryout tray pass through.

"There might be a drop or two left," Sarah laughed and continued on her way out.

Marcus then held the door for his wife, the Shermans, Elodie, and the Rennigers to enter ahead of himself.

"Well, now the line will be out the door!" Will exaggerated, happy to welcome his Cedar Street neighbors.

"Oh, I see my boss here." Ava waved to Pastor Jefferson, seated near a window and already sipping his coffee.

"We could have church. I see the Farmers and Joe Jacobs, too," Marie noted.

"Who's dat couple over dere?" Marcus asked Will, pointing to the Grimes.

"That's Evelyn and Bert Grimes. They're a sweet couple on my route down Tamarack Street," Will answered.

While his friends got in the order line, Marcus went over to the Grimes table and introduced himself. He intended to make himself a regular at his friends' establishment.

"I imagined we'd be taking today's cash receipts, spreading them on the bed, and rolling in them," Will teased his wife after their first exhausting day as business proprietors.

"Ha! Hardly anyone pays with cash anymore," Shelby laughed, tempering Will's expectations. "We made about $65 in actual hard currency. That's not so much to roll around in."

"Well, do you feel you've got your feet under you? Am I good to go back to my day job tomorrow?" Will wondered.

"I think so. It looks like Marcus Van Zant wants to replace you as the Mayor of Latte Da. He stayed for quite some time after his housemates left, and he introduced himself to several customers."

"I couldn't ask for a better replacement. I considered about asking him if he'd like to start a weekly men's Bible study in our upstairs space. What do you think about that?"

"Oh, Will, that's a marvelous idea! I want Latte Da to be used for God's glory and the benefit of His kingdom. That upper room is waiting for its purpose!" Shelby agreed wholeheartedly.

Chapter Thirty-Nine

"Dad!" Lovie shouted from the staircase to Micah, who was watching Thursday night football in the living room with Chase. "I'll be ready for bed in five minutes. I want you to come and tuck me in. And yes, I know to brush my teeth."

Micah heard her footsteps scamper up the remaining stairs. He smiled, pleased with the unusual request from his independent daughter who, since Aunt Shelby had moved out, dawdled and dilly-dallied her way into bed for half an hour after she'd been sent to bed.

When Micah entered Lovie's room, she was pajamaed and sitting on the edge of her twin bed. He flipped off the overhead light since her nightstand light was illuminated, and Lovie swung her legs up on the bed and lay down.

"Did you use toothpaste this time?" Micah asked, approaching and sitting on the side of her bed.

Lovie responded by blowing a puff of minty breath into his face.

"Good job! I guess we're ready to commence with the tucking in." Micah stood, rearranged the covers over his daughter's body, and sat again.

"What was the best part of your day today?" he asked.

"I'm having it right now," Lovie answered with a grin. "We haven't done this in a long time."

"Well, you threw me over for your Aunt Shelby for quite a while,"

Micah chided gently, giving her blonde head a tousle. "I thought you were too big for tucking in."

"I'm not too big."

"That's good information for me," Micah answered, rubbing the stubble on his face.

"Dad, am I an ugly girl? I'm not pretty, am I?" Lovie asked somberly.

"What?! You're my beauty!" Micah reacted, caught off guard. He looked directly into Lovie's round green eyes and, lowering his voice, asked: "What made you ask such a question?"

Lovie hesitated and bit her lip before answering. "Everyone is talking about date nights at Latte Da, and no one's asked me to go with them."

Micah bit his own lip, stifling his mirth. "By 'everyone,' you mean your brother and Silas?" he guessed.

"Yes. But I also overheard Mr. and Mrs. Sherman talking about it today after school. They're going on Saturday."

"I see. And is it important for you to go to your aunt's coffee shop or to have a boy ask you to go? Never mind. Don't answer that because I am the only 'boy' who will take you to Latte Da for a good number of years. I'll take you on Saturday night, alright?"

Lovie's face lit up with a full-faced smile, and she nodded in agreement.

"It's a date!" Micah leaned forward to hug his daughter. Then, he turned off the bedside light.

"Dad?" Lovie said before Micah stood, searching his face by the ambient light shining in her room from the hallway. "Do you remember when Mrs. Van Zant's grandson, Ethan, visited, and we played with the puppies? He didn't like me. I don't think he thought I was pretty."

Micah sighed and looked at Lovie sympathetically. He was both shocked and saddened to witness how, at only eight years old, his daughter attributed a boy's dismissal of her to a lack of physical beauty.

"Of all the reasons Ethan might not like you, if that's even true, it's definitely not because you're not pretty. You're gorgeous, like your Momma was. But Lov, you must know that pretty isn't every boy's top priority. Some boys like sporty girls, or popular girls, or girls who are interested in the same hobbies they are. You can't be everyone's favorite. To be everyone's favorite, you'd have to pretend to be a hundred things you're not. Don't do that. Just be yourself, and someday, when you're a lot older, some boy will think you're pretty great the way you are. And then, they will ask me if they can take you to Latte Da, and I will say 'no!'"

"Daaaaddy!" Lovie whined and grinned. "You have to say 'yes' sometime."

"Uh, no, I don't. See how easy it is for me to say 'no?' No, no, no! I can do that forever," Micah insisted, kissing Lovie on her cheek. "Goodnight, sweetie. Don't forget we have a date Saturday night!"

Micah left Lovie's bedroom door ajar as she preferred and returned to Chase and the football game downstairs.

"What'd I miss?" Micah asked before he could see the score on the television.

"Zilch. Neither team can make a first down, and they're punting back and forth."

"Okay. Well, your sister and I have a date at the coffee shop this Saturday evening. She tells me everyone's talking about 'date night' there," Micah sat next to Chase, fishing for his son's admission of interest.

"It's pathetic that my little sister has a date to go there before I do, even if it is just with you," Chase grumbled, scrunching his face at the television screen.

Micah turned his body to face Chase. "Is there someone in particular you have in mind you'd like to go with who wouldn't be pathetic?"

Chase kept his gaze on the television, but a smirk tightened the corners of his mouth. "Maybe," he responded.

"Her name is 'Maybe'?" Micah teased. "How unusual."

"Look, Dad," Chase turned to meet his father's eyes. "Unless a guy has a job, he's got no money to take a girl to the cafeteria vending machines, let alone to Latte Da. I already asked DeShawn McBride about a job at his business, but I have to be 15. I've got a year to wait. But I also want to save money for a car. I don't know how guys do it!"

Micah chuckled at his son's dilemma, but not for too long. He remembered the angst of being a 14-year-old high school freshman and struggled to decide whether to offer financial assistance to jump-start Chase's dating prospects or leave it alone. He sighed and wished for Dahlia for the millionth time since she'd died. Single parenting was a tough job, especially tonight.

"Go! Go! Go!" Chase screamed at a running back on the television, his attention diverted.

Micah, thankful for the parental reprieve, joined his son in rooting for their team.

Chapter Forty

A week after Christine asked Luther to use his resources to find more information about their half-brother, Bradley, he called her back to report what he'd learned.

"Hello?" Christine answered her cell phone at the dining table where Bradley had just served her lunch.

"It's not good, Christine," Luther began.

With Bradley sitting at the table next to her, she cut Luther off. "I'm sorry, this isn't a convenient time. I'll have to call you back," she responded and pressed the end call button.

Bradley set his jaw. His sister did not receive many calls, and he'd never seen her brush one off so quickly. His curiosity piqued.

When she'd finished her salad with glazed salmon, Christine ascended the staircase to her bedroom. Although she'd discarded the walking boot weeks ago, she still took the stairs more slowly than she used to before her parking lot fall. When she reached her room, she closed the door behind her and locked it. Bradley, who'd hustled up the back staircase and into the guest room across from Christine's bedroom, heard the lock click and knit his brows, agitated. He was sure she was hiding something from him.

As she'd done previously when she wanted to speak to Luther in absolute privacy, Christine ensconced herself in her ensuite bathroom and covered the floor register with a towel.

When she called her brother back, Luther did not make his sister leave a message for the first time in years. He picked up her call after the first ring.

"He was sitting right next to me!" Christine blurted without introduction when Luther answered.

"Okay. Well, as I started to say, it's not good news. Bradley has worked in restaurants all right, but his longest tenure in any place was courtesy of the California State Prison system. He spent ten years in Los Angeles for grand larceny and worked in the kitchen. He's done lesser stints in the county jail for domestic assault. His current wife – number three – has a restraining order in place, and there's a warrant on a larceny charge," Luther disclosed.

Christine gasped. "What do I do now?" she pleaded.

"I told you before we even discovered his history: He's got to go!" Luther reiterated his position.

Christine put a hand to her worried head. "What if that's easier said than done?"

"I'm sure that will be the case. He'll need incentive, and that's the price you pay for your hasty decision. Consider it an investment in your future peace of mind," Luther suggested without sympathy or an offer of further involvement.

Christine pressed the end-call button, leaned against the marble double-vanity for support, and wondered about the best course of action. She didn't suppose she could get rid of Bradley in the same manner she did when he was a youth by ruining him with drugs. *"That would take too long anyway,"* she mused. *"It's going to have to be cash. We'll start small."*

She heaved a sigh of exasperation and flung the towel from the floor into the laundry chute. Before leaving the bathroom, she checked her face in the ornately framed bathroom mirror. Christine knew she hadn't shed tears, but she checked her face for less obvious signs of distress that her half-brother might detect. She patted her cheeks to restore the color that had drained from them.

When she returned downstairs, she found Bradley washing the lunch dishes in the kitchen sink and observed him critically as she stood unseen in the hall just outside her office. He was broad-shouldered and every bit as tall as their father had been in his prime, about 6'1", she guessed. He would be a formidable physical challenge for any woman if he should decide to get aggressive, and it gave her pause to know he had a history of doing so. Still, Christine realized her problem would not resolve itself, and she felt her checkbook gave her more leverage than Bradley's imposing frame afforded him.

After he'd put the last piece of silverware in the dish drain and hung the dishrag to dry over the faucet, Christine requested his company in her office.

"Bradley, I'd like a word if you don't mind," she announced crisply.

"Sure thing," he answered. He knew she'd been eyeing him, having seen her reflection in a silver-plated water pitcher sitting in the dish drain.

Bradley settled himself on the settee in her office while Christine repositioned her tapestry-upholstered desk chair to face him.

"I believe my time of convalescence is complete. You have been a great help to me during a time of need, though you've also benefited from the temporary arrangement. However, I'm sure our usefulness to one another has run its course, and I'm asking you to make other arrangements for your living," Christine dictated her demand in a steady voice.

"You're putting me out?" Bradley whined. He deliberately rounded his eyes and pouched his lower lip.

"We're both adults, Bradley, and we're moving on," Christine chastised his childish expression and reframed his conclusion.

"Though technically, I would be the only one moving," Bradley griped and threw up his hands. "I have nowhere to go, Sister. And right before the holidays, too!"

"I don't particularly celebrate the holidays myself, so you wouldn't be missing anything here," Christine shot back. "And I hear people are leaving California, so the rental market may be softening. You have reliable transportation now," she reminded while suggesting a destination.

Bradley was trying to think on his feet. He considered that he didn't have to aim for permanence. Perhaps his sister would negotiate if he gave a little or pretended to.

"That's true," Bradley conceded. "I'm very grateful for the replacement vehicle you provided. And to tell you the truth, I kind of miss California. The trouble is, this is a heck of a time to drive through the Rocky Mountain passes, which already have snow. They won't open again until Spring," he lied. He missed neither California nor mentioned the southern desert route.

Christine, delighted to hear her half-brother say he missed California, couldn't think of an immediate solution to the problem of the closed passes, and while she hesitated, Bradley pounced on the opportunity to deepen her confusion by scrambling his messages.

"I guess you're right. I'm glad I came back to Faircourt, reconnected with you, and could help you out when you needed me. But, it's probably time to head back home," he tried to sound conciliatory and sincere. He stood, stretching to his full height and taking a few steps toward his sister until he towered over her chair. Then he added in a low voice, "I'll be leaving at the end of February."

"I'll give, I'll give you $10,000 to get settled if you leave now," Christine stammered.

"No," Bradley flatly refused and headed for his bedroom to watch television.

CHAPTER FORTY-ONE

"The seasonal decorating committee has arrived," Marie chimed as she walked in the back door of Latte Da, arms laden with Fall decorations.

"And Marcus!" Marcus added, disassociating himself from the seasonal decorating committee, which consisted of only Marie and June.

"Good morning, neighbors! You can use the upstairs space to spread out and assemble your decorations before placing them in the cafe," Shelby suggested, looking up from the oven where she was removing steaming cranberry orange muffins.

June and Marie headed up the staircase, and Marcus walked to the ordering counter.

"Good morning, Five. I'll have a double Cuban coffee," Marcus requested, reaching for his wallet.

Five held up her hand in protest. "I've been told your money's no good here since you befriend the customers."

"Is dat so?" Marcus flashed a toothy smile, delighted his efforts were recognized and appreciated. He pushed his wallet back into his rear pocket.

While she prepared the espresso, Five continued to chat. "Can I ask you a question?"

"Sure!"

"You live in a houseful of other people. Do you really need more friends?" She chuckled nervously, suddenly aware of how personal her question sounded.

"No. I don't," Marcus answered forthrightly. And then he nodded toward the early customers seated in the cafe and added: "But dey do."

Five tilted her head in responsive reflex as if a change in her physical perspective could help her comprehend the older man's unexpected answer. Her eyes softened, and she responded: "You're a very kind man."

"Please tell dat to Grant Renniger next time you see his mean mug," Marcus laughed.

In a few minutes, Five handed him his coffee, and Marcus sat on the sofa near the window, striking up a conversation with a 30-something guy with a man-bun.

"How does he do that?" Five wondered aloud to Shelby, who was putting muffins in the pastry case.

"Catch me up. Do what?" Shelby asked.

"Start talking to strangers."

"Oh," Shelby chuckled. "He was a pastor before he retired. He's used to talking to people. But I believe he's genuinely curious about people, too."

"I'm curious about people, well, to a degree. But I don't plop myself next to them and try to be their new best friend." Five was playing defense and offense.

"Why not?" Shelby challenged, temporarily suspending muffin arranging.

"You don't either!" Five retorted as she dumped discarded grounds into the compost bin.

"True," Shelby agreed. "But we were talking about you, not me."

Five stuck the portafilter under a stream of rinse water and considered her answer.

"I walk a tightrope between wanting to be invisible and wanting to have friends," Five admitted.

"Bright pink hair isn't exactly an invisibility cloak," Shelby pointed out.

Five smiled and raked a hand through her pink tresses, acknowledging: "Yeah, that's the part of me that wants to be seen, I guess."

"Everyone needs to be seen," Shelby sympathized.

"So, what do you think of these?" Marie interrupted.

She held up four 6" glass vases from Dollar Town with stems of artificial autumn leaves inserted. Behind her, June followed with four more vases.

"Oh, sweet! They're perfect for the tables. Go ahead and set them out," Shelby instructed.

"We have a large autumn wreath for the front door and two smaller wreaths for the counter front. There's also a pretty cornucopia to decorate the top of the pastry case. They'll only be up for a couple of weeks till Thanksgiving is over. But then we'll get to do it all again for Christmas!" Marie enthused.

The ladies set the bud vases on the tables, chatting with patrons who occupied a few of them. Then, they returned upstairs to retrieve the oversized decorations.

"How nice to have our own...what did she call them?...seasonal decorating committee," Five remarked.

"Decorating is kind of Marie's thing, and since her house is pretty well set, she says it scratches an itch to come here and fluff us up," Shelby explained. "I don't have any knack for it myself. Now, if you need a sweater or a pair of mittens knitted, I'm your girl!"

"I didn't know you knitted! My grandmother knitted things for us when I was a kid. I don't know how many pairs of mittens I lost before she got the idea to attach them with a little crocheted rope through the sleeves of my coat. I always thought she'd teach me someday, but she got a bad cancer and was gone just days after they found it. I can't say how many times I wished I'd had something she made – just to take it out and hold it, knowing her hands held it."

"You had a grandmother you loved, then?" Shelby asked, and without waiting for affirmation, added with a small smile: "Me, too."

"Hey! Do you need help with those?" out of the corner of her eye, Five noticed June struggling with an armload of wreaths.

"I wouldn't mind," June admitted, stopping to let Five relieve her of the two smaller ones.

As Five took the wreaths from her arms, a beam of morning sunlight shone through a side window and across her face. June stared at her a moment.

"What pretty hazel eyes you have, Five. They're light brown around the pupil and fade into a fern green. I've never seen eyes quite like yours," June remarked.

Five smiled shyly. "Thanks. I never knew they were hazel until I was 20, and a lady at a makeup counter in a mall department store told me. My family always said they were brown, so I thought they were. Nobody more than glanced, though."

Five turned away and placed the smaller wreaths on the counter while June went to hang the large one on the front door. As June opened the door, a customer entered and Five returned to her station behind the counter, ready to take an order. As she stood waiting, it struck her: June had looked at her and noticed her eyes were hazel, not brown. She had been seen, not because of, but perhaps despite, her pink hair, which grabbed all the attention.

CHAPTER FORTY-TWO

Lovie bounced down the stairs, her blonde tresses swinging in a ponytail that she did all by herself, wearing a pink sweatshirt dotted with silver stars, newish blue jeans, and pink high-top sneakers.

"Ready for our date at Latte Da, Dad!" she announced excitedly.

Micah, wearing a white dress shirt, navy/gold/white striped tie, tan dress pants, and a navy sport coat, stood at the front door, a poochy frown on his face.

"Is that what you're wearing?" he asked, disappointed.

Lovie stopped on the last stair and noticed her father had dressed up. She froze, not knowing what to say or do.

"Don't you have a dress?" Micah suggested.

"I have the one Aunt Shelby bought me last Easter, but it's too small now. I grew over the summer. The only other one I have is my junior bridesmaid dress from her wedding. Do you want me to wear that?" Lovie questioned.

"That may be a little too much. Besides, that was for a summer wedding. You need something with sleeves for this time of year."

Lovie's face flushed. She didn't understand why her dad persisted in asking about a dress he knew she didn't own. She began to fear she wouldn't be going on a coffee date after all.

"Dad, I don't have another dress – with or without sleeves," Lovie looked him in the eye.

"Wrong!" Micah smiled at her. "Go check the closet in Aunt Shelby's old room."

Lovie turned and ran up the stairs like a jackrabbit. Micah heard her emit a joyful shriek when she opened the closet door. Five minutes later, Lovie descended the stairs again. This time, she wore a warm knitted sweater dress. The top of the long-sleeved dress had alternating stripes of pink, brown, cream, and orange, and the skirt was solid brown. Her pink high-top sneakers matched the pink stripes perfectly, her cream socks peeking from the tops.

"That's my beautiful girl! Now we're ready to go," Micah complimented, opening the front door and ushering her out the door with a flourish of his arm. Over his shoulder, he yelled to Chase, absorbed in a video game in the living room: "Don't burn the house down while we're gone, son!"

"I'll try my best," Chase grunted while he blasted aliens to smithereens.

"Look who's here at Date Night!" June gushed as Lovie and Micah walked into Latte Da and next to the table where she sat with Cal.

"Hi, Miss June and Mr. Cal! Dad got me a new dress!" Lovie took a step backward to display her outfit to the neighbors.

"You look like an Autumn Princess," June offered her approval.

"Dad has cleaned up nicely, too," Cal remarked, extending his hand to shake Micah's.

Releasing Cal's hand, Micah noticed the plates in front of the Shermans. "They have pie?"

"Sure do. Shelby said she gets them from Flour and Flake for Friday and Saturday evenings, and the workers there get coffee from here during the week." June explained.

"Glad to see my sister is supporting other Main Street businesses, and vice versa. Well, we had better get in line for some of that pie, right, Lov? Good to see you guys!" Micah responded and began walking toward the order counter.

"How are the puppies doing, Mr. Cal?" Lovie was curious.

"They're growing like weeds," Cal reported.

"Good! Well, gotta go. Bye!" Lovie waved, then skipped after her dad.

"Five, this is my brother Micah and my niece, Lovie," Shelby introduced her employee to the family she was pleasantly surprised to see.

"Nice to meet you," Five responded avoiding looking directly at Micah, focusing on Lovie.

Lovie gawked at Five's bright pink hair, her mouth agape.

"Like her hair?" Shelby prodded her niece.

Lovie slowly nodded her head up and down.

Five laughed. "I'm thinking about going with flames next – bright red with blue and yellow tips. I'll use some gel to make it spikey. What do you think about that? Wouldn't it be cool if my head looked like it was on fire?"

Lovie's eyes widened, and she looked at her aunt, horrified but not wanting to disagree.

"She's kidding," Shelby assured with a chuckle. Then, turning to Five, she sought confirmation. "You are kidding, right?"

"You never know," Five responded with an impish grin. In her peripheral vision, she noted Shelby's good-looking brother was smiling.

"So, what can we get you two?" Shelby asked.

Micah read the countertop chalkboard sign listing five pie flavors and decided: "We'll have one piece of blueberry and one piece of cherry pie, a medium decaf coffee – black, and a hot chocolate with whipped cream."

He pulled a credit card from his jacket pocket, ready to tap the machine, when Shelby stopped him.

"This one's on me, little brother," Shelby offered.

Micah looked down at Lovie before responding to his sister in a low voice. "I'm on a date with my girl and trying to do the whole nine yards. If I don't pay, I've only gone eight yards."

"In that case, it'll be a hundred dollars," Shelby teased.

"I want you to take my money, but I don't want you to take all of it!" Micah retorted, laughing and tapping his card to the machine before the price changed.

A teen employee behind the counter put their pie and two forks on a tray. Five added paper cups of brewed decaf and hot chocolate to it.

"Come back and see us again!" Shelby invited with a smile, ready to turn her attention to the next customers.

Micah and Lovie found an empty window-side table for two and sat down.

"I ordered two different pies so we could try both and vote on which is best," Micah explained to his daughter.

They each tried bites of both pies and pretended sips of coffee and hot chocolate cleansed their palates between bites.

"The cherry is better," Lovie insisted.

"I agree. Cherry wins," Micah nodded.

Lovie looked around and noted the Shermans were gone; another couple had taken their spot.

"Lots of people come on dates here," she observed.

"And how's your date going so far?" Micah winked at her.

"This is the best date I've ever been on, Dad!" Lovie answered, wiping cherry pie filling from her mouth with the sleeve of her new dress.

Chapter Forty-Three

"I expected the day before Thanksgiving to be dead!" Shelby locked the door and slumped onto the cafe couch after the last customer exited at 4:05 PM.

"Ha, they fooled you!" Five laughed as she sprayed disinfectant and wiped down the tables. "Did you notice it was mostly men or young women who aren't responsible for the holiday cooking? Most of our customers today were probably trying to stay out of the way at home."

"I've got to get home and start cooking myself. Well, I have to get the birds soaking in the brine, anyway. But that means I'd have to stand up again, and I think my tush has melded to this couch. I feel like I could just pull up my legs, get horizontal, and take a nap right here," Shelby yawned to emphasize her point.

Rap! Rap! Rap! Ava knocked on the front door, bundled in a blue wool coat and with a gloved hand resting on the handle of a wheeled cart.

Shelby looked up and exclaimed, "Oh! I forgot Marie was coming to help decorate the upstairs room for tomorrow."

"Stay where you are. I'll let her in." Five moved to the door and unlocked it.

Ava pulled in a draught of cold air along with her cart as she entered the warm cafe.

"The second-string decorating help has arrived!" Ava announced herself and removed her gloves. "Marie is indisposed this evening, so she sent me to do her bidding."

"Ava, I'm so sorry. I have to run home and get the turkeys into the tub. It will take me about an hour before I can get back here," Shelby apologized.

"Shelby, go do your turkey thing and stay home. I can help Miss Ava scatter some decorations upstairs," Five offered.

"Five, remind me to give you a raise when we're rolling in the dough," Shelby stood up, gave Five a quick side hug, and headed toward the service area to retrieve her purse and coat. "I'll see you girls tomorrow!" She shouted over her shoulder and exited the back door.

"That's a cool little cart to carry your boxes and bags from your car," Five admired its utility.

"Thanks. And it's pretty low-tech, so not much can go wrong, unlike our van, which gave up its ghost today. Marcus says the transmission is gone, and it's so old it's not worth sinking money into fixing it. So, I schlepped this stuff in my trusty cart from our house. Good thing it's just four blocks away," Ava explained with candor.

"I need to get one of those. I haven't had a car for over two years, and it's a pain walking everywhere and buying groceries two bags at a time. I had to give up buying milk – too heavy. And summer watermelon, which I love? Forget that."

"That explains how you keep a trim figure – between bustling around this place and walking errands. Maybe there will be an upside to being without gas-powered wheels for a while," Ava consoled herself.

Five smiled at the compliment from Shelby's kind neighbor. "Ready?" she asked, leading the way to the upstairs room. She grabbed the axle of the cart to bear most of the weight of carrying it up the steps while Ava held the handle end.

When they reached the top of the stairs, Five flipped the light switch, illuminating the space already partially illuminated by streetlight spilling through the uncovered, extra-large upper windows. Ava removed her coat and commenced unpacking the cart, setting decorative items on an eight-foot folding table against a wall that would serve as the buffet table. Three more identical tables were lined end-to-end in the middle of the room for the family-style Thanksgiving meal.

"I guess the first thing to do is put down these tablecloths – or tableplastics, as the case may be," Ava directed. "Then we can put down the burlap runner, faux pumpkins on top of that, scatter these silk fall leaves, and add the fairy lights last."

Ava stepped back to admire the way Five artfully placed the fairy lights.

"Five, you're really good at arranging those. They would have looked like globs if I'd done it," Ava commented. "So, tell me how you came to be named 'Five,'" she added casually.

Five hesitated. The personal question was unexpected, and she needed a moment to weigh her answer. It was impossible to measure how much to say on such short notice, so, taking a deep breath, she decided to pull back a bit of the curtain of her past and see how it went from there. Subconsciously, she placed a hand on the table as if to steady herself.

"To tell you the truth, I named myself Five – it's all legal and stuff. My parents put 'Audrey Rose' on my birth certificate at my grandma's suggestion, but it didn't really fit me. It has a lot of baggage. Like it comes with an expectation to be feminine and perfect. 'Five' is kinda stripped of any of that. It's pretty bare-bones, right?" she laughed nervously. "I mean, what expectations can a person have of a girl named 'Five?' Besides, I was the fifth grandchild of my grandma, so at least there's some meaning to it. Made it my legal name when I turned 18."

Sensing the girl waving a white flag of surrendered self-esteem, Ava drew closer and asked: "What did your parents think of the change?"

Five laughed. "Didn't care. My grandma was disappointed, though. She still called me Audrey until she passed four years ago."

"And now that you've lived with the name 'Five' for these years since you were 18, any regrets? Does it suit you better?" Ava wondered.

Five now leaned against the table. "Hmm. I don't hate the name Audrey Rose like I used to when I was younger. But it'll never fit me. I'll never be perfect, and I don't want to be frilly-feminine. Five works!"

"Can I make a comment about what you just said?"

"Haha! Most people don't ask," Five chuckled and nodded.

"It's a little jarring to hear you say, 'I'll never be perfect,' because that's an impossible goal for anyone. No human can be perfect. Why do you expect that of yourself?"

Five looked at a streetlamp outside a window, searching for her answer. "I guess 'perfect' is the wrong word. I should have said 'innocent' instead. I lost my chance to be innocent," she risked being clear.

"Aww. Can we sit?" Ava, understanding, offered a chair to the young woman, and she accepted.

Ava continued, speaking gently. "There are so many ways of being broken by others in this world. The hurt leaves its mark and changes us. But how we've been hurt doesn't have to define us or be the last word in our lives because Jesus offers us hope we can be so much more than we'd ever imagined. Our identity can be fixed as a child of the eternal God of the universe if we can take our focus off the evil that's been done to us and consider the evil we've committed against Him. Five, we can't change the past or the people who've hurt us. What we can change with His help is our response to God's simple call to repent and believe. When we do that, there's a cosmic change in our identity."

"Repent of what? Believe what?" Five asked, frustrated by her ignorance.

Ava explained the gospel to her slowly. "We repent of our sins. Sins are the things we do in disobedience to God's word. We apologize for committing sins in the past and ask for His help to reject sin going forward. We believe that Jesus is God, the Father's only son, He lived a sinless life on earth, and died on the cross to bear the justified wrath of the Father for all our sins. The certainty of Jesus' resurrection is our certainty that we'll be resurrected and united with Him at our death. When we repent and believe, we are adopted by God as Jesus' brothers and sisters and given the Holy Spirit to help us live lives that honor Him through obedience. The Holy Spirit living in us assures us we belong to God and are His children. Have I explained what it means to repent and believe in a way you understand, Five?"

"I guess. But how do you know what God considers sin? And how do you know Jesus is God's son and that his death was enough to cover the tab for everyone's sin? There are a lot of religions out there that don't believe in Jesus." Five was skeptical.

"You're right," Ava agreed. "But there are two things we can do if we want to know God. One, we can ask Him through prayer to reveal Himself to us, and two, we can examine the evidence in the Bible to see if what is written is true."

"I should probably get a Bible someday," Five shrugged. Then she stood. "Guess we better finish up here so you can get home before you miss your supper."

Ava gamely agreed, and the women decorated the buffet table and taped twisted streamers of yellow, orange, and brown crepe paper across the ceiling. As they worked, Ava prayed God would root the gospel message in Five's heart.

CHAPTER FORTY-FOUR

"Find your seats, everyone! The food is ready, but before we eat, let's give thanks to God," Will instructed as host of the late afternoon Thanksgiving dinner.

As the guests searched for their name cards at the place settings, Ava approached Five and slid a pocket New Testament into her hand.

"So you don't have to wait for 'someday,'" Ava whispered.

Five smiled and put the New Testament into the pocket of her baggy jeans.

When all the guests were seated around the long table, Shelby asked: "Doesn't this room smell wonderful? Thank you, everyone, for your delicious contributions. Shall we hold hands to give thanks for this and all our other blessings?"

Everyone reached for their neighbor's hand, and Will prayed with specific gratitude for each guest's situation: *"Lord, we serve a good and kind King, and today we give You special thanks for Your abundant blessings. In this past year, You have restored health to us (Cal and Elodie) and mended fractured friendships (Silas and Chase.) You have blessed us with new life (DeShawn, Mariana) and healed our families (Micah, Lovie, Sam, and Bobby.) God, we thank You for providing for our physical needs (Shorty, James, and Five) and helping us build bridges with others (Marie and June.) You also gave us wisdom when needed (Marcus and Ava.) And, Lord, I am particularly blessed for the gift of my godly wife (Shelby.)*

But Lord, you have also put Your hand of discipline on us (Farmers) and taken away things that were important to us (Grant.) For these things, too, we give thanks, knowing that discipline assures us we are Your children and we can trust Your wisdom above our wants.

For these and all Your blessings, we bless You in return. Now, we thank You for this food. May it strengthen us to honor You and do Your will. Amen"

"Since honor is also due our elders, we'll go through the buffet from oldest to youngest," Shelby instructed.

"She's talkin' to you, Calcium. Lead the way!" Elodie razzed with an elbow into Cal's arm.

Cal stood without hesitation. "Don't need to tell me twice!" he chortled and headed toward the buffet table. "Come on, Bobby! It pays to be an old dude today."

Lovie frowned when she figured out she'd be the last to get her food. But she brightened when she realized no one would be behind her critiquing her choices and portion sizes.

As plates were filled and everyone returned to their seats, the conversation volume around the table increased. Old friends, now-familiar neighbors, and new acquaintances wove a ring of friendly discussion and comment.

Will to Patty Farmer: "I can't tell you how glad I am that you and Tom are here today. I'm sure it's not easy, but you both are rare examples to the church of biblical restoration. You encourage my faith, and I'm so proud to be your friend."

Patty Farmer to Cal Sherman: "I don't recall that we've ever been formally introduced, but I recognize you from church. I'm Patty Farmer. I've been at Grace Fellowship Church since I was two weeks old, and I'll be buried next to my parents in the cemetery there. Cradle-to-grave member, I am."

Cal Sherman to Elodie Ford (whispered): "This turkey is okay. The gravy helps. Wish it were your fried chicken, though. Shelby has a lot to learn about cooking birds. If you repeat that to anyone, I'll have to deny it. And people will believe me because everyone knows you're hateful, and I'm a puppy-lovin' sweet old man. Haha."

Elodie Ford to Chase Norman: "I hope when you're an old man someday, you don't wear white tee shirts under blue jean overalls every day of the week. It'll make people think you're not smart. Believe me."

(Bewildered) Chase Norman to Silas: "You've probably figured it out by now, but we've got some interesting neighbors on Cedar Street. You never know what they're going to say. Sometimes, the best thing to do is just nod and hope they move on to something relevant."

Silas to Marie Renniger: "You guys wouldn't happen to be considering upgrading that stock tank pool of yours to something bigger, would you? A big yard like yours needs a nice in-ground pool, don't you think?"

Marie Renniger to DeShawn McBride: "Your wife looks positively radiant, DeShawn. I'd have given my eyeteeth to carry off a pregnancy as beautifully as she does. I looked simultaneously swollen and pinched – like a goldfish that jumped out of its bowl and wasn't discovered for a day or two."

DeShawn McBride to Shorty: "You be sure to get seconds if you want 'em. There's plenty of food, and the pies haven't been put out yet. There's no need to be shy around these folks – they're good people. You'll see."

Shorty to Ava Van Zant (whispered): "I'm Shorty. I work for the McBrides. I feel out of place here, but the eatin's good. Do you know all these people?"

Ava Van Zant to Bobby McBride: "This is our second Thanksgiving that we've shared, Bobby. I hope we make it a continuing habit. I love a big Thanksgiving with lots of people and very little work because we all share in it. And just think, next Thanksgiving, one more McBride will join us! She might be old enough to have a bit of pumpkin pie."

Bobby McBride to Five: "I hear you're the secret ingredient of Latte Da. Will and Shelby speak highly of you. That's my daughter-in-law Mariana over there. She's expecting my new granddaughter, Julia, in February."

Five to Marcus Van Zant: "Marie mentioned you're the coffee pour-over king. We can't do those for customers – it takes too long. But would you mind showing me your process sometime when you're in the shop? I'd love to learn."

Marcus Van Zant to James Daniels: "I'm Marcus, and you're James I heard. Which stuffing did you go wit, da plain or da fancy one? Grant – he's da one sitting two places to your right – he made da ladies make dat plain stuffing, and I hope dat no one but him eats it so we don't have to cater to him again next year. Do you like da Cowboys?"

James Daniels to Mariana McBride: "The guy on the other side of me doesn't want anyone eating the plain stuffing. Wish I had known that before I loaded up on it. At least my turkey is on top of it, so it's covered. Did you know we weren't supposed to eat the plain stuffing?"

Mariana McBride to Grant Renniger: "My father-in-law watches me like he's guarding the Queen's crown. When the pies come out, would you mind getting me a giant slice of the pumpkin pie? Cover it with whipped cream so he can't see it's an enormous piece. Eating for two, you know."

Grant Renniger to Sam: "Your brother Silas gave up on basketball this year. Too bad. Do you play any sports? Golf, by any chance?"

Sam to Lovie Norman: "For the first time in my life, I'm not sitting at a kiddie table, and I get put next to you! Is mashed potatoes all you're eating? You're weird, kid."

Lovie Norman to Micah Norman: "Dad, Sam said I was weird. I don't care if he said that. Dad, can I have pink hair? I can wait to get tattoos."

Micah Norman to June Sherman: "You don't want to trade places with me, do you? Is that allowed? Between Lovie's wild ideas and the turkey tryptophan kicking in, my brain is fried."

June Sherman to Tom Farmer: "I bet you're wishing right now that you had stretchy pants on. Don't make that mistake next year. Wear sweatpants next year, enjoy your food, and be comfortable. I wear stretchy pants every day and I'm always comfortable."

Tom Farmer to Shelby: "Shelby, thank you."

Shelby to Will: "Last Thanksgiving, you asked me to try a coconut snowball with you at Latte Da. This Thanksgiving, you're my husband, and we own Latte Da. I'll never get over how God has blessed us. I love you with all my heart, Will."

Chapter Forty-Five

"Good idea to walk home with that big Thanksgiving sittin' on our stomachs. A little exercise should help the digestion," Bobby affirmed Elodie's suggestion as he held Latte Da's back door open for her.

As they began their walk down Main Street, Bobby held his left arm in front of his torso, bent at the elbow. He assumed Elodie would tuck her hand in the crook of his arm as she had done when they started walking together. When she slipped her hands into her ivory wool coat pockets instead, he reminded himself their walks had started for "medicinal" purposes. Now that her back was healed, they were merely social strolls. So, he put his hands in his coat pockets, mirroring Elodie's posture.

"How many times has your birthday fallen on Thanksgiving Day?" Elodie was curious.

Bobby chuckled. "Three or four. Ah, you remembered my birthday."

"Of course. I thought someone would say somethin' this afternoon, and we'd all sing to you. But that didn't happen," Elodie frowned.

"I exacted a pledge from DeShawn and 'Lil Momma not to say anything. Everyone was there for Thanksgiving, not to make a fuss over me. But the kids made me a nice breakfast this morning and gave me a new recliner for my bedroom. It rocks, too! That's going to come in handy in a few months."

"That's one little girl who'll never be put down, will she?" Elodie mused, shaking her head.

"Haha. You're not wrong. I'm like a kid waiting for Christmas over this baby."

"So, what's your 'grandpa name'?"

"Pap. That's what Fendi and Prada, my granddaughters in Florida, already call me."

"Pap smear!" Elodie blurted, unfiltered. Then she started laughing.

"What did you say?!" Bobby demanded, stopping in his tracks and raising his eyebrows to their limit.

For a full half-minute, Elodie could not control her laughter. She stood with Bobby on the sidewalk, holding her middle, tears beginning to roll down her cheeks.

"I'm sorry! I'm sorry!" she choked out as her fit subsided. Regaining some composure, she elaborated on her apology. "This is Cal's fault! My mind has gotten in a rut of constant word association, trying to come up with alternate names to call him. When you said the name "Pap," it was just what came to mind." The laughter started up again, though more subdued.

Bobby huffed and began walking, crossing Main Street onto Cedar Street. Elodie quickened her pace to catch up.

"I'm really sorry. That was rude. Funny, but rude," she chuckled.

"That is the un-sorry-ist apology I ever heard! And you are not pinning this on Cal," Bobby insisted, the edges of his mouth resisting a smile. "You are a piece of work, Elodie Ford, you know that? You've ruined my grandpa name! Now, instead of hearing my precious grand-daughters' voices when they call me, I'm gonna have your nonsense ringing in my ears. How am I supposed to un-hear what you said? Tell me!" he scolded, attempting to be convincingly vexed with her.

"You're right! You're right!" Elodie was at last sincere. "I'm so sorry for lettin' my mouth run before thinkin'. That's Cal rubbin' off on me, too. No, no," she corrected herself. "This is not anyone else's fault but mine. I am sorry for ruinin' your grandpa name, and I beg your forgiveness. See, I'm beggin' here and not just regular askin'."

Elodie tugged on Bobby's arm to encourage eye contact. She softened her expression with pleading eyes and a pout when he looked at her.

"I'll forgive you on one condition," Bobby offered while pulling his phone from his back pocket.

"What's that?" Elodie asked, curious.

"You put that pleading expression back on your face and let me take a picture of it."

"You've got to be jok..."

Bobby knitted his eyebrows together, and Elodie knew he was serious.

"If you see Bigfoot in the wild, you take a picture as evidence. If Elodie Ford looks contrite, you take a picture to prove you didn't imagine it," Bobby insisted.

Elodie sighed and stopped walking. "Well, okay. But let's get this done quick."

She stood still and repeated her previous expression while Bobby snapped a picture. He'd intended to get multiple shots, but Elodie didn't hold the pose after the first one.

"Okay. Deal's a deal. You're officially forgiven," Bobby smiled his big mega-watt McBride smile that used to bother Elodie so much. He'd noted he'd been getting away with it in recent months.

They walked a block down Cedar Street in amicable silence.

"I have a birthday present for you," Elodie offered meekly.

Bobby stopped walking, closed his eyes, and pursed his lips, inviting a kiss.

"Get on with yourself!" Elodie roared. She refused his joke but laughed at it.

"Well, let's have whatever else it is then," Bobby chuckled and held out his hand.

From her coat pocket, Elodie pulled a small box wrapped in blue and white gingham paper with an orange curling ribbon frill.

"Oh, a legit present!" Bobby took the gift from her hand. "Want me to open it while we walk?"

"Only if you can do it and not trip and fall down," Elodie was pragmatic.

"Let's find out if I can," Bobby responded, carefully pulling off the ribbon and unwrapping the package.

Bobby removed the box top and saw a red leather clip on a bed of white fluff. He fumbled with the box, then lifted the item, noticing some letters stamped around it.

"It's magnetic. Pull the two ends apart," Elodie instructed.

"*Friends are the family you choose*," Bobby read. "That's very sweet, Miss Elodie. I hope we are friends. But what is it?"

"It's a bookmark! The magnet ends clip together and hold the section of the book you've already read or the section you haven't read. Whichever. There's something else under the white stuff," Elodie instructed.

"Ah, a gift card to the bookstore!" Bobby held it in the air.

"Yup. Now you can buy a couple of books and use your new bookmark. Get you some mysteries, adventure, or books about babies – whatever you want."

"That's nice. I like your gift," Bobby beamed, organizing the bookmark and card in the box.

When he had finished the task and put his hands back in his pockets, Elodie wove her arm through Bobby's to continue their walk home.

"We are friends," she confirmed softly.

Chapter Forty-Six

"Neighbors!" Shelby greeted Ava, Elodie, June, and Marie, who approached the Latte Da order counter on Friday's date night. "Thought you'd have seen enough of this place after yesterday."

"Yesterday, you didn't serve coffee," Ava reminded.

"True," Shelby agreed. "We took the day off from making coffee."

"Understandably so!" June was quick to reassure. "Our guys are doing whatever they do on Friday evenings in the Garage Cave, so we figured we'd support our favorite coffee shop. We're not running the risk of its being up for sale again. Not on our watch!"

"You guys are the best," Shelby gushed. "What can we make for you?"

The ladies gave their orders, paid, and stepped to the end of the counter as they waited for Five and her teenage assistant to prepare their drinks. In a coordinated flurry of activity behind the counter, they pressed coffee, steamed milk, and added syrup flavors to concoct the revived Coconut Snowball coffees. With the order completed, the assistant barista placed a tray of cups on the counter before the ladies.

"Oh! Can I have a cup of ice water, too?" Marie asked.

The girl turned around with the empty tray to fulfill the request, unaware that Five was directly behind her, intending to say hello to her new friends. She hit Five hard in the chest with the tray.

"Ooooo. Owwww!" Five erupted and turned away with a grimace.

"Are you okay? I'm so sorry, Five! I didn't know you were there!" the stricken girl apologized profusely.

"I'll be fine. Need a minute, though," Five replied, taking deep breaths. "Shelby, I'll be right back," she announced, heading for the ladies' bathroom and untying her Latte Da apron as she scurried away.

Since there weren't any customers at the order counter for the moment, Shelby followed Five. "Going to check on her," she relayed to the assistant as she walked away.

Shelby walked into the ladies' room and found Five with her arms wrapped tightly around her chest, apron flung on the sink counter, and tears rimming her eyes.

"Got you good, did she?" Shelby asked, her own face twisted in sympathetic pain.

"Sure did," Five groaned. A tear dripped onto her cheek.

Shelby thought she saw panic in Five's tight expression. "Five, are you okay?" she asked.

Five looked her employer and friend in the eye. "I've been watching a lump in my breast," she confessed.

"No!" The word escaped Shelby's lips before she had the presence of mind to temper her reaction. "How long have you been watching it?"

"Almost a year now," came Five's flat reply.

"And you haven't seen a doctor?"

Five shook her head, indicating she had not.

"Sweetie, they don't get better by watching them. You've got to see a doctor," Shelby insisted.

"I don't have one or the means to pay for one."

"We're going to figure it out," Shelby said as she wrapped the young woman in a motherly hug.

Five's private worry spilled over its embankment, and she allowed herself to sob on Shelby's welcoming shoulder.

"Do your parents know?" Shelby asked after a few moments.

"I wouldn't tell my parents if they were the last people on earth," Five pulled away, hotly adamant.

"Okay, okay. I didn't know," Shelby soothed but didn't understand. "We'll just figure it out."

Five grabbed her apron from the counter and swiped at the tears on her face. After disclosing her immediate problem, Five composed herself and explained to Shelby what she was entitled to understand, even though Shelby hadn't asked.

"My older brother abused me when I was young. My father recorded it and sold it online. He went to prison for five years, but my mom took him back. I'll never return to that house where they think I'm the problem."

"Of course you won't. I'm so sorry, Sweetie, but I'm glad you told me so I can understand how to help. You must know you are not without family. I'm your family. Will's your family. Got it? We'll figure this medical thing out together."

Five took a deep breath and then another. She felt like she'd just set down a heavy load.

"It's not that I'm not grateful for your kindness. I am. But how do you just pick someone out to be family and then make their problems your own? The real world doesn't work like that," Five was cynical.

Shelby smiled and leaned against the sink counter. "I get it. Two years ago, I would have said the same thing. I'd had some hard breaks, made some poor decisions, and thought the world was pretty heartless. But my life changed when God came into it. When I understood what a mess I was, I stopped expecting others to be better than they could be. You wouldn't believe what a relief that was. Jesus took away my guilt and shame for things I'd done – not things done to me, sins of my doing! – He took that, and I was different because His Spirit lives in me. Now, when I know the right thing to do in a situation, that's what I do, and I trust Him to help me with the details. That's walking by faith. You need family, Five. You're so independent, but you can't do everything alone.

Deep inside it feels right to become your older sister and God will help me figure it out."

Five listened but said nothing in response.

"You take your time here. I'd better get back to the order counter," Shelby smiled and walked out of the ladies' room.

Instead of going back to work, Shelby retrieved her cell phone from her purse and walked up the stairs to the second-floor space, still festooned with Thanksgiving streamers from the previous day. She dialed a number and waited for an answer.

"Mariana, it's Shelby. I need a big favor. Can you get an emergency appointment with Dr. Buffington for Five? She's had a lump in her breast for almost a year."

Chapter Forty-Seven

"You ready for today, Calypso?" Elodie asked as Cal paced the main hall of the house.

"Yes and no," Cal muttered glumly. He stuffed his hands in the pockets of his overalls and continued his circuit of the hall.

In contrast to Cal's sullen mood, June played a bouncy rendition of *Wonderful Grace of Jesus* behind the living room's pocket doors. Elodie wasn't sure if she was trying to lift her husband's spirits or expressing personal gladness regarding the day's business. Today, the puppies were going to their permanent homes.

"Ready or not, here come the first takers. I'll let Grant know. I think he's in the basement anyway," Elodie advised and disappeared.

Cal opened the front door before the Norman family reached the porch. "Hi, guys!" he tried to sound cheerful.

"We've come to take Hero home!" Lovie skipped past Cal.

"We decided his name last night – Hero. The black male puppy is the one we want," Chase informed.

Micah looked at Cal and held up a puppy collar and leash set – blue with a line of white bones down the center.

"They've vetted the entire litter and have spoken their choice," Micah announced with a shrug and a grin.

"I'm glad that one's not going very far. He's the sweetest boy. Go on down to the basement," Cal invited.

A few minutes later, the Norman family walked out of the front door with a blue-collared, wriggling black puppy held snugly against Chase's chest.

"I want to hold his leash!" Lovie wailed insistently as Cal closed the door behind them.

"Don't you have some kind of project to work on in the Garage Cave?" Elodie inquired, noting Cal's forlorn expression. "Maybe you shouldn't be here when people are pickin' up the pups."

"You might be right, but I don't have any projects at the moment," Cal lamented.

"Then how 'bout you take June and me Christmas shoppin' at the outlet mall? It's a nice day for it," Elodie suggested.

"You want me to fight for a parking spot at the outlet mall on Thanksgiving weekend and then get jostled in the crowds fighting for tokens of peace and goodwill? Ha!" Cal scoffed.

June threw back the pocket doors and exclaimed: "A capital idea! If you can find the parking spot, you can stay in your truck and nap while Elodie and I shop. If you're agreeable, we'll take you to lunch afterward."

"Give me ten minutes to get ready!" Elodie shouted, rushing up the staircase before Cal could answer.

"Where are you going with your hair on fire?" Marie asked as Elodie passed her and Ava in the upstairs hall.

"June and I are gettin' Calvinator out of the house before he breaks down over losin' the pups. He's takin' us shoppin' at the outlet mall."

Marie and Ava exchanged interested glances.

"Can we go?" Ava asked, hopes and eyebrows raised.

"The more the merrier, I say!" Elodie answered brightly. "We have to chip in for the driver's lunch, though. Bus leaves in ten minutes."

"Are you sad to see dem go?" Marcus asked Grant as Jonathan Jefferson and his family pulled out of the driveway with one of the two white and tan puppies.

"Not a bit! They're cute, but they've been a lot of work for Mercy and me. Marie complained she could smell puppy piddle up in our bedroom through the registers even though I did my best to keep on top of it."

"It'll be nice dat Mercy can come back upstairs wit us. I got used to her coming into da study in da morning to say hello to me."

"Well, she won't on Monday morning. She's got an early appointment with the vet to get spayed. Not taking any more chances on a second round of puppies."

"Who's dis pulling up?"

"That looks like Tom and Patty." Grant opened the door and waved them in.

"We're having a special on puppies," Marcus joked as the couple entered the house.

"They're down in the basement. Follow me, and you can pick one out," Grant led the way.

"Four left, huh? Do you have a chair?" Tom asked, looking around the basement.

Grant produced a folding chair hidden behind the furnace and set it up near the puppy corral. Patty, Marcus, and Grant watched as Tom took a seat and laid each puppy, in turn, on its back in his lap.

"This one!" Tom pointed to a black girl. Noting the puzzled expressions around him, Tom explained: "We want a calm dog, not too hyper. You can get a good idea of their disposition if you lay them on their backs and see if they relax or flail around. This black one is the calmest of the lot."

"I just learned something!" Grant exclaimed, impressed with Tom's knowledge.

"It's been a long time since we've had a dog. It'll be nice to be greeted every day with unconditional love," Patty shared, her soft voice almost a whisper.

"Well, we'll get out of your hair and take our Bernice home," Tom said, picking up the little black puppy he'd selected and handing her over to his wife.

As the Farmers led the way up the stairs, Grant caught Marcus' attention behind their backs and silently mouthed 'Bernice,' making a sour face. Marcus grimaced in agreement.

"You have people at your front door," Patty announced, the first to see familiar faces through the front door window. She waited for Grant to open the door to greet them.

"It's the Jacobs Family come to get your puppy, right? Come on in, Joe, everybody," Grant welcomed the family into the house.

The Jacobs children hurried past the adults in the hall to say hello to Marcus, whom they recognized from Vacation Bible School and an occasional Sunday School class substitute.

"Joe and Allison, this is Tom and Patty Farmer and their puppy, Bernice. The Farmers go to church with us," Grant introduced the couples who did not seem familiar with one another.

"We know who they are," Allison spat, walking past them toward her children down the hall. Joe followed on her heels.

"Sorry," Patty apologized meekly to her host, opened the front door, and escaped.

Stunned by the Jacobs' display of rudeness, Grant laid a hand on Tom's shoulder. "No, I'm sorry," he whispered to Tom, who hurried after his wife.

Sitting in the passenger seat of Grant's black sedan, Marcus held the remaining two puppies in his lap as they drove out to the country to deliver them to the Eggleston Farm. Grant filled Marcus in regarding the frosty reaction of the Jacobs to meeting the Farmers.

"I don't understand it, Marcus. If all believers have the Holy Spirit indwelling them, how can we be so hateful to one another?" Grant wondered.

"We all indeed have da Holy Spirit, but it doesn't mean we're all at da same maturity level. Joe and his wife are new believers. It's been my experience dat often, new believers have an arrogance of expectations. Dey excuse dere own previous sin because it happened before dey were saved. Dey know dey still give da Enemy minor victories, but dey imagine dey'll never fall for any of Satan's bigger traps, and oders shouldn't eider. Dey lack da humility dat comes wit maturity. God will teach dem in His time."

"Pride goes before destruction, and a haughty spirit before a fall," Grant quoted Proverbs 16:18

"Dat too," Marcus acknowledged with a nod.

Chapter Forty-Eight

"Two songs. Just two songs like last year," Marie coaxed the friends and neighbors gathered in front of 306 Cedar Street on their way to the Faircourt Christmas Tree Lighting.

"Awww," Chase and Lovie moaned in unison.

"Every bit of kindness we show Christine Williams softens her heart. I know it does!" Marie insisted to the reluctant participants.

"I'd like to see her heart soften, that's for sure. I'm in!" DeShawn agreed enthusiastically. "Come on, Freshman!" he urged Chase.

The group, bundled in winter coats, hats, and mittens, followed Marie and DeShawn across the street to stand in front of Christine's grand white clapboard house. June hummed the pitch for the first note of *O Come, O Ye Faithful*, and the song commenced as fine snow fell on the singers.

Passing through her entrance hall, Christine heard the song immediately. Instead of opening the front door to acknowledge her neighbors' effort, she pulled back the curtain from a living room window to acknowledge them with hesitant reserve. Marie alone detected the slight hint of pleasure at the corners of Christine's mouth. In contrast with how she hid in an upstairs window when they caroled last year, this reaction was a significant leap forward.

As the group began their second song, *Away In A Manger*, Bradley stomped down the main staircase and threw open the front door.

"Get out!" he snarled at the carolers. "Mrs. Williams does not like her peace disturbed. Have you no respect?"

He did not see his sister in the living room enjoying the attention her neighbors paid her. That was Bradley's problem with the situation. He understood outside influences could complicate his plans. Therefore, he determined to keep his sister isolated from the attention of well-meaning do-gooders who might intervene on her behalf.

He'd acted impulsively, but his quick, observant scan identified this group as Christine's immediate neighbors, which was unfortunate. He'd planned to recruit them as allies. But what was done was done. The upside was these people wouldn't likely interfere on her behalf if they knew they'd face growling opposition.

The carolers, not needing repeated berating, beat a hasty retreat toward Main Street.

"How dare you speak for me!" Christine snapped like a whip.

Bradley flinched at his sister's unexpected appearance and reproach. He quickly found his footing.

"I'm stunned, sister. I was merely trying to protect you. Isn't that a big part of why you invited me to stay?" he defended himself while stepping closer to her.

"You thought I needed protection from Christmas carolers outside my house?" Christine scoffed.

"Among the group was the felon who lives across the street and with whom, I believe, you are particularly concerned. Is he now allowed on your property? I was not made aware of the status change." Bradley was smug.

Left speechless, Christine breezed past Bradley and climbed the staircase to her bedroom. She would have slammed the door, but for the nagging suspicion her half-brother would react in offense. Bradley's promised departure at the end of February couldn't come soon enough for her.

"I do not have good vibes about that brother of hers," Marie admitted to Grant as they strolled with their friends. "We were not disturbing her peace. I could tell she was touched."

"He seems a little controlling, I think," Grant agreed, his nose red from the cold.

Walking in front of the Rennigers, DeShawn and Mariana could hear their comments. Mariana leaned into her husband's shoulder and whispered: "Maybe that hateful woman is finally getting a taste of her own medicine. Might be good for her."

"Dad, we're going into Latte Da, right? Aunt Shelby said they were giving out small cups of hot chocolate with mini marshmallows. We're going, right?" Lovie badgered her father.

"Yes, we can stop. But remember, this is her business, and she and Uncle Will will be swamped. They're expecting tons of people like last year, so they won't have much time for us. Don't get your feelings hurt, alright?" Micah cautioned, jerking the zipper of his parka closer to his chin.

Micah looked down at Lovie and noticed she was sucking on a lock of hair that she'd pulled from the confines of her fuzzy knit hat.

"What are you doing?" he asked in a low voice.

Embarrassed but caught in the act, Lovie explained. "When it's super cold out, I can make my hair freeze like a popsicle. It's fun. I do it when I wait for the bus in the morning or on the playground at recess. Addy showed me, now I do it too."

Micah made a sour face but said nothing. He hoped it was a passing fascination.

As the group turned onto Main Street, with the Van Zants leading the way, Ava noted to her husband: "Looks like they're having a party upstairs at Latte Da and forgot to invite us!"

"Dey've rented it out tonight. I was dere dis morning, and Five mentioned it. She said dat room is booked solid for da evenings till past New Year's," Marcus informed.

"That's wonderful for Shelby and Will! I'm so glad they're making that space a profit center," Ava rejoiced for their friends.

"I've already got tree, maybe four men interested in a Tuesday morning Bible study after da New Year. I want to see if June is interested in leading a women's study dere."

"Why June? Why not me?" Ava objected.

"Do you want to lead a women's Bible study in addition to your job?" Marcus asked, already sure of the answer.

Ava demurred with a little grin. "No."

"Dat's what I tought. You just like to be asked so you can say 'no'."

"I don't like saying 'no.' But I do like being asked," Ava tucked her gloved hand in the crook of her husband's arm.

"Look at that," June nudged her walking partner, Elodie.

A flock of children surrounded a woman dressed as Mrs. Santa Clause, who was passing out candy canes in front of Flour & Flake Bakery.

"I'd like to have that job next year!" Elodie remarked, her hands stuffed in her ivory wool coat pockets.

June chuckled. "You can be anything you want to be when you grow up, dear."

The group roamed the small downtown area for an hour as the falling snowflakes grew fatter and heavier. The older neighbors were inclined to head for home in the deepening snow, but gamely waited until Santa arrived on a Faircourt firetruck and threw the switch that lit the massive blue spruce Christmas tree in front of the courthouse. Christmas season had officially begun.

"Dad, look!" Lovie demanded in a whisper as they headed for home. She proudly displayed a lock of blonde hair, frozen straight and stiff as an arrow.

CHAPTER FORTY-NINE

"Marie! Come and sit. We're ready to start," Grant urged his wife, who was sprinkling the center hall with Christmas decorations she pulled from a large plastic tote.

"Sorry," Marie apologized, taking a seat on the couch between Grant and Elodie for Thursday Meeting. "I've never been so late getting decorations out. Where have the days since Thanksgiving gone?"

"Cleaning the basement after the puppies cleared out took a chunk of effort and energy," Ava reminded, blowing a stream of cool air over the mug of hot chamomile tea in her hands.

"You also spent an evening at Latte Da swapping out the Fall decorations for Christmas before the town tree lighting," June added.

"It seems da older we get, da faster dis earth spins," Marcus reflected somberly, rubbing his silver chin whiskers.

Cal smiled. "Remember when you were a kid, and summers lasted forever?" he asked.

"I was always happy to go back to school to see teachers and friends I'd missed," Elodie agreed.

"Now it all flies past so quickly. Seems like last Christmas was just a little bit ago," Marie insisted.

Ava rested her mug on a blue-jeaned leg and mused: "I wonder if we'll have any concept of time in eternity?"

"I can't be dogmatic about it, but if there's no sun in the new heaven and earth, how would time even be measured? I think our concept of time will end. Then again, perhaps it'll be replaced by tracking the passage of regular events. Maybe there will be scheduled feast times or something like that," Grant guessed.

Elodie wilted dramatically over the arm of the couch, having reached her tolerance threshold for eschatological speculation. "Is this seriously our topic for Thursday Meetin' tonight? I'd rather help Marie with her decoratin' or go bake somethin' with June."

"Don't you like to think about what eternity will be like, El?" Ava wondered.

"No, I don't. It makes my brain mushy. All I need to know is that Jesus will be there, and I'm good," Elodie asserted.

Marcus released an involuntary snort and tried to mask it with a rapid stream of words.

"Okay, den. Da only actual agenda item I'm aware of is dat we need to choose names for our Christmas gifts like we did last year. Ava, do you have da slips of paper?"

"I have them!" June acknowledged, lifting a bowl from the floor beside her chair.

June stood and walked around the room, holding the bowl in an outstretched hand so everyone could pick a folded slip with a concealed name. She retrieved the last one for herself and returned to her seat.

"Can we open them now?" Elodie asked, curious to see whose name she drew.

"Sure. But remember," Marie began and looked directly at Cal. "The name on your slip is to remain a secret."

"I did not mean to reveal that I had Grant last year. It was the new medicine talking. We're going to let that little mistake go, right, Marie?" Cal pouted in defensive complaint.

"Let what go? I've forgotten already," Marie agreed, feigning confusion.

Everyone opened their slips, and the only obvious reaction was a quick laugh, which escaped Cal's restraint. All eyes fastened upon him.

"What? I didn't say anyone's name!" Cal insisted, eyebrows furrowed.

That was technically true. However, the name on the paper he drew, which elicited his visceral response, was his own. They hadn't considered or discussed what to do in the event that should happen. But given the sharp reminder of how he'd blurted the name he drew last year, Cal decided to keep his quandary to himself. He refolded the paper and stuffed it in the bib pocket of his overalls.

"Is that it? Are we done here? Can I go back to decorating?" Marie wanted to know.

"Just one more ting," Marcus added. "I don't want to put you on da spot, June. But I wondered if you'd consider leading a community women's Bible study some weekday morning at Latte Da. Any weekday morning, dat is, oder dan Tuesday. I'll be leading da men's study on Tuesdays beginning after da first of January. Shelby is eager to use da upstairs space, and she's offered it for free Bible study space."

"A women's Bible study," June repeated the request softly, mulling it.

She was already teaching the four-year-old Sunday School class at Grace Fellowship Church but would readily acknowledge it took little preparation time. June would enjoy the challenge of deep study necessary to lead a class of adult women as Marie did.

"You don't need to give an immediate answer. Pray about it," Marcus added.

"Okay. I will. But I wouldn't even know how to go about gathering a group of women outside of our church," June admitted.

"I've rounded up some men just by spending time at da coffee shop and talking to dem."

June frowned. That was not a practical option for her. She had home duties Marcus did not. He understood.

"I have a capital idea! I could try to round up some interested women for you when I'm dere. Also, I bet Shelby would let us put a poster in da store window to advertise both Bible studies," Marcus suggested.

A subtle smile replaced June's frown. "I'm going to ask God to show me if that's a commitment He wants me to take on. It's a big honor to serve Him that way, but it is also a big responsibility. I need Him to sift my motives and assure my mind. The last thing I want to do is glorify myself and have all that work burn up when it's tried by fire at the judgment."

"Amen!" Marie encouraged with volume in her voice. Her shout startled Mercy, who had been napping at Grant's feet.

"Now, are we done? Marie and I have work to do." Elodie stood before she received an answer.

"Da meeting's adjourned," Marcus relented.

"Marcus, would you bring the tree down from the attic? Grant, can you get the box of outdoor lights from the garage and put it on the porch? Then you'll be ready to string the bushes out front tomorrow," Marie directed.

Cal beat a retreat from the living room before Marie could pin him with a task. Besides, he was already mentally occupied, wondering what to get himself for Christmas.

CHAPTER FIFTY

"Good mornin', Calcutta, Grant." Elodie acknowledged the guys at the breakfast table.

"Mornin'," the men answered in unison.

"Don't know what you all have goin' on this afternoon, but it won't be goin' on in here. So, heads up about that. Patty Farmer and Lovie have been invited over to make Christmas cookies and treats with us ladies," Elodie explained as she repositioned a bobby pin in her braids.

"We're all for staying out of the way while you're making treats," Grant reassured.

"Just remember us when it comes to taste testing afterward," Cal urged, twitching his eyebrows playfully.

Elodie shook her head in disbelief at him. "Do you ever run out of your insulin supply? For a person with diabetes, you've got a ferocious sweet tooth."

Cal simply shrugged and grinned.

"It's nice of you ladies to include Patty, but won't her husband miss her on a Saturday afternoon?" Grant wondered.

Elodie stepped behind the kitchen island to pour herself a cup of coffee. "Not unless he planned to ask her to help him at the church today. Patty says Tom likes to work on Saturday afternoons. It's one less evenin' he has to drive home in the dark."

"I didn't know Tom was back working at the church," Cal said, surprised.

Elodie took a seat at the kitchen table. "Maybe that was the goal – people not bein' all in the details of how he was payin' the church back. Tom apologized, and that should be enough. Anyway, I only know cause Ava said she's relieved not to be doin' the cleanin' anymore. Patty's been open with us about it, too. Been a few weeks now."

Grant, finished with his tea and banana muffin, wiped his hands on his jeans, and stood to clear his place. "Changing the subject, or rather, returning to the previous one. Will you ladies be making those peanut butter cracker sandwiches dipped in white chocolate? I love those things and could eat my weight in them."

"That might be a reason not to make them," Elodie remarked, looking over her glasses at Grant and focusing her gaze on his waistline.

"I beg you not to suck the joy out of Christmas. Those things only show up once a year," Grant pleaded.

"Why is that?" Cal aided Grant's cause. "You ladies could make them for other holidays, too - Easter, Father's Day, opening day of duck season."

Grant chuckled and made a fist for Cal to bump in solidarity of their mutual appreciation for the cracker/peanut butter/white chocolate confection.

"Because then they wouldn't be a treat, they'd be a treatment," Elodie protested.

Their hopes deflated, Cal puckered his face while Grant trudged to the sink.

Elodie softened and offered a concession. "You can probably count on them for Christmas and maybe a sample tonight if you stay out of the kitchen this afternoon."

"Okay, girls! This is the to-do list: frosted sugar cookie cutouts, raspberry thumbprints, gingerbread men, peanut brittle, rocky road fudge, and white chocolate dipped peanut butter crackers," Ava read from a list of recipes she'd printed out for distribution.

"Lovie and I will take the cutouts," June held out her hand to receive the instruction sheet she didn't need to consult.

"I'd like to do the thumbprints," Patty Farmer requested shyly.

Ava stepped forward, giving Patty the printed recipe and a warm, genuine smile.

Elodie chimed in: "I've got the gingerbread men – my specialty. Don't need any recipe. You can keep that, Ava."

"Well, I'm candy – peanut brittle and fudge," Ava kept the remaining sheets.

"That leaves me with the peanut butter crackers. No recipe for those," Marie chuckled. "Just slap them together, dunk in white chocolate, and throw on some sprinkles. Delicate assembly, but not rocket science."

"Everyone grab an apron from the pile on the table. The ingredients are organized at the stations you see around the kitchen. Patty and Elodie, you'll each have one of the double ovens since June pre-made her cutouts last night. I think that's everything but the Christmas music to work by," Ava instructed before momentarily disappearing into the dining room to switch on the stereo.

A moment later, *Blue Christmas* poured from the dining room speakers, and Ava, Elodie, and June braced for Marie's predictable outrage.

"Aggh! That is the worst Christmas song ever recorded," Marie groaned.

"The female background singing is obnoxious and cringe-worthy!" June repeated a line of complaint about the song she'd heard many times from Marie's lips over two decades.

"Whose brilliant idea was it to write a depressin' Christmas song?"

Elodie took up the very familiar rant.

"Even Elvis' voice couldn't save that monstrosity of a song!" Ava finished mimicking Marie.

"All true! All true!" Marie laughed at the good-natured ribbing from her friends.

"Really? I like anything by Elvis," Patty ventured to admit while focused on tying apron strings behind her back.

Marie sighed, sensing she had her work cut out. "But have you really listened to *Blue Christmas*? It's a crime against Christmas music!"

The rise in volume of Marie's voice had no effect on Patty or her opinion of Elvis. She leaned back against the kitchen island counter and declared: "Elvis could sing a grocery list and make it sound like pretty poetry."

"That's right," June nodded in agreement with Patty. "The only Elvis albums my dad allowed in our home were his gospel ones. But when I was 13, like all my other girlfriends, I wanted to be Elvis' teddy bear." She giggled at the recollection.

Elodie snorted but shared: "An auntie gave me the 45 single of *Can't Help Falling In Love* for my 12th birthday and I played it on repeat in my room till my momma yelled up the stairs for me to play anything else before she snatched me bald-headed."

"*In The Ghetto* always made me cry," Ava confessed, pouring chocolate chips into a double-boiler on the stove. "I loved his voice."

Marie saw she would make no headway turning Patty against the Christmas song she detested since Elvis was involved and June, El, and Ava had rushed to his defense.

"Actually, the very first present I gave Grant when we started dating was a cassette tape of Elvis singing *Marie's The Name of His Latest Flame*," Marie admitted reluctantly.

Lovie, confused by the ladies' conversation swirling around her, licked green icing from her finger and asked: "Who's Elvis?"

CHAPTER FIFTY-ONE

In the fading light of late afternoon, Bradley sat in a far corner of the parking lot of The Oxmoor Center Mall, watching well-to-do Louisville women bustle through the doors of an upscale department store. Although his SUV wasn't running, Bradley's sweaty hands gripped the steering wheel as he contemplated the risk he needed to take.

In the weeks since Christine had offered him peanuts to leave Faircourt, he had thought he'd be able to chip away at her resolve with a charm offensive or, perhaps, increase her perceived dependence on him for protection. Neither had materialized. His sister referenced the hastily negotiated end-of-February departure deadline with nagging regularity.

Bradley needed a grand gesture that would appeal to Christine's vanity. He had to 'wow' her with an impressive present. The problem was his billfold contained a driver's license and lint, and Christmas was a week away.

"They're called crimes of opportunity, but go-getters create their opportunities. Only chumps wait for things to happen." The words of a long-ago jail cellmate ran through his mind as they often had over the past few decades. Bradley shifted into go-getter mode, wiped his palms on the tops of his trouser legs, and stepped out of his car. He removed his thrifted overcoat and tossed it in the back seat before shutting the door.

Bradley strolled through a mall entrance in his white button-down shirt and gray slacks, his wavy gray hair combed back. He looked like a boss to the twenty-something mall employees and the mature but seasonal workers. In less than twenty minutes, he walked out again. This time, he carried a shopping bag from the upscale department store. Inside the bag was the designer purse of a well-to-do, but unfortunately distracted, woman.

Once he was back in his vehicle, Bradley resisted the urge to rifle through the purse immediately. He made his way from the edge of the parking lot to Shelbyville Road, trying to avoid mall security cameras getting a shot of his rear license plate. A few miles down the road, he pulled into a garden center shuttered for the winter and parked to examine the contents of the red leather purse stamped to resemble crocodile skin.

He pulled out a zippered pouch containing make-up, a cell phone, a hairbrush loaded with brunette hair, a curiously long receipt from a drugstore, a souvenir key ring from St. Croix with a luxury vehicle fob and house keys, and finally, a red leather wallet that matched the purse. Inside the wallet were a Kentucky driver's license, half a dozen credit cards, a health insurance card, and $97 in cash, which Bradley deposited into his billfold.

The cash wasn't enough for a present that would 'wow,' so Bradley considered his options. Four of the six credit cards were store-specific. The other two were American Express and platinum VISA. He could use these online since he had his victim's driver's license with the required zip code. However, an online purchase would require shipping lead time, which Bradley didn't have. Riskier still, it would require providing a shipping address, which would lead an investigator right to Christine's door.

In the ambient light of the retail district, Bradley scanned the scattered purse contents on the passenger seat. His eyes rested on the set of keys. Without her keys, his victim wouldn't be able to drive home right away. Bradley decided to drive to the address on the license, let himself in with the keys, and expand his self-made opportunity. He punched the address into his vehicle's GPS and followed its guidance to a two-story, gray-painted brick house with black shutters and a circular drive on the northeast side of town.

"Come on, Big Boy. You've done this before. Just like riding a bike," Bradley gave himself a mental pep talk. He wiped his palms on his trouser legs again and got out of the car, stolen keys in his pocket.

Other houses along the street had interior lights, illuminating rooms now that the sun had set. This house had no visible interior lights. Still, Bradley played it safe and approached the garage's side door as he pulled the key ring from his pocket. He had his choice of three keys that might fit. But before he tried any of them, he turned the handle just in case. In his experience, this was the door people often forgot to lock. Sure enough, the handle turned, and Bradley stuffed the keys in his pocket.

Slowly, Bradley advanced inside the garage, where a late-model BMW was parked. From inside the house, he could hear a broadcast sports event coming from a television, and he muttered a low curse. It was time to make a quick decision. Should he leave with nothing, or take what he could from the garage and risk a confrontation with the man he presumed, inside the house?

"You've come this far, Big Boy," Bradley reasoned to himself.

Assisted by the light of his cellphone flashlight, Bradley opened the vehicle door and fished his hand under the driver's seat, searching his personal preferred place to stash contraband. Bradley pulled out a large Colt revolver.

"Paydirt! This will be worth something," he mused.

Bradley noticed a bag of state-of-the-art golf clubs against the wall and slipped the gun into it. He picked up the bag gingerly so it wouldn't rattle and draw the attention of whoever was in the house, and departed, closing the door behind him.

Although fueled with adrenaline, Bradley willed himself to drive slowly from the affluent neighborhood to the Gene Snyder Freeway and down to a pawn shop off Dixie Highway. He brought in the golf bag slung over his shoulder and was approached by the proprietor.

"Looking to pawn or sell?" a sloppy forty-something man with a wad of tobacco tucked between his gum and cheek asked, looking over the new golf clubs. His shirt displayed a plastic nametag that read "Frank".

"Sell. The wife and I are downsizing. Going to be moving into an in-law apartment at our daughter and son-in-law's home in Twin Falls, Idaho. These were a retirement gift from the office, but we won't have the space for these, and my degenerative back won't let me play anymore anyway," Bradley lied.

Frank looked Bradley up and down, noting the button-down shirt and dress pants. He'd been in the business 25 years and pegged Bradley as trying too hard with the overload of details.

"I got something else in here." Bradley reached his arm to the bottom of the bag and pulled out the Colt, giving Frank a flash of anxiety before realizing he wasn't being robbed.

Bradley handed the gun over by its barrel end.

"Colt Anaconda. Nice. No room for this either?" Frank asked with discernible sarcasm, turning over the weapon and inspecting it.

"You want to buy this stuff or not?" Bradley cut to the chase.

Frank shrugged. "It'll sell. Suppose you left your ID at home? Well, never mind that."

Five minutes later, Bradley Hall walked out of the south-end pawn shop with $1,600 cash in his hand. Added to the $97 of cash from the woman's wallet, he now had the means to delight his sister, if not 'wow' her.

CHAPTER FIFTY-TWO

Shelby arrived at 6 AM to a darkened coffee shop. Five had always arrived and turned on the lights a few minutes ahead of their scheduled preparatory hour before Latte Da opened to the public at 7 AM. Shelby flipped the light switches, hung up her coat and purse, and preheated the oven to bake the scones while wondering if Five was all right. After Shelby slid the tray of scones into the oven and set the timer, hurried footsteps approached from the stairs.

"Shelby!" Five screeched when she reached the service area. "I logged in to Dr. Buffington's office portal and got my test results! It's a benign fibroadenoma! Benign!"

Shelby rushed to Five to hug her. "What a relief! That's the best news!" she whispered in Five's ear.

Shelby sensed her friend's body relax in her embrace before it began rolling with sobs.

"I was afraid I was going to die," Five choked out the words she had never spoken aloud.

"Oh, sweetie," Shelby soothed in a motherly tone, making gentle circles in the middle of Five's back with her hand. "It was a terrifying thing. Of course, you were afraid," she added as tears of sympathy and relief formed in her own eyes.

Still holding Five, Shelby swiped at a tear running down her cheek. Aware of the movement, Five pulled back to look at her and was startled by Shelby's tears.

"No one's ever cared about me like you have. If it weren't for you, I'd never have gotten to see a doctor or found out I don't have to be a worried hot mess anymore. Thank you for being such a good friend to me."

"I'm not your friend. Remember what I told you? I'm your family – me and Will. Friends come and go, but family stays," Shelby smiled and swiped another fallen tear.

"Do you mean that? I mean, really? You mean it?" Five couldn't help her skepticism.

"I mean it. That's why we expect you to be at our house on Christmas morning. You're family, and you belong with us. But don't imagine you have the better end of the deal. Will and I have our problems and issues, like everyone else. And we're sinners – there's that. Can deal with it?"

Five grinned with her entire face. "I can deal with it," she assured.

Shelby took a few steps and removed a carton of creamer from the refrigerator to fill the self-serve carafes. Five filled the coffee brewer and stocked the canisters of roasted beans for the custom coffee orders.

"Ava Van Zant gave me half a Bible at our Thanksgiving dinner," Five restarted the conversation. "I've been reading it."

Shelby reacted spontaneously with incredulous laughter. "Half a Bible?"

"Just the new part," Five explained as best she could.

"Oh! She gave you a New Testament. I get it," Shelby tapped herself on the head with her palm. "I should have known that. It's all still new to me, too. So, what are your thoughts about what you've read?"

"I started at the beginning and got through the first five chapters until I ran into a wall. Haven't been able to get past it, so I stopped reading."

Shelby leaned against the prep counter, giving Five her full attention. "What can't you get past?" she asked, curious.

"I was talking with Ava, and she said you don't have to be perfect to belong to God. I remember that distinctly because she called me out for saying I wasn't perfect. But Matthew says that when Jesus was preaching, He told people they must be perfect because God is perfect. It can't be both, right?" Five asked, picking up an apron under the counter.

Shelby's mind swirled with uncertainty. She didn't know how to explain theological issues as her husband did, and she wished Will was with them instead of on his way to the post office. Will always knew the answers to Bible questions. She decided just to say that.

"Will could explain better than I can. We can ask him about it when he stops in at lunchtime today. All I know is God's standard is perfection because He's holy. I also realize we can't live up to that. But Jesus did," Shelby responded, explaining what she could. "And that's why Jesus had to die. He took the punishment we deserve for our sins, and if we repent and believe, He'll save us from having to bear our own punishment."

"Ah, that makes sense. Miss Ava told me the same thing – that we have to repent and believe." Five took a slow breath and continued. "You know, before I heard the results of my test, I knew if I died, I'd go to hell."

"You'll still die and go to hell someday unless you repent and believe," Shelby blurted, instantly mortified by her lack of finesse. "I mean…" she began to revise her comment.

"No, you're right," Five admitted before Shelby could temper her words.

Shelby dropped her shoulders, relieved her bluntness hadn't caused offense. Now emboldened a bit, she challenged: "Do you want to do something about that?"

"I'm not sure what to do," Five whimpered with honesty.

Shelby grinned. "I do! Come on, let's go sit on the couch, and we'll pray."

"Don't I need to do this in a church?" Five was startled but followed her friend, who was already headed into the cafe seating area.

"Nope. In fact, this is where I prayed to receive salvation – just about this time a year ago! If it worked for me here, it'll work for you," Shelby spoke, moving with purpose toward a physical location and spiritual objective.

The women sat side-by-side on the couch.

"I'm going to pray first, and then you're going to pray," Shelby instructed.

"But, I've never!" Five panicked, her eyes wide and heart pounding.

"That's why I'm going to pray first. We're just talking to God, and He doesn't pay as much attention to our words as He does to what's coming from our hearts. He knows what's there."

Sitting on the couch with Five's hands in hers, by the soft light of the cafe emergency bulb, Shelby bowed her head and prayed:

"Lord, I'm so grateful to You for the good news that Five's lump is benign. That's such a blessing and relief to us. But, Lord, we know that You also want Five to be well and alive spiritually. I ask You to hear her prayer of repentance and belief and adopt her as Your daughter. Amen."

Keeping her eyes closed, Shelby gave Five's hands a little squeeze. Nervous and unsure of herself, Five opened her eyes to look at Shelby for guidance. But Shelby maintained a posture of expectation that Five would pray. And so she did.

"God, I have no idea what I'm doing, but I'm doing it, and I hope You can make sense of my words and see what's in my heart like Shelby said. All I want to say is I'm sorry for all the things I've done that made You sad or mad. I know Jesus had to die to make it right with You, and I'm really sorry about that. But I believe in Him. He can save me from the hell I deserve, and I hope He will. Amen."

Five opened her eyes again to see Shelby looking back at her this time.

"Did I do it right? I don't feel anything different." Five asked, worried.

Shelby smiled. "If it was from your heart, then it was just right. And it's fine that you don't feel different. Salvation isn't about our feelings; it's believing God is true to His word no matter how we feel. That's walking by faith."

"But shouldn't something be different?" Five wondered.

"Girl, everything is different. Three minutes ago, you were an enemy of God, and now, you are His beloved child. Three minutes ago, you were a captive to your sin nature, but now, you're sealed by the Holy Spirit of God and empowered to overcome sin. Those are enormous changes!" Shelby exclaimed.

Five, grinning, repeated the phrase Shelby used, which was a medicinal balm to her heart: "His beloved child."

After a moment's reflection, Five bounded off the sofa and did a little energy-releasing jig around it to Shelby's amusement.

"It's going to be weird to make coffees today. Now, it seems like a holiday or something – like I should celebrate a big deal," Five announced.

Shelby jumped to her feet and grabbed Five's shoulders. "Let's make it a holiday! We still have to make coffees though, because it's our job. But I'm going to run to Big Mart and get some helium-filled balloons and a big cake we can share with our customers. We'll celebrate your "Big Deal Day" and you can tell anyone and everyone exactly what that means. Sound like a plan?"

"Sounds like you're making it a Big Deal!" Five smiled shyly, but agreeably.

Chapter Fifty-Three

The Cedar Street neighbors walked home in a gaggle after Christmas Eve service at Grace Fellowship Church, including Bobby, Micah, and Lovic, who didn't usually attend church but were persuaded for special occasions.

"I was happy to see Five come to our service," Marie said, walking alongside Shelby.

"She's a sister in Christ now. She prayed for salvation at the cafe with me two days ago, just like I did with you last year," Shelby beamed.

"Seriously? That's wonderful news! I can't wait to tell Ava. She shared the gospel with Five a few weeks ago," Marie rejoiced.

"And she gave Five half a Bible," Shelby chuckled.

Marie knitted her brows. "What?"

"She gave her a New Testament, but Five called it half a Bible."

"That's cute," Marie giggled, paying careful attention to the slush on the sidewalk and her foot placement.

"Well, she's getting a whole Bible from me and Will tomorrow when she comes for Christmas," Shelby confided.

Marie patted Shelby's shoulder. "I'm so glad you were the one to help birth Five into the Kingdom. What a blessing for you to have that privilege. And I'm so proud of you."

Shelby groaned. "Marie, if you'd been a fly on the wall, you wouldn't have been proud of me. I didn't challenge her to count the cost of following Christ like you did with me. I just lost my mind and forgot what I should say. I gave the sorriest, the most raggedy gospel presentation ever, and it was a miracle that any of it made sense to Five. On top of that, I told her she was going to hell when she died! Can you believe it? I was anxious because Will wasn't with me, and he could do it so much better. My mouth just said stuff. It had to be the Holy Spirit working in spite of me. He turned my nervous disaster into something that helped Five and drew her to repent and trust Christ."

"Doesn't that give you confidence?" Marie asked, grinning. "God knows what He's working with when He uses people made from dust to help lead another soul to Him. He fills our gaps and accomplishes His will with a perfect result despite our glaring imperfections. If God is drawing someone to Himself, we truly can't mess it up, and that should make us fearless with sharing the gospel."

"We can't mess it up," Shelby repeated softly. "That's encouraging."

"Right?!" Marie agreed, putting her arm around Shelby's shoulders and squeezing affectionately.

The friends sat around the candle-lit dining room table for a late Christmas Eve supper of meat and vegetable stew, fresh-baked sourdough bread, and mulled cider. As soon as Marcus put the 'amen' on his prayer of thanksgiving for the meal, Marie could wait no longer to share her news.

"You all saw Five at church this evening, and I know you were glad. But you'll be even gladder to know she put her faith in Christ for salvation – two days ago. Shelby told me as we were walking home."

"Praise God!" Ava was the first to react with a shout and clap of her hands.

The others followed with their exclamations. "Wonderful!" "Amen!" "It's a merrier Christmas now!" "Dat's what I'm talking about!" "Thank You, Jesus."

"She's a newborn spiritual baby," June noted with motherly affection. "Hey! I wonder if she would come to my women's Bible study."

"Does dat mean you've decided to do it?" Marcus asked, quick to pick up on June's idea.

"It means I've decided to do it!"

"Your study would be on a weekday mornin', right? Five has to work unless Shelby will let her off for an hour," Elodie reminded while buttering a piece of bread.

"There's always Sunday School," Ava suggested.

"Listen to us – already planning Five's discipleship for her," Marie chuckled.

Grant looked up from the bowl of stew he was picking at and said: "Nothing wrong with that. Jesus said to make disciples, not converts."

"Changing the subject for a moment, did anyone notice if Christine Williams was at the candlelight service? If she was there, she wasn't in her usual front row pew," Marie inquired.

"I was greeting at da back door. She didn't come," Marcus informed.

Cal set down his glass and muttered: "That explains why I enjoyed it better than last year."

"Calvert Sherman!" June whispered at her husband in rebuke.

"Maybe she and her brother made other plans," Ava guessed.

"Perhaps," Marie shrugged. "Anyway, I wanted to say Merry Christmas to her, so I was looking for her."

"Are you finding enough to eat in your bowl, Grant?" June noticed him pushing around its contents.

"Not a big fan of stew. I just pick out the meat chunks and eat those. With the bread and butter, it's enough to get me to breakfast," Grant acknowledged half-heartedly.

"So, you like the meat then?" Elodie asked with a smirk.

Grant's eyes widened as he grew suspicious. "Okay. What is it?"

"Add rabbit to the list of meats you like. This is rabbit stew. Somethin' different for Christmas Eve supper," Elodie answered him.

Grant looked helplessly at his wife for sympathy for his unwitting participation in a new dish with an exotic ingredient.

"Should have told him it was squirrel!" Cal teased, chuckling.

Marcus joined in: "Or possum!"

Grant put his fork down. "A rabbit is a rodent, just like a squirrel or possum. You don't need to make it worse because it's already as bad as it can be."

"Too late," Elodie insisted, chuckling. "You already liked the meat in the stew."

Marcus read from his phone. "According to da wisdom of da internet, rabbits are not classified as rodents."

"See there, Dear. It's not rodent meat," Marie consoled her perturbed husband.

"Oh, wait!" Marcus continued reading. "Dey were classified as rodents before 1912. Sorry, Grant."

Grant rose from his chair at the table. "I'm going to bed to wait for the vomiting and diarrhea to commence, which will pave the way for Angel of Death. But you all have a Merry Christmas Eve," he hypothesized dramatically.

The friends listened to Grant's footsteps through the hall and up the stairs, Mercy padding along behind him. When all was quiet, they resumed their conversation and the supper, which may or may not have included rodent meat, depending on one's timeline.

CHAPTER FIFTY-FOUR

Mariana, perched under the living room Christmas tree, extended an arm to hand her father-in-law a present. When he didn't reach for it, Mariana noticed he wore a faraway expression.

"Dad, is something wrong?" she wondered.

Bobby shook his head. "Oh, Miss Banana, don't you worry about me. I was just thinking about how different today is in this house compared to last year. Last year, this house sat empty during the holidays. I was in Florida, DeShawn was, you know..." Bobby still couldn't make himself say 'prison' out loud. "And I had no idea about you, much less that you were family!" But this year, here we all are with Little Julia on her way and everything! I'm not sure my heart could hold any more happiness."

"I know what you mean, Dad," DeShawn echoed from his seat on the floor opposite his wife. "And you know what else occurred to me? I can't imagine how this moment could have come together in any other way than the hard way it did. Would we be as grateful if it all came to us without the years of longing, missing, and hurt? Or would we take what we have now for granted, or worse, be disappointed?"

"I am beyond thankful for the two of you and the home I have here," Mariana added somberly. "It's like God took my sorrow-filled life and started adorning it with treasures and jewels. It's richer than what I dared to hope for." She patted her baby belly.

DeShawn beamed at his wife. "We can't be this thankful and not give thanks to the One who sovereignly worked for our good when we were unaware."

He took his wife's hands in his own and prayed out loud:

"Dear Father, from Your high and holy throne, You sent Your Son to come as a baby, grow as a sinless man, and sacrifice His life to pay for our sins. You have met our most pressing need for salvation, and still, You bless us with more good gifts: family who love us, friends to come alongside us, and the miracle of new life. See our grateful hearts and be blessed by the praise we offer You in Jesus' name. Amen."

"Amen," Bobby repeated softly, to DeShawn and Mariana's surprise.

Five sat on the couch at Will and Shelby's on Christmas morning, wearing a second-hand red dress from a Main Street consignment shop and inhaling the pungent evergreen boughs surrounding her. The live tree in the living room, lit with hundreds of white lights, lent its perfume. Shelby also bedecked the staircase banister with greens, the doorways, and nearly every available flat surface.

"Smells like a pine forest in here," Five noted. "How do you make the scent last?"

"Is it too much?" Shelby asked suddenly self-conscious.

"No, no! It's surprisingly fresh, that's all. I mean, your tree's been up a while, hasn't it?"

Will pulled an aerosol can from behind the television. "She gives the tree a daily douse with this," he grinned. "Also, she replaces the branches everywhere else every few days. You should see the pines in the backyard! They look like they've been to a barber on his first day on the job."

"They were out of control and needed it," Shelby defended herself before changing the subject. "Before my brother's family comes over for brunch, I thought we'd do our little gift exchange."

"Okay," Five agreed, taking the small gift bags at her feet and handing a gold one to Shelby and a silver bag to Will. "You go first," she instructed Shelby.

Shelby set her bag on the coffee table before her and rubbed her hands on her cream-colored corduroy slacks. She pulled out some white tissue paper and a large candle scented like freshly mowed grass.

"I know you like nature scents. Obviously. Hope this helps you make it till Spring," Five smiled.

"I'll be lighting this on New Year's Day!" Shelby squealed, delighted.

"Now yours, Will!" Five ordered.

"I hope it's a basketball!" Will teased as he opened the bag, much too small to contain a basketball. "Socks!" he announced, holding them aloft.

"I heard you complain your feet get cold on your route. These babies are heated and rechargeable. They even have a tiny remote control!"

"Whoa!" Will exulted, examining the package more carefully.

Shelby handed Five a box wrapped in white paper stamped with green wreaths, red berries, and gold bows. "This is from both of us," she explained.

"It's almost too pretty to open. But I will!" Five announced, giddy.

She tore the paper and opened the box to reveal a red-leather bound Bible with gold-gilded pages. Lifting it gently, Five turned the front cover and read a handwritten inscription:

For our forever sister, Five. May the study of these pages impart wisdom, comfort, and holy joy. With affection and love, Will & Shelby.

"Now you have a whole Bible!" Shelby giggled.

"Thank you. Thank you so much," Five whispered, not taking her eyes off the gift and continuing to turn the pages.

Lovie woke her father and brother up at first light with the announcement: "Santa came! Santa came! Get up! It's time!"

Understanding that trying to hold back Lovie from Christmas morning's present opening would be an exercise in futility, Micah and Chase donned their bathrobes and slogged their way to the living room. Mechanically, Micah plugged in the Christmas tree lights while Chase turned on the Christmas With The Chipmunks CD - the family tradition.

Micah segregated the pile of presents under the artificial tree, pre-lit with colored lights, into collections for each child and gave the go-ahead to unwrap. The children tossed wrapping paper, bags, and boxes aside, which puppy Hero assumed was his go-ahead to further destruct. He took them into his mouth with playful growls and shook large bits into smaller bits.

Within 20 minutes, Lovie and Chase had opened their presents and identified their favorites – Chase's a retro leather bomber jacket he'd admired in the mall, and Lovie's a building block set to construct a princess castle complete with figures and furniture.

"Okay, let's get the mess picked up, then we can have hot chocolate and a bagel with cream cheese. There are still three hours until we go to Aunt Shelby and Uncle Will's for brunch. And don't forget to get your presents out of Hero's reach," Micah instructed.

"Aggh!" Chase yelled as he turned to heed his father's warning.

Hero was already chewing a sleeve of his brand-new leather jacket.

"I remember you said you didn't do much for Christmas, but I got you a little something." Bradley handed Christine a small Tiffany-blue gift bag with a silver Tiffany logo.

Christine, at the kitchen breakfast table, pushed aside her toast and received the bag, intrigued. She removed a small box from the bag and opened it to reveal a thin gold chain with a tiny ruby gem affixed in the middle.

"From Tiffany's, as you can see. It's your birthstone," Bradley pointed out proudly.

"Thank you," Christine acknowledged politely but with more understatement than her half-brother expected.

She resumed eating breakfast, and when she noticed Bradley had not moved away, Christine added: "As you remembered correctly, I don't really observe Christmas. Just another day."

Bradley understood she was dismissing him, and he seethed as he retreated up the rear staircase to his bedroom. He realized Christine hadn't made an ounce of effort to get him even a token gift – after all he'd risked for her! As he replayed their interaction in his mind, she didn't seem appreciative, let alone impressed with the present meant to wow. Bradley muttered curses upon her and vowed he'd be well-compensated for his gesture, with or without the woman's cooperation.

"Okay, California, you're next!" Elodie encouraged Cal to retrieve the present with his name from under the Christmas tree.

Without searching, Cal went straight to the present he'd bought, wrapped, and placed himself. Taking it back to his seat, he tore open the wrapping paper and opened the shoebox containing a pair of black athletic shoes he promptly displayed for his friends.

"Look! I've got a pair of those nifty shoes I can slide my feet into standing up. Don't have to bend like a pretzel to put them on!" he boasted.

"Those are real nice, Cal. Who are they from?" Ava inquired.

Cal looked around sheepishly.

"Who was Cal's secret Santa?" Marcus surveyed the faces of the friends.

"I drew my own name," Cal admitted at last.

"You what?!" Marie was incredulous. "You're not supposed to be your own Santa!"

"Well, you told me I couldn't tell whose name I drew, didn't you? Made kind of a special point of it as I recall," Cal objected to the rebuke.

"But I didn't mean..." Marie started.

Cal held up his palm to stop her. "It's fine. Got just what I wanted, and I have no complaints about my Santa," he laughed.

"Hmm. I want to draw my own name next year," Grant muttered jealously.

Chapter Fifty-Five

"Hello, kids! Merry belated Christmas!" G-Lu opened the door of her independent living apartment at Pleasant Pond Retirement Village to welcome Grant and Marie. "Come in! Come in!" she swept them in after receiving a hug from each.

"Merry belated Christmas!" Marie returned the greeting and set a large holiday bag half-filled with wrapped gifts for her mother-in-law next to a small coffee table adorned with a retro-style, battery-operated ceramic Christmas tree.

"Nice tree, Mom," Grant complimented.

"I thought so. Dottie Battles renewed her pursuit of Jonah Fineman and was chucking her Christmas decorations in favor of Hanukkah decor. I was happy to take this off her hands," G-Lu explained, satisfied with her bargain. "I imagine you ran Christmas out of your house like a vacuum cleaner salesman," she chuckled, turning toward Marie.

"You know it!" Grant confirmed. "Marie cracked her whip and had everyone de-Christmas-ing yesterday – day after Christmas like always."

"And we're all ready for the New Year to arrive – like always," Marie asserted, straightening her shoulders. "Curious to see what Santa brought a good girl?" Marie changed the subject, nodding toward the gift bag on the floor.

"Naturally. But do you think we could go downstairs for lunch first? I woke late, skipped breakfast, and now I'm ravenous," G-Lu confessed, pulling the sides of her navy cardigan together but not buttoning them.

"You're the boss," Grant assured her, taking his mother's arm to support her in case her blood sugar was low. He led them out of the apartment and toward the dining hall.

"I'm delighted to hear you say that, son," G-Lu grinned and patted Grant's arm with her free hand. "Staff and resident volunteers are thin this week between the holidays, so I volunteered you to call our bingo after lunch. We start at one o'clock."

Grant's eyebrows flew upward. "You what?! I've never called a bingo game in my life!"

He shot a helpless glance toward Marie, seeking sympathy and rescue. He found neither in her expression, which was instead decidedly amused.

"Far as I know, it's not as complicated as brain surgery. Once we had a resident's visiting fourth-grade grandchild call the numbers," G-Lu recalled, meaning to encourage.

"It would be his honor to serve you and your neighbors by calling the numbers for your bingo game. Wouldn't it, Grant?" Marie was grinning at him, no help at all.

Grant frowned at his wife and sighed. "I'll try my best," he relented.

After a lunch of club sandwiches and fruit salad, G-Lu led Grant and Marie to the activity room, where a dozen residents waited expectantly on either side of an 8' table. G-Lu had hyped her son's visit and created an expectation among her neighbors of a benevolent yet charismatic man who might remind them of a particular incarnation of James Bond.

She pointed Grant to a card table at the front of the room on which a small steel cage filled with numbered balls sat. To the right of the table was an easel with poster-sized tear-off sheets of bingo numbers, which the caller would cross off with a chisel-tipped red magic marker.

"Don't let a kid make you look bad, Grant. Remember, I have to live here," G-Lu admonished in a whisper before taking a seat at the player's table across from Marie.

Grant stood beside the card table, turned the cage to mix the balls, and pulled one out. "Let's get this party started!" he shouted awkwardly.

Several players reached for their hearing aids. "Don't scream at us!" an old man wearing a Cubs baseball cap yelled back in complaint.

G-Lu lowered her head, and Marie giggled, putting her hand over her mouth.

Grant lowered his volume and called out, "Fifty-seven!"

"You have to say the letter so we know the column. Say, 'G-57,'" a white-haired woman corrected.

"It's written on the ball along with the number. Don't take lazy short-cuts," added the old man, who'd previously told Grant not to scream.

"Either you have a 57 on your card..." Grant huffed before curbing his rebuttal.

Marie shot a mortified glance at her husband, and G-Lu put her hand on her forehead.

Grant crossed off G-57 on the sheet and pulled the next ball. "I-29," he called, slashing a red line through the number. There were no complaints or suggestions from the players, and Grant welcomed the silence.

He pulled a third ball and marked the sheet. "N-33!" Grant felt he was finding his rhythm.

"B-2," he called, and then ad-libbed: "2-B or not 2-B." He chuckled at his joke.

Everyone at the table looked up with an icy stare, including Grant's wife and mother. Grant nixed any further spontaneous attempts at humor.

"O-74," he called flatly.

"You forgot to cross off B-2. Now cross off O-74 while you're at it," a bald man stage-whispered to Grant, who did as instructed.

"I-16," Grant said miserably, crossing off the number on the sheet.

"Bingo!" a woman wearing her glasses on her forehead shouted.

"Whew," Grant exhaled, relieved to be finished. He tore the tracking sheet from the pad and wadded it up. "Well, that was a riot," he noted sarcastically, heading for the exit.

"Where are you going?" G-Lu demanded.

"Bingo was called. We're done," Grant explained. "Let's go!"

"That was one game. We play ten. Do you leave after one hole of golf? No, you play all 18," G-Lu countered.

Fifty-five minutes later, Grant was overjoyed to hear 'bingo' shouted for the tenth and final game. As he departed the activity room with Marie and G-Lu, the woman wearing forehead glasses rushed to Grant's side and cooed soothingly: "It's a harder job than it looks, but you really got the hang of it at the end there."

Back in his mother's apartment, Grant slouched into the reading chair. "Mom, promise me you'll never volunteer me to call any more bingo games. I'm not cut out for it, and I pretty much hate it."

"I promise," G-Lu agreed before adding lightly: "I'm sure you'll do better at being the DJ for our after-dinner dance party this evening. We start at six o'clock."

Chapter Fifty-Six

"Hey, boss. Can I come in?" James Daniels asked after rapping on DeShawn's open office door.

"Sure can! Have a seat," DeShawn invited over the rattle of the space heater he was using to supplement the small building's inefficient furnace that needed maintenance or replacing.

James shook his hands at his sides and sat in one of two chrome chairs upholstered with nubby black fabric on the opposite side of DeShawn's desk.

"Got big plans for New Year's Eve tonight?" DeShawn asked cheerfully, noticing James' anxiety.

"No. No plans. Shorty likes to go to bed early, and the television being on bothers him. Guess I should just come out and say what I'm here for: I'm giving you my two-week notice. I visited my aunt and uncle in Tuscaloosa over Christmas, and they've invited me to move down there with them. They're giving me my own space in their finished basement, and my uncle's going to get me an apprenticeship with his electrical contractor's union. Says that would be a good career start for me. I could even support my own family someday."

DeShawn nodded. "He's not wrong. We'll miss you here, but it's a great opportunity. I'm happy for you, James, and I wish you God's best."

His difficult task over, James relaxed his shoulders and stood. "You'll be glad to know my aunt and uncle go to a big Baptist church in

Tuscaloosa. I'm going to go with 'em and check it out."

"That's great. I hope you keep asking questions. Just remember, decision day must come before Judgement Day, and that can come at any time, my friend," DeShawn warned.

"I know. Thanks for everything you've done for me – the job, a place to stay, and our discussions. I appreciate it." James thrust out his hand, and DeShawn stood, walked around his desk, grabbed the offered hand, and drew James in for a man-hug.

While Sam and Silas played video games in the living room, Will roasted coffee beans on the back porch. He sat in a collapsible camping chair, bundled up against the frosty night air, trying to decide whether he was smelling or tasting the rich aroma pouring from the roaster. He focused on the matter.

"Hey there!" DeShawn shouted, rounding the back corner of the house.

Will jumped to his feet, startled from his reverie.

"You scared the fool out of me!" Will admitted when he recognized DeShawn approaching.

"Sorry, man. You still have some fool in you to spare, though," De-Shawn laughed. "I opened our front door to let Rover in and smelled the coffee. Figured you were out here, and Shelby would still be at the shop. Mariana's already gone to bed, so I figured I'd wander over and hang with you if you wanted the company."

"Have a seat, brother," Will nodded toward another camping chair. "Good thing heart attacks don't run in my family, or I'd have had one," he said, patting his chest and recovering his nerves.

"I'll text you first next time. How's that?" DeShawn offered.

"Yeah, do that if it's the dead of night," Will agreed and checked the time on his phone. "Or if it's only 8:30. Wow, it seems later than that. You said Mariana is already in bed?"

"She's coming up to her last month. Seems to go to bed earlier and earlier now."

"I guess it's reasonable to get tired if you're growing a whole other person in your body," Will agreed as he sat beside his friend.

DeShawn rubbed his hands down his pant legs and exhaled. "Were you ready when Sam was born? I mean, did you worry if you'd be a good father?"

"I thought I was ready. The truth is, I thought I was ready for anything because I knew everything. Young and stupid, I guess. Didn't know what I didn't know – or what I understand now," Will reflected, watching his words become clouds of steam in the cold air.

"See, that's what I'm afraid of for myself. What do I understand about being a father? So, what do you have for me, man?"

"You're asking me for advice on being a dad?" Will laughed. "I think you'd be better off talking to Jonathan. He hasn't messed it up with a divorce like I have."

"I talked with Jonathan, but now I'm talking to you."

"What'd he tell you?" Will continued to deflect.

"Jonathan's got four young boys, a wife, 220 church folks, and zero time for introspection or waxing philosophical about fatherhood. He told me to keep my eyes open and prayed up for when I had to close them. That was the extent of it."

Will coughed and remarked: "And you imagine I can add to that?"

DeShawn stood and rotated his chair, then sat face to face and nearly knee to knee with Will.

"Let me tell you something I've figured out, man. Who knows better the consequences of sin – someone who understands them theoretically from an ivory tower or someone who's lived them in a prison cell for 20 years of their life? And who did Jesus say loves more – the one who's been forgiven little or the one who's been forgiven a lot?"

Will answered the questions with a slight shrug of his left shoulder, understanding their point.

"Don't think you have nothing to say about fatherhood because you've made some mistakes. From where I sit, if you've learned from your mistakes, you definitely have something to say. So, you keeping it to yourself or what?" DeShawn challenged.

Will looked over his shoulder into the empty kitchen, knowing his sons were in the living room beyond. He turned back to DeShawn and looked him square in the eye.

"My...my biggest regret," Will choked and stammered. "The biggest mistake I made was letting the church be the primary center of my sons' religious education. If I could go back and do it all again, I'd make sure they learned at least twice from me what they learned in Sunday School and Youth Group. They would understand church education is only a supplement to the truth they receive at home – the truths they see modeled at home. What they got was the opposite because I was too busy. I'm trying to do better now, but they're with me so little, and Sam is so..."

Will stopped speaking and turned toward the fuming roaster.

DeShawn sat back in his chair. "I got you. I feel that. My baby girl is going to benefit from what you shared with me. You had something to say, and I thank you."

Though his throat was constricted with failure and regret, Will managed a grateful smile for DeShawn's encouragement and kindness.

CHAPTER FIFTY-SEVEN

Using the handrail for support, Mariana waddled up to the second-floor gathering room above Latte Da for the baby shower Ava and Marie had organized for her. She was prepared for a simple gathering of her neighbor ladies, a couple of coworkers from the doctor's office, and a few women from Grace Fellowship Church who were friendly to her and DeShawn. She'd expected nothing more than a pink and white frosted sheet cake and sparkling punch for refreshments.

However, with floral assistance from Patty Farmer and the baking talents of June and Edith Eggleston, the ladies created a beautifully decorated, pink rosebud tea party-themed soiree. Mariana's breath caught in her throat when she reached the top of the stairs and got her first glimpse of the room.

The eye-catching centerpiece of the décor was a semi-arch of muted rose and cream-colored balloons of varying sizes placed in front of the large corner window. Interspersed among the balloons were pink silk peonies with soft green foliage. To the right of the balloon arch was a cream-skirted buffet table laden with gifts covered in baby-girl pink wrapping papers. To the left of the arch was another buffet table covered with platters of tea sandwiches, pink macaroons, white chocolate-dipped strawberries, pitchers of iced peach-flavored tea, and white cupcakes meticulously frosted with delicate pink rosebuds.

In the foreground were five round tables with cream-colored plastic tablecloths, each with seven place settings of floral paper plates on pink paper doilies, disposable crystal stemware, and rose-gold plastic utensils. Ceramic teapots, borrowed from a few of the attendees, served as table centerpieces. These were filled with a mix of pink roses, pale yellow chrysanthemums, and light green eucalyptus stems, which Patty could get from her floral job at cost. Varying shades of pink ribbons and fairy lights intertwined at the base of the teapots.

As feminine and frilly as the room was decorated and as exquisite as the refreshments were, something more unexpected overwhelmed Mariana. Every place setting was occupied except for the ones designated for herself, Ava, and Marie, who had accompanied her up the staircase.

"There must be 30 people here!" Mariana whispered over her shoulder to the ladies.

"Thirty-five, including us," Ava whispered back.

Mariana took several steps forward and gushed: "How beautiful! I've died and gone to girly heaven." She rubbed her baby belly absentmindedly, sharing her delight with the little one growing inside.

As co-hostesses of the baby shower, Ava and Marie led a prayer of petition for the safe arrival of baby Julia and thanksgiving for the luncheon. Then, they directed the ladies to take their plates and follow Mariana through the buffet line. Marie switched on a Bluetooth speaker paired with her phone and a playlist of soft instrumental lullabies.

"Marie and Ava, you've gone way beyond anything I could have imagined a baby shower to be. I can't even think of a proper way to say thank you. I'm just floored. And there are so many women from GFC here! Did you bribe them to come?" Mariana wondered, astonished at the turnout.

Ava placed a hand on Mariana's shoulder and looked her in the eye. "No one was bribed. Everyone came because they wanted to come. I know you keep your head down at church, fearful that no one wants you there or cares. I hope you see this afternoon, that's just not true. All these women are here to rejoice with you."

Mariana looked around and beamed at the ladies who celebrated her baby daughter's impending arrival. Indeed, they all looked happy to be there.

"Sometimes we project our fears onto others and see them playing out scenes we've scripted for them. But when we turn off our projector, we can see what's truly there," Marie winked at Mariana to soften the words she hoped the younger woman would take to heart.

After the women finished their luncheon, Ava stood to ask: "Who's ready to see what's in all these packages?"

The question was answered with applause, and Mariana was led to a chair next to the gift table to unwrap the bounty of presents for baby Julia. One by one, she opened adorable layette outfits, necessary supplies, and all manner of infant paraphernalia.

All eyes were on Mariana, except for June's. June's eyes were on Shelby, and she recognized the agonizing struggle the childless woman was trying to manage. When Shelby stood and attempted to escape unnoticed down the stairs to the women's restroom, June followed several steps behind.

June opened the Ladies' Room door and found Shelby had already released the floodgates of her tears and was sobbing at the sinks. June rushed to embrace her.

"I know it hurts. Go ahead and let it out," June soothed in her ear. "I don't know how you lasted so long up there. You're stronger than I ever was. I couldn't even set foot in a baby shower till I was well into my fifties, and all hope was gone."

"Oh, June! I have no one to blame but myself. My twin babies never had a beautiful shower given for them with a community of godly women to celebrate their existence. They never drew a breath because their mother was a selfish coward who destroyed them. Why didn't I protect them and love them like Mariana loves her Julia? I can't even tell you how much I hate myself right now," Shelby sobbed on June's shoulder, pained by wounds of regret that refused to heal.

June held Shelby tightly as she released her frustration and pain. When she felt Shelby's shoulders sag from the expenditure of emotional energy, June said softly: "All children, born and unborn, are created in the image of God as eternal beings. That's why I believe your babies are with Jesus – right now, as I speak. And if that's so, then you are still your children's mother – the earthly mother of children you'll be reunited with in eternity."

Shelby stopped crying. June had her attention and took her by the shoulders, giving space to look at one another's faces.

"You understand that since you're an adopted child of God, every sin you've committed – the blood of Jesus covers EVERY SIN. You're forgiven, and He will never condemn you because Jesus was condemned in your place. Hating ourselves for sins Jesus has paid for doesn't help us feel better and doesn't help our children. But I have an idea that might comfort you - it's what I'd do in your situation. I would buy them a cemetery plot and a memorial stone – to mark their existence and importance and to have a place to grieve or celebrate them, depending on the day. They wouldn't be my shameful secret. They'd be loved children I'd look forward to embracing someday in the grace and goodness of God's kingdom."

Shelby didn't respond with words, but a light appeared in her eyes, and a trace of a smile spread on her lips. She'd spent years only grieving what she'd thrown away. Now, she might nurture the hope that remained.

Chapter Fifty-Eight

Marcus clapped his hands together as he stood before the ten men assembled around the table in Latte Da's upstairs gathering room on a bitterly cold Tuesday morning. It was the inaugural session of the Men's Community Bible Study – a day Marcus had looked forward to for the past two months as he recruited participants in the cafe below.

"Tank you all for coming to da Men's Community Bible Study. We're going to start wit a deep dive into da letters of John over da next several weeks. Dis is not da Gospel of John in da front of da New Testament, but da letters he wrote dat are found in da back. I want to begin by noting da fact dat John is an old man when he's writing dese letters. He's a senior citizen like many of us. And da theme of da letters he writes as an old man is love – Christ's love for us and da love believers should have for one anoder. He talks about love so much dat he's earned da nickname "Da Apostle of Love."

But as a young man, Jesus gave John and his broder, James, a different nickname. He called dem "Sons of Thunder." When John was a young man, according to Luke 9:51-56, he asked Jesus if he could call down fire from heaven to make human toast out of da residents of a Samaritan town who refused to roll out da welcome mat for Jesus and his disciples. Dat wasn't very loving."

So, dere seems to be a change in attitude and priority from John's youth to his senior years. Has dat been true in your life? In what ways have you changed from your youthful self?"

Marcus was pleased his question ignited a flurry of comments from the men assembled around the table before him, most of whom he'd only recently met. The exceptions were Cal, curious to experience his friend and housemate's teaching ability, and Tom Farmer, who still hadn't secured daytime employment.

Marcus' method was to prime the mental pump of his students with a question they might easily answer from their current knowledge base or experience before challenging them to think more deeply. Now that he had the men's minds engaged and relating to the author of the short epistles, Marcus delved into background issues before tackling the text of the first chapter and its doctrinal test for believers.

"Has it been an hour already? Seem like you were just getting started," a white-haired man complained as Marcus wrapped up, closing his Bible. He was a regular at the cafe who, Marcus learned, had been widowed the previous Spring.

"I'll have more to say next week. You'll be coming back, den?" Marcus asked, delighted with the man's grievance.

"You might consider doing this twice a week instead of just once," the lonely man suggested. "That way, it wouldn't be so long in between."

Five bit her lower lip from behind the service counter as she watched Ms. June march up the back stairs to Latte Da's second-floor gathering room to lead the first session of the Women's Community Bible Study. It would start in 15 minutes.

Five had wanted to join the Thursday morning Bible study since the poster went up in the store window three weeks ago, but out of concern for shop staffing issues, she hadn't had the nerve to ask Shelby for the one hour per week off. She told herself that Sunday School, church service, and the weekly teaching podcast Will told her about were a good start for someone just starting her discipleship journey.

But as she made orders for women with Bibles tucked under their arms – women she knew would be taking their coffees upstairs and listening to Ms. June teach and be able to ask her questions – Five reminded herself the worst Shelby could say was 'no.' So after she decorated the last latte with a steamed cream heart, Five made her appeal.

"Shelby, I don't want to take advantage. I mean, we're not busy between 10 and 11. It's only once a week. I could figure out a way to make up the time." Five was having difficulty getting to her point.

"Go ahead," Shelby encouraged with a grin, discerning what Five couldn't ask for directly. She was delighted by the girl's desire to learn about God.

Five whipped off her apron, threw it on the counter, and dashed to get her Bible from her apartment across the hall from the gathering room.

"We're going to be studying the little letters of First, Second, and Third John," June explained as Five slid into a seat at the table.

"Sorry I'm late," Five whispered. She opened her Bible to its index to locate the letters as others turned directly to them.

June nodded at her with a welcoming smile and continued. "These brief letters from the Apostle John focus on identifying false teaching and false teachers. But before we get into the meat of the text, I hope you'll indulge me in a tiny rabbit trail. I learned something new about John this week from reading the Gospel of Matthew.

I always knew that John and his brother James were the sons of Zebedee because that's how they're identified in the gospels when Jesus calls them to leave their fishing nets and their home in Capernaum and follow him – they're 'the sons of Zebedee.' I also knew that John was frequently back in Capernaum after he left his father's fishing business because Jesus used Capernaum as the home base of his ministry. But I was reading Matthew's crucifixion account, and here's what caught my eye in chapter 27, verses 55-56:

There were also many women there, looking on from a distance, who had followed Jesus from Galilee, ministering to him, among whom were Mary Magdalene and Mary the mother of James and Joseph and the mother of the sons of Zebedee.

John's mother had also left home to follow Jesus, and she witnessed the crucifixion in Jerusalem! Seeing that family connection at the cross just touched my heart – to realize that John's mother was there for Jesus, but she was probably also a comfort to her son who was there while the other apostles had fled. Maybe her presence helped encourage him to stay," June explained.

"That is a sweet connection. I never knew that either," remarked 40-something Phoebe, who attended the Catholic church in Faircourt but saw the poster in Latte Da's window advertising the Bible study. She had a desire to learn more about the book while her children were at school.

Elodie, there to support June, cocked her head and commented: "I wonder if it was awkward for John's biological mother when Jesus told John that Mary was his new mother and responsibility."

Five giggled and regretted it, covering her mouth with her hand. June frowned at Elodie and concluded her rabbit trail with haste.

"Would someone like to read the first four verses of chapter one of First John?" June asked. She resolved to be more cautious regarding following tangents away from the text as the week lacked sufficient time for preparing the lesson and herself for anything that might pop out of Elodie's mouth.

Chapter Fifty-Nine

The warm air blowing across Kentucky from the south on a mid-January Sunday pushed the temperature to 64 degrees by late afternoon. In nesting mode, Mariana moved through the house, opening windows to let the freshening breeze pass through the rooms. DeShawn, in a short-sleeved golf shirt, picked up sticks and twigs in the yard knocked loose from the trees by the wind. He noted the noses of daffodil buds popping up in the left front corner of the house's foundation plantings just as they had when he was a kid. And he remembered his momma's joy when she'd spot them. "Spring is on its way!" she'd announce to the family. DeShawn stared at the little green swords poking up from the ground, caught up in the bittersweet memory.

Kitty-corner from Christine Williams' house, Bradley was pulling into the Tamarack Street driveway. He walked around the SUV's passenger side to assist his sister from her seat, as she expected her half-brother to do. Christine was gutting out the last weeks of Bradley's stay, looking forward to his return to California and the peace of her former solitude.

Releasing his sister's hand and shoving the passenger door closed, Bradley suggested chipperly: "You're going to miss me in a few weeks!"

He was hoping for a sign he'd made even a little progress in reversing the expectation he must depart.

Christine stood still, smoothing the front of her cashmere sweater, which had rumpled under the pressure of the car's seatbelt. Then she looked Bradley in the eye and responded tersely to the comment, determined to reinforce their agreement: "I think not."

It was too terse, too much for Bradley to accept. The combative reflex he'd used against his estranged current wife and previous wives roiled to the surface and, with a closed fist, he sent Christine sprawling onto the driveway with a blow to her jaw.

The slam of the car door had broken DeShawn's reverie, and he looked in his neighbor's direction. He was stunned to witness Bradley strike his sister and then stand menacingly over her.

"Mariana, call the police! And an ambulance!" he shouted through the open window.

DeShawn bolted toward the scene across the street without a plan, only knowing he had to intervene for Christine's safety.

From the corner of his eye, Bradley saw DeShawn coming for him. He knelt over Christine and spat under his breath: "You're going to thank me for this."

"You need to step away from her right now," DeShawn demanded, standing at his full height, chest expanded, muscled arms flexed above Bradley's head.

Bradley rose slowly, with a disturbing half-smile on his face. Christine tried to rise but winced instead and resigned herself to her prone position. She put a hand to her face, touching a tender jaw with a rising bruise.

"Don't try to move, Miss Williams. An ambulance and the police are on their way," DeShawn soothed.

Christine locked eyes with DeShawn for a moment, and she nodded.

"Good! I'm glad the police are coming. My sister has always feared you'd do something like this, and now, you have," Bradley sneered at DeShawn. "I think you'd better be the one to step away."

DeShawn's facial expression melted into disbelief, and his hands grew clammy. Was this older man intending to set him up for the assault? He took a few steps backward as instructed and let his situation sink in.

Bradley knelt at his sister's side once more and whispered: "A little bruise is a small price to pay for getting rid of the murderer across the street, right?"

Mariana bustled toward the commotion as fast as she could, considering she was heavily pregnant. She observed Christine on the ground, Bradley kneeling beside her, and her husband standing back, looking stricken. Approaching sirens wailed faintly in the distance. Mariana, concerned most by the look on DeShawn's face as he stared at the brother and sister, went straight to his side.

"What happened?" she urged a response from her man.

DeShawn turned toward his wife and muttered: "They're going to say I did it – that I hit her."

"What? No!" Mariana shrieked in disbelief.

"It's their word against mine," DeShawn added. "You know she hates me. This is how they send me back to prison."

Mariana let the words settle in her heart, and fear rose as she imagined returning to the years of visiting DeShawn at the Kentucky State Reformatory. This time, she would effectively be a single mother. She began to weep softly. For a moment, she contemplated urging DeShawn to run.

A police cruiser arrived on the scene. With no sense of urgency, an officer emerged and walked toward the injured woman and the man tending her. Bradley said some words to him, and DeShawn stepped closer to engage in the conversation.

The officer backed him off: "Stay where you are!" and continued to talk with Bradley while making notes on a pad.

At last, an ambulance pulled behind Bradley's car in the driveway, and paramedics scrambled to aid Christine. She could not speak to them, though she guarded her jaw with a hand and released frequent painful moans. The paramedics loaded her onto the stretcher and whisked her away toward LaGrange Hospital.

Marie heard the commotion of police and ambulance sirens and saw the emergency vehicle lights twirling on the Tamarack Street side of Christine Williams' house. She did not have a direct line of sight to the people and stood at her bedroom window, vacillating for several minutes before deciding to engage and check if she could assist her friend. The ambulance pulled away just as she crossed Cedar Street and Marie approached the McBrides.

"Is Christine alright?" Marie inquired anxiously.

"I saw her brother punch her face, and she fell. I ran over to help. They're telling the police I did it," DeShawn explained flatly.

Marie gasped in horror and then looked at Mariana, who buried her face in her husband's shoulder.

"Dear Jesus, let the policeman see the truth. Shine the light of truth over this situation, please, dear Lord," Marie petitioned in a whisper as she laid a hand on Mariana's arm.

The policeman approached the little group and asked: "Who witnessed the incident here?"

"I did," DeShawn spoke up.

"What about you ladies?" the officer demanded.

Marie shook her head no.

"I didn't witness what happened myself, but I called 911," Mariana offered.

"Then I'll ask you ladies to step back to the curb while I speak to this man," the officer directed, pointing toward Cedar Street.

Marie and Mariana turned and walked to the assigned spot out of earshot of the officer's conversation with DeShawn. They watched as DeShawn explained, with gesturing hands, what he witnessed from his yard and the subsequent turn of events at Christine's. The police officer listened and spoke to DeShawn. The ladies saw DeShawn drop his head and nod in the affirmative. And then, they watched the officer handcuff DeShawn, put him in the back of the police cruiser, and drive away.

Chapter Sixty

Marie escorted Mariana into the friend's house kitchen with a motherly arm draped across the shaking woman's shoulder for security and comfort.

"We have trouble," Marie announced to her housemates, who were assembling sandwiches for supper around the kitchen island. She tried to strike a balance in her tone, communicating urgency and calm control. Every eye was on Mariana, who had obviously been crying.

"DeShawn was in his front yard and saw Bradley strike Christine in their driveway, knocking her down. He told Mariana to call 911 and then ran to Christine's defense. But the next thing he knows, they've accused him of assaulting her! The police just arrested DeShawn and took him away," Marie explained to an audience of widening eyes and dropping jaws.

"That's what those sirens were about? I didn't pay them any mind," Elodie regretted.

Grant reached for the cellphone in his back pocket. "I'm calling Joe Jacobs!" he announced decisively.

"Mariana, I'm so sorry this is happening. Why don't you sit down? You've lost your color," June suggested, ushering her from under Marie's arm to a kitchen chair.

"Did anyone else witness what happened?" Ava wanted to know.

Marie and Mariana shook their heads.

"Hello, Joe, it's Grant Renniger. We have an urgent situation we need your help with. Please call me when you get this message," Grant relayed to the attorney's voice mailbox.

"I didn't see Joe and his family in church dis morning," Marcus recalled.

"Now what?" Cal asked.

Marcus threw up his hands. "Now we wait for him to call back."

"And pray!" June reminded.

Marie sat at the table next to Mariana. "I knew that brother of hers was trouble, and I told Christine so," Marie reflected. "I just can't believe she'd go along with bearing false witness against DeShawn."

"Can't you? You've seen her outbursts against my husband," Mariana challenged, trembling with fear.

Marie had to acknowledge the point. "Yes," she said simply.

"I don't understand why she allowed a man who would strike her and then lie about it to live under her roof in the first place," Ava commented.

"I don't either," June agreed.

"I do!" Elodie disagreed. "If you ever lived alone as a senior adult, you'd understand it can be worrisome and scary. If somethin' happens to you, who's goin' to know about it? I read once about an 80-year-old widow who died in her bathtub, and they didn't discover it till nearly a year later. The bathwater was goo!" Elodie explained, adding the latter detail for dramatic effect.

"Eww!" June reacted, pursing her entire face.

"I'm tellin' you, a person might overlook a lot in a companion just so they don't have to die alone," Elodie recalled the fear that used to grip her mind.

"Joe Jacobs will help us," Grant stated, eager to steer the discussion back to the immediate issue.

"Bobby!" Mariana suddenly recalled. "DeShawn's daddy should be told what's happened. He was napping."

"I'll go tell him," Elodie volunteered. Her lime-green skirt swished behind her as she turned to go.

Elodie rapped on the closed door of the former dining room converted to Bobby's bedroom. When no audible response came, she knocked louder and cracked the door open.

"Bobby!" she whispered into the room where faint daylight skirted around the blinds.

He seemed sound asleep, so she walked over to his bed and gently shook his T-shirted shoulder.

"Bobby!" she repeated in her normal conversational volume.

"Huh? What? Who's that?" Bobby asked groggily, pushing himself to a sitting position.

"Bobby, it's Elodie. I have to talk to you."

Groggy, but aware enough to realize this wasn't a social call, Bobby responded: "Okay. Go into the living room, and I'll be there in a second."

When she closed the door, Bobby rose from the bed and donned the black jeans draped across the footboard. With a growing sense of urgency, he slid his feet into leather slippers and hurried to meet his friend in the living room.

"What's going on?" he asked as he approached Elodie, who was standing by the front window. He began to wonder why his son hadn't woken him to say Elodie wanted to see him. Her turning up in his bedroom was strange.

"Bobby, DeShawn's been arrested," Elodie got to the point.

Bobby smiled, not taking her seriously. "Quit playing like that, girl!"

It took him only a second to read her serious expression and realize she wasn't playing.

"He saw Christine Williams' brother hit her, and she fell. He ran over there to protect her, but now they've claimed to the police it was DeShawn that hit her," Elodie explained.

Bobby placed a hand on Elodie's arm to steady himself as her words sunk in. She led him over to the couch to sit.

"This is a dream, right? I'm not awake and I'm having a nightmare," Bobby speculated before another concern overtook his thoughts. "Where's Mariana?"

"She's over at our house. They've called Joe Jacobs but had to leave a message 'cause he didn't answer. He'll call back, though," Elodie assured.

Bobby sighed. "I hate that witch!" he spat with no need to identify the object of his vitriol.

"Christine Williams is not anybody's favorite," Elodie sympathized.

"Someone should burn her out!" Bobby continued to rage, his hands balled into fists at his sides.

"Hold on now, Someone! Do you want to share a cell in that jail with DeShawn? You've got Mariana and baby Julia to think of now, too."

Bobby's fists were shaking, but he held his tongue.

Elodie took Bobby's trembling hands in her steady ones. "I'm here for you. I'm gonna be here with you – me and our household. We're your friends, and we're gonna sort this out. The truth will set DeShawn free."

It was Bobby's impulse to argue with Elodie's assertion that the truth would set DeShawn free. But he'd seen his friends' faith work out in ways he'd never imagined possible. Maybe their faith and their God would come through this time for him.

"I hope you're right about that," Bobby relented, frightened and faithless.

Chapter Sixty-One

Mariana and Bobby sat glumly at their kitchen table, turning over spoonfuls of oatmeal that neither had an appetite for. As far as they knew, Joe Jacobs was still out-of-pocket, and it seemed prudent to carry on with their routines while they waited for help. Both were dressed for work.

"Don't you worry, little momma, DeShawn's not going back to prison. Miss Elodie told me the truth will set him free." Bobby did his best to believe the words he spoke.

Mariana smiled and wondered if her father-in-law knew he was citing scripture. For a moment, she forgot her pressing trouble and considered the impact of the continual drip of a Christian witness on Bobby by their neighbors, herself, and DeShawn.

"It doesn't look like this oatmeal is going anywhere but the trash can. I hate to waste, but maybe we'll both have more of an appetite for lunch." Mariana suggested at last.

"Probably so," Bobby agreed, letting go of the spoon and any pretense of using it.

Mariana stood and reached across the table for his bowl. She halted, and drew a quick breath.

"What's the matter?" Bobby asked, concerned.

Mariana grimaced and looked at the floor. "I'm pretty sure my water just broke."

Sure enough, her light blue scrub pants were turning dark blue, and there was a growing puddle at her feet.

"It's too early!" Bobby protested, standing to his feet.

"Babies have their own calendar. And it's just two weeks early. At my OB visit last week, my doctor said this might happen," Mariana tried to calm Bobby's anxiety.

"What do we do?"

"I'm going to call in to work and tell them I won't be coming in. Then, I'm going to call my OB doctor and let her know I'm going to the hospital. Do you want to drive me?" Mariana invited.

"Yes! Yes!" Bobby agreed excitedly.

"Okay. I'm going to make my calls and pack my bag. Why don't you call the detail shop and tell Shorty to put a sign on the sales office door that you're closed for a family emergency?"

"Oh, that's a good idea. Didn't think of that," Bobby admitted.

"And bring a book! It's probably going to be a long day," Mariana shouted over her shoulder as she hurried upstairs to change her clothes.

It was just before 10 PM Sunday when Joe Jacobs returned from a weekend family trip to Nashville, connected with Grant Renniger, and learned of DeShawn's situation. Joe arrived at the hospital in LaGrange early Monday morning, accompanied by a uniformed police officer, to speak to Christine Williams.

Joe knocked once before entering the single room. Christine was lying inclined in the bed, eyes closed, but awake. She turned her head at the sound of footsteps entering her room and recognized Joe and his associate.

"Hello, Mrs. Williams, I'm Joe Jacobs. I've been retained to represent DeShawn McBride, so you're not obligated to answer my questions. I want to make sure you understand that. You and I attend the same church, though I don't think we've ever been formally introduced. This is Officer Swanson. He responded to the call at your house yesterday. Do you remember him?" Joe asked.

"Um hmm," Christine grunted in affirmation.

Joe noticed the whiteboard on the wall to the left side of her bed. On it was written: 'dislocated mandible and intracapsular fracture left femur, closed.' Questioning Christine was going to be a challenge even if she cooperated.

"I see you've suffered a dislocated jaw. I'm sure it's still quite painful. Would you be able to write your responses to a few yes or no questions?" Joe requested.

Christine nodded, and Officer Swanson handed her his pad and pen.

"Mrs. Williams, did DeShawn McBride assault you yesterday?"

Christine wrote her answer on the paper, taking longer than a one-word response would merit. She finished and turned the pad toward Joe. "No - he came to help me," it read.

Joe raised his eyebrows and looked at Swanson. This was going much better than he had expected.

"Did someone else assault you?" Joe asked.

Christine wrote quickly: "Yes."

"Can you write the name of the person who did this?" Joe pushed.

Christine did not hesitate. She wrote furiously: "Bradley Hall"

This time, Officer Swanson asked, "Do you wish to press charges against your brother, Mrs. Williams?"

"Half-brother – yes, I do," Christine corrected in her answer.

"In that case, I'll be paying Mr. Hall a visit this morning," Officer Swanson assured as he retrieved his pad and pen from Christine.

"Thank you very much for your honesty, Mrs. Williams. It will help my client very much," Joe concluded.

Christine grunted and waved her hand around, indicating she wanted the writing instruments again. Officer Swanson obliged.

"Thank him," Christine wrote carefully on the pad, turning it toward Joe.

"I will, Mrs. Williams. I will," Joe smiled.

The two men closed the door as they left Christine's room and walked to the elevators.

"Gotta admit, I was curious to finally meet Christine Williams after years of answering cease and desist notices her brother, Luther, churned out for her," Joe confessed. "Glad she changed her mind about pointing the finger at my client."

"She didn't change her mind necessarily. Her brother, er, her half-brother, was the one who gave the statement yesterday. He was the one who claimed Mr. McBride slugged his sister. She never said a word. Guess she couldn't with a dislocated jaw," Swanson corrected.

"Well, all right then, she's cleared it up now. Let's fill out some paperwork and get my client released, yeah?" Joe suggested.

"Let's do that. And as soon as I'm done, I'll be bringing in Bradley Hall to take his place," Swanson assured. "I'm not going to claim I didn't knock my own sister down a time or two when we were kids, but I can't imagine behaving like that as a grown man with a sister pushing 80 years old."

"Inexcusable," Joe agreed as they stepped into the elevator.

Chapter Sixty-Two

The soft notes of June playing *It Is Well With My Soul* in the living room accompanied Marie into the study. She'd come to visit with the Van Zants, who occupied the room – Marcus, seated in his usual spot behind the desk, and Ava, foot tucked under her bottom in one of the crewel-work upholstered rocking chairs.

"Have you connected with Mariana yet?" Ava questioned as Marie entered.

"No! I texted her over two hours ago to tell her about our conversation with Joe Jacobs last night, but she hasn't responded yet.

"Maybe she's having a busy day at her job," Marcus suggested.

"Hopefully, she's at least read it, and her mind is relieved. That's what's important," Ava added.

Marie sat in the rocking chair next to Ava. "Joe promised Grant that he'd keep him updated on any progress. No word on that front either."

"Wrong!" Grant corrected as he entered the study. "Just got off the phone with him. He went with the arresting officer to LaGrange Hospital and spoke with Christine Williams. She corroborated DeShawn's claim and told them it was Bradley who had assaulted her. Joe thinks he can have DeShawn released sometime this afternoon."

"Praise the Lord!" Ava shouted.

The piano music in the living room stopped, and June slid the pocket doors open and leaned her head into the hall.

"What are we praising the Lord for?" she asked those in the study.

"Christine fessed up. It was her brother who hit her," Marie interpreted Grant's words.

"So, DeShawn's in the clear?" Elodie came trotting down the hall from the kitchen.

"Dese walls have ears everywhere!" Marcus chuckled at the responses from people who were not part of the conversation in the study.

"Let's face it. We all keep our ears open in this house," Ava acknowledged. "But yes, El, Joe Jacobs is trying to get DeShawn released today."

"Anyone tell Bobby yet?" Elodie wondered.

"I texted Mariana a while ago that we got a hold of Joe last night. But I haven't heard back. Marcus thinks she might just be having a busy day at work. I didn't text Bobby, and neither of them has the update about Christine as far as I know," Marie offered.

"Bobby, Bobby, Bobby," Grant sing-songed. "You sure concern yourself with keeping him clued in." He looked at Elodie with a grin.

"What's that to you? Someone should clue you in to minding your own business!" Elodie snapped.

"Oooo, hit a nerve, did I?" Grant laughed.

"Pish," Elodie dismissed.

"Grant, please don't give her grief about Bobby. Her concern is an improvement over her former hatefulness, don't you think?" June pleaded.

"Don't worry 'bout me, June. I can crack another rib or two of his if I need to as an admonishment. In Christian love, of course," Elodie chuckled.

Grant instinctively touched his side where Elodie had broken two ribs administering the Heimlich maneuver on him last year. He quit teasing El about Bobby.

Elodie pulled her phone from her apron pocket to call Bobby and saw his text message.

"They're at the hospital! Bobby's at Louisville General Hospital with

Mariana. Her water broke this morning!" Elodie announced. "He sent this an hour ago, and I didn't see it."

"That explains why she hasn't answered my text," Marie exhaled.

"Oh! I hope Joe gets DeShawn out in time for the birth!" Ava exclaimed.

Grant reached for his phone. "I'll text Joe to let him know there's an extra element of urgency."

"Say, where's Calla Lily, June?" Elodie asked, noticing his absence in the excitement.

"Ha! He's at the same hospital. He had a check-up scan and appointment this morning at the crack of dawn." June looked at her watch and frowned. "Aww, he's probably on his way home already. Let me check."

June retrieved her phone from the top of the piano and used a GPS tracking app to identify Cal's position.

"Nope! He's still there. He hates it when they schedule his appointment early in the morning, and the doctor doesn't show until hours later. I'm going to text him to hang around and take Bobby to lunch in the cafeteria. I've heard that first babies take a while, and Bobby could use moral support."

"Bobby, Bob...," Grant began singing and halted.

Elodie smirked at him. "I like how you did that, Grant. The fruit of the Spirit is self-control."

"This is a pleasant surprise, Cal. Glad it worked out you were here. I've just been sitting outside Mariana's room most of the time. They gave her something to get the labor going, and there's a lot of checking and monitoring that neither one of us wants me to witness," Bobby grimaced.

"Well, I got another pleasant surprise for you. DeShawn should be here sometime this afternoon," Cal was pleased to share.

"You serious?" Bobby desperately hoped it was true.

"Grant's lawyer friend got Christine Williams to tell the truth. Supposed to get DeShawn released pretty quick."

"Aw, man! Woo! I bet you guys prayed about it, didn't you?" Bobby asserted with a sharp clap of his hands.

Cal's face grew hot, and he wished Bobby hadn't asked so directly. He meant to pray for DeShawn but hadn't. Now, it was a minor miracle Bobby wanted to give credit to God for answered prayer, and he'd either have to lie to encourage Bobby's faith or tell the truth and honor God.

"I'm ashamed to say I fell asleep before I finished my prayers last night, but I'm certain my Junie prayed," Cal admitted, embarrassed.

Bobby didn't seem deflated by the confession. "Well, that's good," he beamed, digging into the hamburger before him, his appetite revived.

After lunch, Cal kept Bobby company in the maternity waiting room, spending a few hours watching a succession of people suing one another in petty courtroom dramas on the television. At 5:05 PM, DeShawn rushed past them and into Mariana's room. And at 7:14 PM, 7 lb 2 oz Julia Elena McBride entered the world screaming at the top of her lungs.

Chapter Sixty-Three

"Don't anybody get too close to me 'cause I'm feelin' a cold comin' on," Elodie instructed as the friends assembled in the living room for Thursday Meeting. She pulled a chair far out into the entrance hall where she would still hear the conversation and plopped listlessly onto it.

"Wish you'd said that 45 minutes ago when I was practically sitting in your lap at the supper table," Cal complained.

"Nobody's getting sick! I forbid it!" declared Marie, scanning the group with a pointed finger. "Mariana just came home with the baby today, and it'll take weeks for colds or flu to run through this house. Little Julia will be saying her first words before we can visit if any of us gets sick."

"I've already seen her," Cal bragged smugly, pressing thumbs against his overall suspenders.

"We know. You don't have to rub it in," Ava chided him and slouched against the back of the couch.

"She's just the prettiest little thing," Cal continued, insisting on rubbing it in.

Ava rolled her eyes. "We can tell you've been sitting close to Elodie – some of her sass rubbed off on you."

"Another reason no one is allowed to get sick is because Christine Williams has been transferred to Faircourt Rehabilitation Center, and

I intend to visit her on Saturday. I won't be allowed if I even catch the sniffles," Marie warned.

"They gonna dry ole Christine out and put her on the wagon in that rehab?" Cal chuckled at his deliberate misunderstanding.

"They're going to help her while her broken hip heals," Marie corrected. "What's gotten into you, Cal? Did someone change your meds again?"

June intervened. "I can see why you might think that. He's certainly in a mood this evening. But he's just happy, that's all."

"Why are you so happy, Calcutta?" Elodie stretched her head in from the hall.

"Besides being the first one in this household to set eyes on our tiny new neighbor, I also got the first decent report from my doctor in years. He said my scan was clear, and I have no new malady taking the cancer's place. I'm stable as a six-legged table!" Cal grinned.

Grant initiated a round of applause, and everyone joined in.

"Dat's wonderful news, Cal!" Marcus rejoiced.

"It's been so long since I had good news about my health. I didn't even really hope for it. I'm glad the Lord saw fit to give me a season of respite from the struggles," Cal confessed.

"Thank You, Lord," June whispered. She welcomed the respite, too.

"Tom Farmer got some good news today, too," Marcus remembered. "DeShawn had an opening at da detail shop and hired him."

"Oh man, that is good news. He's been looking for a job for a while," Grant sympathized.

"It's hard to find a job when you're over a certain age," Ava commented, leaning on the arm of the sofa, her chin resting in a cupped hand. "I wonder if he'll be doing the interior cleaning young James was doing before he left. That might be hard on Tom physically."

"DeShawn already filled dat position. Dis is a new position, taking orders and cashing people out."

Grant rubbed his chin thoughtfully. "I wonder if it's a good idea for Tom to handle cash."

"Maybe that's why DeShawn's giving him that particular position – so he can prove himself in that area," Marie speculated. "At any rate, I'm sure DeShawn will monitor the receipts. He seems to be doing very well with his father's business."

Cal sat forward in his chair to comment. "I can't help but wonder about Bradley Hall. That's one guy who won't have any second chances or opportunities to prove himself. Old Christine Williams and I never had much to do with one another after our scrappy introduction over where I parked my truck. Still, I would never wish a violent brother like Bradley on anyone."

"Joe Jacobs says Luther Hall will make sure he does time in a Kentucky prison before he's sent back to California, where they've got a warrant out for him," Grant revealed.

Marcus scratched his whiskers. "I wonder what's going to become of dat vehicle his sister bought him."

"I thought you and Ava had gotten used to walking everywhere and given up the search for a replacement vehicle," Marie chuckled.

Ava grimaced and exhaled. "We haven't given up. It's just the more money we can put away from my job, the better vehicle we can buy, and the longer it will last. Hopefully. We're being patient."

"That makes good sense," June encouraged.

"I must admit, da walking has been good for my waistline, too. So dere's dat."

"Well, is this all we have for Thursday Meeting this week? It's been a lot of chat and not much business," Grant observed.

"Ava, you seem lethargic. Are you coming down with something too?" Marie inquired.

Ava sat up straight to correct the perception. "No, I'm fine, thanks. I got an email from a friend back at our old Bloomington church today, who passed along some sad news that's made me a little glum. She told me Beulah Francis died – do you remember meeting her? – you met her once. She was a lovely white-haired widow who mothered and spoiled Marcus and me like we were the children she never had. I'm happy she's with her Savior, but this world seems a little colder and dimmer knowing she's not in it anymore."

"I wish I remembered her," Marie pursed her face. "But I'm sure that is a loss for you both. I'm sorry."

"She was a mentor regarding hospitality, which reminds me of something else. What do you all think about inviting Five over some evening for dinner? It would have to be a weekday evening since she works late at the coffee shop on Fridays and Saturdays, and we don't have a formal supper on Sundays."

"We're overdue to have her," Marie readily agreed.

"She's coming to my Bible study. I'd like to get to know her better," June seconded the suggestion.

"Elodie, do you have any ideas for what we could make for her?" Ava asked, pitching her voice toward the hallway.

There was no response.

"Elodie?" Ava repeated her name.

Still receiving no answer, Ava stood and took a few steps to look into the entrance hall. Elodie's head was tilted forward, chin against her chest, and she was softly snoring.

"She's asleep in the chair!" Ava giggled into the living room.

"Aww. She said she wasn't feeling well," June whispered, guarding Elodie's rest.

"Ava! Remember that time at summer camp when you, me, and El fell asleep in the cabin and missed supper? The camp director supplied pots, lids, and spoons from the kitchen to the rest of the campers, and they surrounded us and scared us half to death. We could reenact that for El!" Marie suggested with a devious grin, hoping to distract her grieving friend.

Marcus lifted his right hand and raised the index finger. "A capital idea!" he enthused.

"I couldn't imagine a meaner thing to do!" June objected.

"I couldn't imagine a funnier thing to do. But that's why everyone loves you, June, and they're so-so about me," Marie chuckled.

"I love you, Babydoll," Grant winked at his wife. "Maybe we can just leave her there all night instead."

CHAPTER SIXTY-FOUR

DeShawn plodded down the staircase close to midnight with his fussing, squirming daughter in his arms. Dead-tired, he headed for the kitchen to make Viper Strike triple-caffeinated coffee so he'd be able to stay up with Julia so that Mariana could sleep. He'd mentioned to his wife at dinner that she seemed a little grouchy and received a blunt education that it's a symptom of sleep deprivation, as well as crying, which Mariana proceeded to do. DeShawn got the hint that his wife needed a break.

Rounding the hallway from the staircase, DeShawn met his father emerging from his bedroom.

"Looks like nobody's sleeping in this house. You okay, Dad?" De-Shawn semi-whispered.

"I'm good. I heard you coming down the steps with Julia, and I thought I'd like to take a shift with her. You've got work tomorrow," Bobby offered as he pulled the belt of his plaid flannel robe into a knot.

"Yeah, but so do you."

"Son, we both know your star is rising at the lot, and mine is setting. That's all good – how it should be. It's about time I think of retiring, anyway." Bobby held out his arms to receive Julia, and DeShawn carefully transferred her into his arms. "Helping with this little angel could be my new part-time retirement job."

Bobby patted Julia's bottom gently as he spoke, and she passed a bit of gas. She continued to squirm a bit in Bobby's arms but was significantly less fussy.

"Oh! So that was the problem!" DeShawn chuckled. "How'd you know that, Dad?"

"I didn't know it because she and I don't speak the same language yet.' But I try one thing after another until I hit on the correct remedy. Got lucky on my first try. I'm glad you got to see she's in good hands, though. So, will you leave her with me and go back upstairs and get some sleep?"

"She's all yours! Mariana just fed her, so she should be good on that front for a while. Thanks, Dad," DeShawn answered. He gave his daughter a gentle kiss on her forehead and headed back upstairs.

Bobby took Julia into his bedroom, opening the window blinds to let the moonlight from a full moon in a clear sky create a natural nightlight. Then he loosened his robe's belt before sitting with the baby in the rocking recliner he'd been gifted for his last birthday. He lifted the footrest and bent his legs so his feet pressed down. Then he placed Julia on his elevated thighs so they could gaze at one another.

"Well, good evening, Miss Julia," Bobby spoke softly to the tiny girl who was rolled up like a ball in a pink swaddling blanket sprinkled with fluffy white jumping sheep.

"Thanks for making me look good in front of your dad back there in the hall. I appreciate that. I know he sees I'm not the sharpest knife in the drawer anymore – the years are taking a toll on your Pap's concentration and memory. But you won't mind that, will you? Naw, you'll think your old Pap knows everything – at least for a while, haha."

Wide awake, Julia watched her grandfather's lips moving and listened to the soothing sound of his bass voice.

"Sure hope your Mam can look down from heaven and see the little dolly I've got in my lap named for her. Let me tell you, she was one intelligent lady. She was book-smart in school – always at the top of her class. That's where I met her in the fifth grade when her family moved to Faircourt. Always had her nose in a book when the other girls were jumping rope or playing with strings on their hands. Not your Mam! She loved books and reading. I can still picture my Julia as that girl at school – wearing a blue dress with gray trim her momma made.

Let's see, what else can I tell you about your Mam? Oh, she was more than book-smart. She had sense, too - always sensed when people were lying, knew when to spend and when to save money, and she understood what to say to make people feel good about themselves in any situation. About the only dumb thing she ever did in her life was hitch herself to me 'cause she was too good for me and didn't realize it. I sure wasn't going to tell her! And that's the only smart thing I ever did. My Julia was a good woman – a good wife and an excellent mother. I hope you grow up to be just like her. I don't know if I'm supposed to say that, but I hope it because you'll get along fine if you turn out like her. Well, except for the sickness at the end. I certainly don't wish the cancer on you – or anyone.

If I were totally honest, I might have wished cancer on that awful neighbor of ours, kitty-corner across the street. You steer clear of her – that Christine Williams! She got your daddy out of trouble last week but put him in it in the first place, too. She's been purely hateful to him since he came home from...well, I'll let your daddy tell you about where he was for a long time when you're older. Anyway, your daddy lets that old woman's spitefulness roll off his back like it's nothing to him. I don't understand that, but I'll tell you I admire it. It's probably something your Mam would have done. Probably got it from her."

Bobby could feel his legs growing stiff from staying too long in the same position. He lifted baby Julia into the crook of his arm and lowered the footrest. She continued to gaze at him.

"Thankfully, all the rest of our neighbors are decent people. Across Tamarack Street next door, we've got seven folks who have cared about you before you were even born. They're praying people like your daddy and your momma. 'God-fearing' my momma would have called them.

They've been good to me and your parents, and they'll be good to you, too.

You know, little one, I'm glad you'll be growing up in this house. It's not a fancy house, but it's solid, and there's a lot of love inside and surrounding it. That wasn't true two years ago. Two years ago, I was just taking up space inside these walls. But so much has changed. Started spending my Friday nights in the neighbor's Garage Cave and made some good friends. Then your daddy came back and brought your pretty momma with him. And then, of course, they brought you here, and we're getting acquainted with one another now, aren't we? You don't know this yet, but you and I are going to be buddies. Yes, we are. But don't think I'm going to be spoiling you! Haha. Well, maybe a little here and there, and that'll be our secret."

Bobby raised the index finger of his free hand and tenderly stroked Julia's soft baby cheek. Next, he fluffed the wispy curls of her thin black hair, and as he did so, the eyelids over her muddy-blue eyes drooped.

"Oh! I see what's happening here," Bobby whispered. "There you go, baby girl. You close your eyes and go to sleep now. Your Pap's got you snug as a bug in a rug here. We're just going to put our feet up, and both of us can rest."

Bobby pulled the footrest back up, shifted Julia to lie on his chest, and leaned back to recline them both. He tapped her swaddled bottom several times before the two of them drifted off to sleep in the comfy chair.

CHAPTER SIXTY-FIVE

Christine Williams demanded a private room at the Faircourt Rehabilitation Center and was awarded one on the strength of her belligerence and bank account. It was larger than the room she'd occupied in the hospital for the first three days following her assault. Perhaps it only seemed so because it wasn't cluttered with assorted monitoring equipment and furniture for visitors.

In any case, her current accommodation seemed an improvement to Christine, though it was just as institutionally colorless as the hospital room. She called her brother, Luther, to inform him she'd been transferred to the local rehab and to request he order a flower arrangement to brighten the lifeless room she expected to inhabit for the next few weeks. She did not expect he would come to visit her and deliver the flowers himself.

"Looks like you figured out a way to get rid of Bradley without going further out-of-pocket," Luther's voice boomed as he entered Christine's south-facing sunlit room.

His joke that Christine set herself up for injury to avoid a cash payout fell flat.

"Ah, you think this place is free? You wouldn't suspect such a bargain if you'd had a dislocated jaw and hip fracture, which are both quite painful. Who knows how long I'll be eating soft foods?" Christine grumbled, minimizing moving her mouth as she spoke.

"I told you to rid yourself of him months ago," Luther could not resist reminding as he placed the arrangement of brightly dyed Gerber daisies on the nightstand.

Christine wrinkled her nose at the flowers. "Did you ask for the most garish arrangement they had?" she said, ignoring the 'I told you so' comment.

"You said you wanted colorful, and colorful is what I got you. You're welcome," Luther pretended he heard appreciation for his effort.

"All right, thank you," Christine conceded the point.

"So, how bad off are you?" Luther asked with softening concern.

"Truth be told, it was not as bad as it might have been. My jaw was dislocated, not broken, and I have a hairline hip fracture that will heal without surgery." Christine turned her face toward the single casement window in her first-floor room and added: "I never thought he would be aggressive toward me."

"You knew he had a history of it," Luther challenged, pulling the room's single chair from against the wall to her bedside and sitting.

"I believed he was angling for a bigger payout. The day you and I spoke, I offered him ten thousand besides the vehicle I'd purchased for him – which I had the presence of mind to title and register in both our names. Anyway, he promised to leave at the end of next month. When the time came, I figured he'd ask for more, and I was prepared to go to twenty thousand, which would have set him up for a fresh start back in California. Now he's sitting in jail with no car and no money. Stupid man!" Christine vented.

Luther thought his sister contributed a share of stupidity in the situation but kept that opinion to himself. It was all moot anyway.

"Let me ask you a question. Has this episode that's played out over the past several months led you to consider downsizing or perhaps moving into an independent living situation where you can have people around?" Luther was planting a seed.

"It has not!" Christine snapped, raising a hand to the jaw she'd thoughtlessly extended.

"I guessed not," Luther chuckled. *"But maybe you'll consider it now that it's been suggested,"* he thought to himself.

Marie saw Christine sitting up in the bed but knocked once anyway on the open door of her room to announce her visit before entering.

"Hello, Christine! My, what pretty flowers!" Marie greeted her neighbor.

Christine looked at the flowers and sniffed. "The adjective I chose was 'garish,' but it lends color to all this beige and white, I suppose."

"Indeed, they do. Do you mind if I sit?" Marie nodded at the chair Luther had left at the bedside and vacated before lunch.

"Please," Christine invited.

"There's some arthritis in my hips. I figure I'll be a candidate for some hip replacements in my future," Marie shared as she sat.

Christine ignored Marie's complaint, which wasn't her problem. "How did you know I was here?"

"You're a big fish in a small town, Christine. You should wonder who doesn't know you're here," Marie stated bluntly.

Christine smiled briefly before she realized: "My house! I don't even know if it's locked!"

"I can ask Grant to check both of your doors if that would put your mind at ease," Marie offered, taking her cell phone from the purse at her feet.

Christine nodded. She hated asking for favors from people who didn't owe her any.

Marie sent a text to her husband and saw it was read.

"You should have your answer soon. But now that we know you're concerned, our household would be happy to keep an eye on your place while you're away. We did that for Bobby McBride when he went to Florida last year. Of course, now he has his son and daughter-in-law..." Marie dropped off, realizing she was treading into sensitive territory.

Christine was unperturbed by the reference to DeShawn and inquired: "He's been released from custody, hasn't he?"

"Oh, yes! The next day, and in the nick of time. His wife, Mariana, delivered their daughter Monday evening, and he was there," Marie informed.

"I'm glad for him. For them," Christine responded, but with a cool reserve at odds with the sentiment spoken.

Emboldened by the first positive words she'd heard Christine utter about their neighbor, Marie ventured further.

"I understand DeShawn came to your defense in the, er, altercation with your brother," Marie spoke, trying to be careful with her words.

"My *half*-brother," Christine bristled before adding: "and yes, he came to help me."

"DeShawn McBride is a good man who made a terrible mistake as a teenager. Pastor Jefferson told you as much, but I realize actions speak louder than words. Do you think DeShawn's actions have spoken for him?" Marie asked pointedly.

"I told his lawyer he helped me," Christine deflected the question.

Marie did not let her get away with it. "I was told you did, and that was a good thing. But that doesn't answer the question I asked. Do you think DeShawn's actions on your behalf have spoken for him?" Marie repeated with clarity.

Christine turned her face to the window to find her response.

"Do you suppose a murderous deed is offset by one good deed?" Christine challenged.

"The first thing that comes to mind in answer to that question is Romans 5:18 -

Therefore, as one trespass led to condemnation for all men, so one act of righteousness leads to justification and life for all men.

Jesus' good deed offset Adam's evil deed, so yes, in principle, it can happen," Marie answered, not missing the opportunity to speak of Jesus.

"I get my sermons once a week from Jonathan Jefferson, Marie," Christine chided lest the experience be repeated.

Marie feigned shock. "Is that all the sermons you listen to? That's barely enough to keep a bird alive! No wonder you're irritable!" And then pivoting to a more cordial tone, she added gently: "The least you could do is thank DeShawn. He took an enormous risk for you without a second thought."

"Hmm" is all Christine would offer in response.

Marie's phone chirped in her hand, and she read the text from Grant to Christine:

> All's well at Christine's front & back doors -locked securely. Tell her we're praying for a speedy recovery.

"That's good news. I appreciate him checking the house for me," Christine said, a wave of relief washing over her.

Marie chatted with her neighbor for several more minutes, inquiring about her injuries and prognosis, before taking her leave. She didn't want to wear out Christine or her welcome. But after Marie's departure, an irritating phrase she used continued to ring in Christine's ear: "The least you could do."

Christine did not want to be known for doing the least she could do.

Chapter Sixty-Six

"Fire up da space heater, Grant!" Marcus, rubbing his icy hands together, pleaded. "We should have done dat an hour ago to take da chill off dese stone walls."

An early February blast of Canadian air had forced Friday night Garage Cave activities into the basement even though it meant taking on the alternate challenge of getting Cal down the stairs. Marcus and Grant managed it without capitulating to Cal's suggestion they place a mattress at the bottom and toss him like a field-bloated watermelon. And although the guys had set up the table and chairs in advance, they'd forgotten to mitigate the chilly dampness in their alternate venue.

"Who's got the snack?" shivering Cal wondered.

"Not me," Bobby shrugged, still wearing his coat. "DeShawn's got his hands full now and no time for baking."

"I wasn't asked. I could have picked something up on the way home from the office if I'd been asked," Micah insisted.

"Will would have brought honey-mustard pretzel pieces," Grant reminisced wistfully.

Cal sat back in his chair and pouted. "This is going to be the worst Garage Cave night ever."

"Just hold on. Let me go upstairs and see what I can find," Marcus said as he stood and headed up the basement stairs.

"Don't forget to check the girl's hiding places!" Cal called after him.

"I hate that Will can't come to Garage Cave nights anymore," Grant complained.

"Shelby needs his help at the cafe on Friday and Saturday nights. Having your own business cuts down a man's time for fraternizing," Bobby reminded.

"Hasn't seemed to cut down yours," Grant challenged.

Bobby grinned. "And it won't because I don't have one anymore."

"You sell up?" Cal asked, surprised at the news and seeking information he knew his wife would ask him.

"Nope. Gave up. I signed the business over to DeShawn this week. It's his now," Bobby explained. "And I am officially retired from McBride Motor Mart."

"He won't have to change the name on the sign," Cal commented.

"Well, congratulations, Bobby! Welcome to the club of the unemployed," enthused Grant.

"Oh, no! I already have a new job," Bobby beamed.

"Unemployment didn't suit you?" Micah wondered.

"I'm going to be a stay-at-home Pap! The pay's not much, but the benefits are great. Baby Julia and I are going to become great buddies," Bobby boasted, delighted with his new vocation.

"I found some onion dip!" Marcus came trudging down the steps.

"And chips?" Cal asked hopefully.

Marcus frowned. "No chips. But I got baby carrots."

"Did you look..." Cal began.

"Yes, I looked in da girls' hiding places. Dere were no chips or cookies, just barrenness and disappointment – plenty of dose," Marcus interrupted Cal's interrogation and placed the carrots and dip on the 6' folding table.

"It's good to eat healthy!" Micah tried to find a silver lining to the regrettable snack for a men's game night.

"Worst Garage Cave night ever," Cal muttered, confirming his previous prediction.

"If no one wants to eat the carrots, why don't we play blackjack and use them for chips?" Micah suggested.

The guys looked at one another, considering the idea.

"A capital idea!" Marcus agreed at last, still not having worn out the phrase.

"Is it, Marcus? It's not still gambling if we play with baby carrots instead of money?" Grant deferred to his friend's professional expertise.

"I don't tink so. It's not like you could trade dem for cash," Marcus speculated.

Micah chuckled and shared a memory: "I once read about a guy who started with a paperclip and, through a series of trades, he ended up with a house."

Amused and inspired, Cal pulled a tiny carrot from the bag and held it in front of Grant's face. "What will you trade me for this, buddy?"

"Nothing!" Grant dismissed, rolling his eyes.

"See? Carrots are not currency. But I've never played blackjack," Marcus admitted.

"It's basically 21. Face cards are 10, aces can be either 11 or 1, and the other cards are their value. Whoever is closer than the dealer to 21 without going over wins," Cal explained.

"I'm dealer!" Bobby offered, pulling a deck of cards from the pile of games available at the end of the table.

"Aww. My idea! I was going to be the dealer," Micah whined.

"Then you should have been faster than me to claim it. So, now you 'was' going to be the dealer is correct," Bobby laughed. "Now, you all get on that side of the table, and Marcus, give me the carrot bag. Gonna start everyone off with six carrots."

Bobby doled out everyone's betting carrots and called for them to place their wager. Marcus pushed a single carrot in front of him; Cal went two; Grant copied what Cal did; and Micah pushed four in front of himself.

"Ooo, big player in the house!" Cal teased.

Bobby dealt the cards – two face-up for the players and one face-up with one face-down for himself. His face-up card was a three.

Marcus had a ten and an eight. "I'll take another," he said.

Micah and Cal winced at the aggressive play. Bobby dealt Marcus a seven, and Marcus pretended to cry, so Bobby scooped away his carrot.

"No guts, no glory," Marcus philosophized.

"Then what was with the one-carrot bet?" Cal mocked.

Cal was sitting pretty with two face cards. "I'll stay," he elected.

Grant had an eight and a six. "Hit me!" he ordered.

Bobby gave him a queen and was confused. Grant pushed his carrots toward him, and Bobby smiled uneasily as he took them.

Micah had a four and a six. "Hit me," he requested.

Bobby gave him a jack and waited for Micah's reaction. But Micah didn't move, and Bobby couldn't calculate his total. He felt his face grow hot. All Bobby knew to do was play his own hand. Since his face-down card was a seven, Bobby felt he should take another, thinking a seven plus his three must be low. But he wasn't certain. He dealt himself an ace and was more confused than ever.

Bobby felt the guys looking at him, but he didn't understand who'd won. Marcus recognized the cues in Bobby's widened eyes and prolonged hesitation.

"Cal and Micah are tied at twenty. What does da dealer have?" Marcus asked as he reached to turn Bobby's face-down card over. "Ha! Da dealer has 21 and wins. Give up your carrots, men!"

Cal and Micah obediently pushed their lost carrot wagers toward Bobby.

"Can I try being da dealer? I tink I'm catching on to dis," Marcus requested.

Bobby's panic melted into resignation, and he sat back in his chair, dropping his arms to his sides and letting them dangle.

"You know I can't do it, and I know I can't," Bobby said flatly to Marcus. "Not even with the pictures of the numbers on the cards. I didn't realize I can't do the math anymore."

Cal, Grant, and Micah now understood what transpired and were lost for words.

"How does dat make you feel?" Marcus tried to draw out Bobby's thoughts, intending to offer whatever comfort he could.

"I feel like it's time to go home," Bobby murmured.

He grabbed his coat from the back of his chair and climbed the stairs.

"Worst Garage Cave night ever," Cal insisted in a low voice.

CHAPTER SIXTY-SEVEN

"Sorry, I'm late!" Cal apologized as he rushed through the back door into the kitchen.

"She'll be here in less than ten minutes!" June reminded.

"Junie, you know fix-it jobs rarely go smoothly. Micah and I had to make an unplanned trip to the hardware store because the blade on my saw was garbage. But we got his rotted windowsill replaced. He just has to paint it. Give me five minutes to change into clean overalls, and I'll be right back," Cal explained as he walked toward their bedroom off the center hall.

"Five minutes, my foot! He's pokier than me," Elodie doubted. She slid two muffin tins of yeast rolls into the oven, set the timer for 13 minutes, and pulled her apron off.

"We need the salad dressing out of the fridge," she processed out loud.

"I'll get them," Marie offered, pulling at the refrigerator door.

Mercy barked sharply in the study and scampered to the front door.

"She's here!" June announced a moment before the doorbell rang.

"I got the door," Elodie continued taking charge. "Ava, pull the salmon fillets out of the fridge. They can go in the oven as soon as the rolls are out."

"Aye, aye, Captain," Ava saluted her kitchen commander.

"Hello, Fiver!" Elodie greeted their dinner guest, making way for her to enter. "You've done something new with your hair." It was impossible not to comment.

"Yeah," Five acknowledged and self-consciously reached for a lock of shaggy light brown hair, twirling it around a finger. "I'm done with the pink hair. It doesn't seem to be 'me' anymore."

"Well, it looks nice. I like it. Come on back to the kitchen; we'll be ready to eat in a few minutes," Elodie invited.

Five unzipped her fern-green hoodie and followed Elodie down the center hall, allowing her eyes to travel over her surroundings. She noted the cozy study through its open doors, the large wooden sliding doors that concealed a room to her left, and the paneled staircase with a fancy carpet runner.

"Your house is beautiful," Five gushed, unused to traditional 20th-century décor.

Elodie turned back toward Five to respond. "Thanks. It's a mishmash of all our things, but it makes a home. We like it."

"Five! Your hair! It's lovely!" Ava enthused over the recent update as the young woman entered the kitchen.

"A natural beauty," June agreed.

"Such a difference!" Marie remarked.

Five blushed. She didn't expect such an effusive reaction to the change she'd made over the last week as she dulled the bright pink with daily clarifying shampoos. It was just last night she'd taken the final step and stripped what was left with commercial color remover.

"Said the pink didn't feel like her anymore," Elodie reiterated Five's comment for her friends.

"Really?" Ava was intrigued and hoped Five would elaborate.

"Someone once told me the pink hair screamed 'look at me!' Well, she didn't use those exact words, but I got the hint. And the more I thought about it, I realized she was right. It was all for attention. Now, I don't want people to look at me and just notice pink hair," Five confessed.

Ava took a step closer to Five and probed further. "What do you want them to notice now?"

"I want them to see Jesus. I don't imagine anyone does yet, but I want to make room for Him. If pink hair gets in the way of that, it should go."

"You're wrong about something," Marie contradicted. "I can see Jesus in you, and I think these other ladies can, too."

June, Elodie, and Ava nodded their agreement.

"If nothing else, at least they can see the natural hair color He gave me," Five demurred with a smile.

The oven timer buzzed, and June moved quickly to exchange the rolls for salmon filets.

"What are we eatin'?" Cal asked as he wandered into the kitchen.

"Has it been five minutes already?" Elodie asked sarcastically, giving Cal a teasing glare over the top of her glasses.

"Well, I'm still not late because Five's not here yet," Cal defended himself.

Standing near the kitchen table, Five waved her hand and said, "Hello!"

Cal looked at her and did a double-take. "Your hair," he began.

"Is not pink!" Five finished his thought and stuffed her hands in her hoodie pockets.

"It's very pretty," Cal followed up sincerely.

Five smiled shyly. "Thank you."

"Calcium, why don't you go tell Grant and Marcus that dinner's about ready? They're in the living room watching The Addams Family," Elodie suggested.

As soon as Cal departed on his mission, Five commented wryly: "Calcium? I thought 'Five' was off beat."

"Elodie calls my Calvert anything that begins with 'Cal' except Calvert. It's her way of showing an unusual brand of affection," June explained.

Five stifled a laugh. "She calls me 'Fiver.'"

"Because that's my 'unusual brand of affection,'" Elodie held a hand up for a high-five, which Five immediately responded to.

Continuing to watch Elodie's movement closely, Five observed her swing her arm backward in an arc after their initial clap up top. She knew what that meant and spun around, meeting Elodie's swing with her own hand at the bottom of the arc for a second clap.

Elodie roared with laughter. "And now, I like you twice as much! None of the old people in this house would know to do that! You're legit street!"

"I could be 'legit street' if someone would show me how," June pouted jealously.

Elodie, Five, Ava, and Marie chuckled in chorus.

"If someone has to show you how, you're automatically not 'legit street.' Is that correct?" Marie guessed.

"Pretty much," Five confirmed with a grin before growing somber. "Don't wish for a street background, Miss June. High/low fives are about the only constructive skill you learn. That, and how to make do when your electricity's shut off."

"Wash your clothes in the sink, cook over a canned heat burner, and go to bed early," Elodie recited spontaneously from memory.

The other women stared at Elodie.

"El, I had no idea you lived that experience," Ava admitted.

"Me neither," Marie echoed.

"Why would you? We've never lived in the same city until recently. And when we were kids at summer camp, I certainly wasn't going to bring it up. It was embarrassin'," Elodie confessed.

Marie shook her head. "You think you know someone after 50-odd years and can still learn something new."

"Who's learning something new? Must be Five because we're all old dogs, and we don't learn anything new," Grant joked, picking up on the conversation as he entered the kitchen with Marcus and Cal.

Ava's hand shot up in the air to indicate she had a question. "Just for clarification, Grant, are you including the women of this household in your characterization of old dogs?"

"Ut oh, I knew dat was going to be problematic as soon as it left your mout," Marcus pushed an elbow into Grant's side.

"I heard dinner was ready. I'll wait in the dining room," Grant side-stepped the hole he'd dug and Ava's question.

Cal and Marcus followed Grant, and the ladies brought in the salmon fillets, vinaigrette-dressed dinner salad, rolls, and two pitchers of sweet tea.

When all were seated in the dining room, June initiated holding hands, and Marcus gave thanks to God for the guest at their table and the food before them. Grant, seated next to Five, passed her the bowl of salad. And as she took it from his hands, Grant remarked to her:

"You've done something different with your hair, haven't you?"

Chapter Sixty-Eight

It was precisely six weeks plus one day from the time Christine Williams left her home in an ambulance until the day she returned to it on a balmy Monday in early March. Her nephew, Eric Hall, dropped her off in her driveway, confident the rehabilitation center would not have released her if she were unable to care for herself.

"Call if you need anything," Eric offered insincerely as he assisted his aunt from the passenger seat of his Audi.

Christine offered an equally insincere smile as she waved him off. Turning toward her house, supported by a walking cane, she let herself in the back door using Luther's emergency key. She had a number of things she was eager to do now that she was back home. The first thing she did was check her watch – 12:10 PM. She'd arranged for her housecleaning help to arrive at 1 PM to purge the house of six weeks' dust, spoiled refrigerator contents, and, most importantly, Bradley's sparse belongings. As far as Christine was concerned, it was all trash.

While she waited for the cleaning ladies, Christine wandered through her house, re-familiarizing herself with her beautiful space and upscale contents, checking that nothing was missing. Satisfied after her leisurely tour, she sat on one of the living room sofas and looked up at the portrait of her ever-young Clarkson.

"I was foolish, Darling, and I might've lost everything you left to me," Christine began speaking to her husband as if he could hear her.

"Although if I could have you back, I'd give it all away without a second thought. What do lovely things matter if you're not here to share them with me? And you know, I was away without any of these things for a while, and I survived just fine. Well, I did have fresh flowers every week. I ordered them myself after Luther brought those dreadful dyed daisies. I know you would have never brought me dyed daisies – your taste was always so refined – just as you are in this portrait...so elegant."

Christine sensed her mood growing morose with longing for Clarkson, so she changed the subject. "You'll never believe what they taught me at that rehabilitation center. They taught me how to order groceries online! I can use the computer to pick out what I want from our local grocery, pay for it automatically, and have it delivered to our house. Isn't that marvelous? I never need to go to the grocery store or carry groceries to the house by myself again. I'm going to do it today, after the cleaners take away the spoiled things, of course. Oh! That's them at the door now. I must go."

Christine let the cleaning crew in through the front door. After instructing them specifically about cleaning the fridge and the guest room formerly occupied by her half-brother, she stationed herself at her escritoire in the home office. But instead of perusing the old gardening magazines as usual, Christine popped the cleverly hidden latch to the secret drawer in her heirloom desk – a drawer that evaded detection when Bradley searched for such a hiding place. From the secret drawer, she removed the title to the used but late-model SUV she'd purchased under duress for her half-brother. She was going to need the title for her planned errand tomorrow.

"Shorty! I need you to come up to the sales office. Now!" DeShawn yelled anxiously into the telephone the second Shorty picked up the call at the detail shop. "You're not in trouble, but I might be," DeShawn concluded and hung up.

Shorty hustled in the back door of the McBride Motor Mart sales office just as Christine Williams, wearing a light brown mink cape, walked with her cane in the front door.

"He...Hello, Mrs. Williams," DeShawn stammered. "I'll be right with you. I just have to address an urgent issue with my employee. Please have a seat in my office if you'd like." He pointed her toward the chairs across from his desk, and she sat to wait for his return.

In the back breakroom, DeShawn grabbed Shorty's arm. "The woman in my office hates me and makes it her hobby to make trouble for me. I need you to hang out across the hall in my dad's old office and keep your ears open in case I need a witness for whatever she's got up her sleeve now. Okay?" DeShawn whispered.

"You got it, boss," Shorty agreed in a returned whisper. He went into Bobby's former office and sat behind a month-old newspaper, propping his feet on the desk. He closed his eyes to listen to the conversation across the hall.

"What can I do for you, Mrs. Williams?" DeShawn asked politely.

"I don't want to take up much of your time, Mr. McBride. There's a two-year-old SUV in the parking lot for you. The keys are on the front seat," Christine informed as she leaned her cane against the desk.

"I'll be happy to take a look at it and give you my best offer," DeShawn assured, rising to his feet.

"You misunderstand. I'm not here to sell the vehicle. I'm giving it to you. Here's the title," Christine explained, pulling the document from her purse and handing it to DeShawn.

Across the hall, Shorty opened his eyes and lowered the newspaper in his hands, disbelieving what he'd heard and trying to catch a glimpse of his boss's face.

DeShawn was speechless as he held the title in his hand.

"You will recognize the vehicle as the SUV parked in my driveway for the past several months. I made a cash purchase for my half-brother before I knew his character, or rather, lack thereof. Neither he nor I have further use for it, and I'd like to give it to you to say thank you for coming to my assistance on that dreadful day," Christine explained.

DeShawn read the title, noting the year, make, and model. "Mrs. Williams, this vehicle is worth at least $30,000."

"I should think so! I paid $35,000 for it five months ago and added less than 2,000 miles since."

DeShawn sat down and pushed the title across his desk. "Mrs. Williams, this isn't necessary. You don't owe me anything. I came over to help because it was the right thing to do – for anybody."

"Very well. I respect that," Christine responded curtly. And then softening, she said with a hint of a smile at the corner of her mouth: "Then consider it a gift for the baby. I understand you have a baby daughter. Congratulations to you and your wife."

Disarmed by the mention of his Julia, DeShawn beamed a wide McBride smile. "For little Julia, I'd do anything, accept anything."

"Ah, named after your mother. Your father must be pleased indeed."

"You could say that," DeShawn continued, smiling.

Her business completed, Christine stood, and pushed the title across the desk. "It's for the baby, then, but I do thank you for what you did. It's the least I could do."

Christine departed, and DeShawn watched out his window as she got in the Renniger's black sedan, and Marie drove her away.

Shorty trudged out of Bobby's former office and grumbled to his boss: "If that's trouble, I want some! If that woman hates you, I want her to hate me, too!"

CHAPTER SIXTY-NINE

The Van Zants, Shermans, and Rennigers lounged on the porch of their Cedar Street home at the unconventional hour of 10 AM, drawn outdoors by the sunshine and warm southerly breeze of the early March morning.

"Prettiest day we've had so far this year!" Cal declared.

"It's nice that all of us are home today so we can enjoy this beautiful day together," June remarked.

"It's a shame El is back in bed." She said she'd open her windows and enjoy the breeze from there. Party pooper!" Marie protested.

Ava tried to defend her friend's decision. "Didn't she go to bed late last night?"

"No. She went to bed early but fell asleep late. I heard her listening to a radio sermon close to midnight," Marcus briefed. "I couldn't tell who was preaching, but his lesson was on da end times. Of course, he was in error."

"Aww. I was asleep. I'm sorry the noise distracted you to that level of detail," Ava sympathized with her husband.

"Oh, I didn't hear all his points. I just assume everyone is in error to some degree on dat subject. I've changed my position a few times over da years, and I'm still uncertain about a few tings," Marcus admitted with a grin.

Grant nodded his agreement. "It's good to hold some theology with humility and remain teachable."

"I can't believe you said dat!" Marcus exclaimed.

"What? You disagree with that?" Grant challenged him.

"I didn't say I disagree. I said I can't believe you said it," Marcus chuckled mockingly.

"Understood. But I retract any implication that you possess a shred of humility," Grant retorted.

"Settle down, boys!" Marie chided the men.

"First warm spring day, and the guys are butting heads like baby goats," June giggled.

"Oh, look! Here comes Bobby pushing a stroller. Must be taking the baby for some fresh air," Ava drew her friends' attention to their neighbors.

Cal leaned over to Marcus, concern stamped on his face. "He's not going to get lost and wander around Faircourt with the baby, is he?" Cal whispered.

"I don't tink so. He's not dat confused," Marcus whispered back.

Relieved, Cal shouted to Bobby when he reached the sidewalk in front of the house: "I see you've thrown Elodie over for a new walking partner."

"Or maybe I have two walking partners now!" Bobby shouted back. "It's a good thing since Miss Elodie's tired this morning anyway," he added, continuing down the street with Julia.

The women on the porch exchanged glances.

"So now Bobby knows El's status in real-time. That's an interesting development," Marie noted, pushing sunglasses up the bridge of her nose.

"They talk on the phone, I understand," Ava added with a hint of mischief.

"If there were an 'interesting development,' El would tell us. They're just friends," June corrected with a gentle reminder.

"I guess," Marie conceded. "At first, we imagined Christine Williams had a boyfriend, only to find out it was a greasy half-brother. Couldn't have been more wrong about that one."

"Speculation is cousin to gossip," Grant recited a favorite saying.

"Kissing cousins!" Cal agreed with an emphatic shout.

"Who's kissing cousins?" Will asked as he approached the porch steps wearing his USPS uniform shorts.

"Speculation and gossip," Grant informed Will before whispering to Marcus: "Told you it was warm enough for shorts!"

"Oh," Will frowned, feigning disappointment. "Thought I was about to be privy to some scandalous tidbit I could pass on to the rest of my route," he kidded.

"I know you can't stay to chat, but we don't see you outside church anymore. We miss you at Garage Cave nights. I hope Latte Da is worth the sacrifice of your man-friends," Grant needled Will.

Will laughed. "It is truly less satisfying than your camaraderie but more beneficial to my bank account. Friday and Saturday evenings are Latte Da's most profitable hours. God is blessing us; overall, the venture is exceeding our expectations. Shelby and I hope to talk our landlord into selling us the house."

"That would be wonderful!" Ava clapped her hands together.

"I wouldn't count Christine Williams out," Marie encouraged, knowing what she'd done for DeShawn and Mariana.

"I'll keep that in mind. Guess I'd better get going. 'Neither rain, nor snow, nor sleet,' you know. Aggh! Almost forgot your mail!" Will climbed the few porch steps and handed a few envelopes to June, who was closest to him, and reached for them.

"And," Will reached into his bag and pulled out a large manilla envelope. "There's one here that needs a signature." Ha patted his chest pocket and retrieved a pen.

"Whose?" Marie asked.

Will looked at the envelope and read: "Marcus Van Zant."

"First time today I was important," Marcus stood and obliged with a signature on the form, which Will tore from the envelope afterward.

"If it gets too warm for you, I know a place that serves great iced coffees!" Will pitched with a friendly wave goodbye.

"That's what it takes to be a successful entrepreneur – always suggesting your product to the market," Grant remarked to his friends.

"But he's not obnoxious about it," Cal agreed.

While the others discussed the qualities and merits of iced coffee, Marcus turned his attention to the envelope he'd signed for. The sender was a law office in the town where he formerly resided, Bloomington, which made Marcus nervous. He unconsciously expected bad news from that city and was glad Ava was distracted in conversation with their friends.

Marcus opened the envelope discreetly, read its contents, and dropped the letter into his lap. His mouth hung agape. Ava was not as distracted as her husband thought and grew concerned as she watched his reaction morph into disbelief. It might have been shock.

"What is it?" Ava asked anxiously, drawing the attention of the others.

Marcus stared blankly ahead and answered: "Our lives have changed."

BOOK CLUB DISCUSSION QUESTIONS

1. DeShawn tells his neighbors Jesus took his sin and shame. What are the consequences of holding on to shame?

2. Unsaved Lovie deals with a puppy's death by saying, "It just happens." What comfort can a Christian offer an unbeliever upon the death of a loved one (not a puppy)?

3. Grant listens to twin sons, David and Daniel, have a confrontation over the phone. What are some good rules for necessary confrontation?

4. Marie reminds Five that everyone has sinful parents. If you could change one thing about your past parenting, what would it be?

5. Pastor Jefferson admits to Grant that he's never seen church discipline successfully completed. Have you? Without sharing personal details about others, what did you learn from witnessing the process? Were you on the "gentle restoration team" as Grant aspired to be?

6. Joe and Allison Jacobs are rude to Tom and Patty Farmer. Marcus notes that new believers can be susceptible to spiritual ar-

rogance. Why do you think that is, and what's the best defense?

7. DeShawn doesn't tell Bobby he's preaching at GFC because he hadn't witnessed any prior spiritual hunger in his father. What are your thoughts about that?

8. Shelby tells Marie that she gave Five "the sorriest, the most raggedy gospel presentation there ever was" and was surprised it bore fruit. Have you ever shared the gospel with someone and learned something surprising?

9. Elodie defends Christine's decision to welcome Bradley into her home and to keep him after she knew he was shady. Why?

10. Christine Williams gave DeShawn (or, Baby Julia) the vehicle she purchased for Bradley. Do you think that signals a change in her heart? Why or why not?

Available November 2025